Books by Emily L. Byrne

FROM

QUEEN OF SWORDS PRESS

Knife's Edge: Kinky Lesbian Erotica
Desire: Sensual Lesbian Erotica

MEDUSA'S *Touch*

EMILY L. BYRNE

Medusa's Touch
Emily L. Byrne

Queen of Swords Press LLC, Minneapolis, MN
www.queenofswordpress.com

ISBN 978-1-7325833-0-6

Cover Design and Interior Layout by: Terry Roy
Star background from vecteezy.com, modified by
Terry Roy

This book is a work of fiction. Names, characters, places and incidents are
products of the author's imagination. Any resemblance to real people or current
events is purely coincidental.

CONTENTS

Contents, *continued*

Medusa's Touch

Emily L. Byrne

PROLOGUE

T HE FIRST SHIPS LEFT EARTH when the air became too thick to breath without filters and the water was nearly gone. They carried the colonists and the supplies they needed to survive the journey to new, unknown solar systems. Each ship was emblazoned with a different corporate logo, designating the crew's sponsor. Each corporation sent its leadership as well as its research and development teams. And its security forces, each one large enough for the core of a small army.

Any corporation with enough credits could sponsor a ship. They were the de facto rulers of Earth by then. They could choose their own destinations, any solar systems their ships could reach and claim. As the generations passed, the biggest corporations expanded, claiming their own systems, their own quadrants. They formed alliances and rekindled old enmities. The Corps Wars that followed were inevitable, at least to those on the winning side.

The Wars rearranged the universe, leaving behind them a loose confederation of worlds dominated by corporate owners and independent operators. The central worlds were linked by a political and economic network that connected the human-inhabited systems under the United Systems Federation. Three hundred years after leaving Earth, humans and the four known alien species were united.

The Wars also created a new cyborg pilot, one who could fly the combat ships by mindlinking to the ship's computer. The links were implanted in the pilot's skull, replacing most of their hair with coiled metal tentacles that could plug into a ship's computer. The mindlink made the medusa ships more flexible and responsive than regular starships, nearly unstoppable in ship to ship combat, except by another medusa pilot who thought and reacted first.

Outside the corporate military, the pilots who choose the medusa operation were few. It was permanent or so they said: once a medusa pilot, always a medusa pilot. And once you got used to having the links, they took on a life of their own, like miniature hands. They defined who you were and how others viewed you. It was more than most spacers wanted, corp or shadow trade.

TiCara X273 was a war orphan on FoxCred Corporate Station, a child of barely thirteen cycles, when she saw her first medusa pilot. By then, she had also seen so many other things that to call her a "child" seemed inappropriate. In the eyes of station security, she was a thief, alley scum who could be used for target practice or worse. Hiding in a spaceship docking bay where she might be seen and captured in order to watch the medusa ships come in was tantamount to suicide.

She did it anyway.

The pilots, when they emerged from their ships, were as alien as anything that she had ever imagined. Their medusas moved independently of the pilots' bodies, like living things. The pilots themselves were strong and well fed, walking slowly in the station's heavier gravity but each step, each gesture, radiating a fierce predatory grace. The stars of a thousand systems shone in their eyes, piercing TiCara's heart until she could dream of nothing else.

Those dreams kept her going, driving her to do anything she had to do to qualify for the corporate starship crews and the medusa operation. Anything at all.

CHAPTER 1

Solar cycle 7, 2345

Pilot-Captain TiCara X273 walked down the station corridor with its red corporate logos and cream-colored walls into Vahn Corp like she owned the entire spaceport and the secur cams and the Eyes weren't watching her every move. She never looked back at them, not even when one of the Eyes scuttled out under her foot, barely dodging away before she stepped on it.

Let the other corps wonder why she was here, why the old man wanted to see her. The speculation would be good for business. If they thought that she was in demand, they would hire her for their own outside jobs, once this one was done. She hid her grin at the thought. Besides, taking another job with Vahn Corp had its advantages.

When she reached the reception desk, Sherin Khan was waiting for her, just like TiCara knew she would be. Not that the rep had ever been anything other than coolly professional when they had met before but TiCara hadn't served as an Ear's pet before she got her medusas without recognizing desire in all its forms. Or, at least what she hoped was desire. The rep's impassive expression made her second-guess her instincts.

If she was being tru, the uncertainty made her awkward and uncomfortable, like a crèche-bred just out of the hold. She covered a wince with a shrug and threw her shoulders back, pulling up every bit of bravado she possessed to wear like body armor before she swaggered up to the rep.

She'd been hoping to get a reaction, any reaction, from Sherin since she first heard the other woman sing in the spacer bars, long before Sherin became Ser Trin Vahn's trusted assistant. And now, here they were, and she was still hoping. The pilot smiled to herself as Sherin escorted her through the lobby and down the short hall to Vahn's office. She wondered if the rep still sang. She hoped she was going to get to find out soon.

The door to Vahn's office stayed closed as they stood before it and Sherin hesitated for an instant before reaching over to the keypad, as if she didn't want to bring the pilot inside. An impulse drove TiCara to step in front of her, standing between the rep and the door so she could look directly into Sherin's liquid dark eyes. Sherin froze, as if she didn't know how to react.

TiCara stepped in, making the distance between them too close for standard corporate communication. They were the same height so TiCara's face was centimeters from the rep's, giving her a close-up view of the other woman's flawless brown skin and her very kissable full lips. Lips that now appeared to be twisting into a grimace of dismay or, perhaps, uncertainty.

TiCara inhaled her nervous discomfort with a small grin and a twisting whirl of emotions that she didn't want to examine too closely. Sherin stumbled back and TiCara, after a moment of hesitation, stepped forward, closing the distance between them like they were dancing. Now to find out what the rep was really thinking. "Hello, Sherin," she breathed. "Starshine girl." She moved her hand up but stopped short of touching the rep's cheek and Sherin moved back out of reach, eyes narrowing in a startled expression.

TiCara gave her a predatory smile and gestured toward the doorway. "Trin Vahn wants me now. But you can have me later. Just hit the green button when you decide you're ready." She waggled her medusas at the other woman and leered.

Sherin looked away, the rapid rise and fall of her chest betraying her agitation. Was it desire? Or was TiCara letting the want that burned through blackhole her brain? TiCara studied Sherin for a long moment, waiting for her to look up and meet her stare, to say something that would tell her what might happen next and what, if anything, the rep wanted from her.

But Sherin stayed silent and looked away and there was a client waiting and credits to be made and cred was too important to lose. At least for now. TiCara smoothed her features into the sobriety appropriate for an important meeting and gestured toward the door behind Sherin.

Sherin spun away and hit the door's old-fashioned secur button with a grimace. She ushered TiCara through, still not making eye contact, then trailed after her to stand in front of the now closed door. Her stance shifted subtly into guard mode, a change that TiCara could sense without turning her head. It surprised her, even hurt her a little. Did Sherin truly think that she was a danger to Vahn?

But now she was letting herself get distracted and she recognized that for the danger it was. Shadow trade pilots like her had bigger worries than chasing the nearest handsome face. She stepped forward, walking slowly with hands clasped before her, through the long white room toward the man she had come to see. Not for the first time, she wondered what the two cloth wall hangings with their depictions of odd creatures and plant life on each side of his desk cost the old man; a good replica of Old Earth embroidered silk was worth more than her entire ship. Originals cost more creds than she could imagine.

Ser Trin Vahn, CEO of Vahn Corp, sat behind his big gray desk looking even more like an Old Earth tortoise than he had at their last meeting, only a half cycle ago. Word from the Eyes was that Eternayouth didn't work for him anymore, that he would die a wizened old man while his seemingly younger rivals outlived him. Or so they all hoped, ghouls that they were.

TiCara was hoping that he outlasted them all, mostly because his credit had always been good. Besides, she liked him better than her other clients, which meant better than not at all. Trusting him was another matter, but then, she was hard pressed to think of any employer she thought she could trust.

She stopped before the desk and gave him the formal United Systems greeting: hand to heart to lips to forehead, followed by a bow. It was more formal than she needed with an established client but she knew it would sweeten up the old man. He was as notorious for formality as for his devotion to the ancient ways that their ancestors had brought to the stars from their home planet. She looked up and he nodded in acknowledgment before he spoke, his voice rasping against her ears, "I have need of your services again, Pilot-Captain TiCara. I apologize for the short notice but this is important."

It must be. Vahn had never gone straight to business when she'd dealt with him before. Nor had he ever mentioned anything that approached urgency. Urgency was expensive, and they both knew it. Normally, he spoke first of interstellar trade, then asked shrewd questions that tried to make her reveal too much about her own operations. Then and only then would he tell her why he had summoned her.

This time was clearly different. He didn't mention Sirius Transport, the shipping corp she currently subcontracted for, only her. Which meant this was an independent deal, risky for both of them. Sirius could cut her contract if they found out. They could do nothing to the old man, of course, not directly. But there were other forms of vengeance for interfering with another corp's contractors while they were under contract: missing licenses, refusals to allow a ship to make port, minor sabotage.

TiCara weighed the risks as she sized up Vahn. Her latest delivery for Sirius had been a success and their rep had let her know that they would like her to make another drop soon, but they had not finalized any details. Sirius might ignore a side job, as long as it was fast and quiet and her ship was available when they were ready.

Vahn gestured for her to sit and a roboserver emerged from a wall panel to place a tea tray with a steaming teapot and small ceramic cups on the desk between them. They each took a cup and sipped. TiCara blinked in pleased surprise: this was greenhouse-grown tea, not the usual imitation made from processed protein. The old man was trying to sweeten her up, too.

They exchanged a few comments about meteorite showers in the Kyrin System and the attendant shipping risks. It was as if he was trying to belie the urgency he had just admitted to feeling. But TiCara knew that it wouldn't last long. She placed her cup back on the tray and he gestured to Sherin. The rep stepped forward and plugged in her portable so that it displayed on the small screen that rose from the edge of Vahn's desk.

Then she stepped aside, her movements slow and reluctant to the pilot's augmented senses. Why was she hesitating? What was going on? TiCara's brain whirled with possibilities.

Perhaps this run would be more dangerous than she had expected when she agreed to this meeting. Vahn was apparently willing to accept the risks, whatever they were, and she found that even more disturbing than his rep's obvious suspicions. Speed and recklessness was something new in her dealings with him. Vahn had a well-deserved reputation for caution and cunning.

She wasn't sure she liked this shift, if that's what this was. Change meant uncertainty, more things out of her control. It was safer in the shadows, back out of the bright lights, back where she controlled the variables. But then, she reminded herself, if she had stayed there, she never would have earned her own ship.

And good cred was good cred. Especially when she owed as much as she did for the *Astra*. She smoothed her surprise and misgivings away with a smile and a sweeping gesture. "Of course, Ser. Any services I can provide are yours." For a price, of course. She left the words unspoken, instead dropping her dark gaze demurely to the red and black carpet that ran under the desk the surrounding chairs, though not without a sideways glance at Sherin.

The other woman watched her employer as if he was the only person in the room, her gaze fixed so firmly on him that her eyes might have been glued in place. Almost as if she was afraid of what might happen if she looked at the pilot instead. TiCara swallowed a sudden burst of optimism and glanced back at Vahn.

Vahn spoke again, his tone taking on an ancient weariness, "You have heard the stories they tell in the spacer bars about Electra 12, have you not, Pilot-Captain?"

TiCara's eyebrows rose, or might have if she still had any. Like most medusa pilots, she had her body hair lazered so that stray hairs wouldn't catch in the medusa coils. But her facial muscles rose upward and the effect was nearly the same in conveying her astonishment. "I have heard some stories, of course. But they also say the asteroid's a myth, Ser."

She thought about tapping into her handheld and doing a rapid search, seeing if there was something new, but there was no time to find anything really useful without appearing distracted, even at top speed. She would have to rely on her unaided memory. Electra 12 was supposed to be an artificial asteroid where something or someone could heal all kinds of human illnesses, perhaps even reverse the effects of human aging, if Eternayouth didn't work on your metabolism. In the bars, they even called it "The Fountain of Youth," after some Earther tall tale.

There were a dozen or so stories about the place, each wilder than the last. Gossip said that the location was known only to a select few, but that the information could be bought for a big enough price. That part sounded tru, certain. They also said that the asteroid was hidden because whatever happened there could potentially trigger another Corps War or that it was neutral territory for the corporations. But nothing TiCara had ever heard or seen suggested that the rumors about Electra were tru, any of them. She looked at Vahn sympathetically now. This might be worse than she thought: only a dying man would pursue a dream as futile as this one.

He gave her a sharp look in return. "I know what you're thinking. It is not a myth, Pilot-Captain, nor am I deluded by my own needs. I have spoken to sources, reliable ones, who tell me that some of the benefits to be obtained from the asteroid's labs are tru, as are the stories about its hidden location," Vahn leaned forward in his chair, his gaze piercing now, "I have paid for and am now in possession of the coordinates. What I want you to do is transport me and my immediate staff there. You will receive the coordinates when we are on board."

This time, TiCara didn't bother to hide her astonishment. Vahn had his own ships, any one of them bigger and faster than her *Astra*. She used her ship for hauling freight and contraband, never passengers. Especially not rich ones. They were hard to please, for one thing, and often other kinds of trouble for another.

She surprised herself by speaking her thoughts aloud, like a raw recruit. "My ship is always available to you, Ser, of course. But why not take one of your own?" A moment later it struck her. Vahn didn't want anyone in his corp to know what he was up to. Chasing after a mirage like Electra 12 made the old man look weak, ripe for overthrow. And if the other corps or even his own subordinates suspected that he was vulnerable, he could lose everything. Which meant that this could be a one-way trip for her and her crew if Vahn wanted to make sure there was no trace of this particular expedition.

Some of her fears must have shown on her face, despite her efforts to discipline her expression. Vahn sounded amused, even paternal, when he spoke again, "TiCara, don't you know me better than that? I will pay well for your search, better for your silence. There is nothing to be afraid of, provided all of us are discrete. Please go and prepare your ship. I ask that you do not tell your crew of our real destination for now. I don't want the Eyes and Ears to learn anything until we arrive on Electra and my treatments have begun."

He paused and gave TiCara an unreadable glance before he continued, "I want to leave within twenty machrons. Sherin will provide you with the navigation coordinates once we are out of port. She and my bondarmin will attend to my needs while you and your crew handle the other logistics. My credit is open to you; take what you need. Consider your silence already paid for. I will make it most profitable for you to bring me safely to the asteroid as well as bringing me home." Then Vahn named a sum that would pay all of TiCara's debts before he leaned back, his eyes closing in a seemingly involuntary gesture of dismissal.

TiCara didn't really believe that he felt that old, that sick. The gesture was meant only to sooth her terrors and she felt ashamed that she needed to see it. But his credit had been good before and Sherin Khan looked almost as good as the credit. This trip would finally be her chance to get close to the beautiful rep. If they made it there and back, wherever "there" really was.

Sherin glanced up, catching her eye, desire clear and unmasked for an instant. TiCara's stomach whirled with butterflies, much to her surprise. That look alone was almost worth all the risks the pilot feared. TiCara smiled, letting her anticipation show. Her medusas moved languidly around her head, as the sensuality of her thoughts traveled through their wiring.

Not that her interest, no, *need*, for this job ended with her desire for the lovely Sherin. Her last few independent jobs had not brought in what she had hoped for, and there was too much competition for shadow trade jobs in Kyrin Spaceport. That was why she was contracted with Sirius now. But if she took Vahn's job, she might not need to subcontract again. And the *Astra* would be all hers, finally.

That was too tempting a notion to abandon: to fly through the stars free of the demands of the corps, to come and go as she wanted, finally free. That had been her dream since she first saw a medusa pilot and fell in love with the possibilities. Now it was within her grasp. If this went well. But even that hope wasn't enough to stop her from asking her next question. "And if your intel blackholes, Ser?"

Vahn tilted his head, eyes slitted as if he needed to weigh his words, weigh her reaction. At last he said, "You will be paid your fee, Captain-Pilot." He waited for her head jerk of agreement and watched her consent to the eyescan on Sherin's pad to sign the agreement before bestowing a wry smile on them both.

That completed, TiCara made the socially appropriate responses to Vahn, doing all that the old man could want by way of a formal parting. Then she followed Sherin from the room, entertaining herself by watching the other woman's body in her form-fitting suit. She looked good. Better than good even.

Maybe even good enough for old-fashioned meatspace sex, something more special than jacking into the VR modules. It had been a long time since she felt that way about anyone, and she let the sensation wash over her, savoring it. She imagined the taste of Sherin's skin, the feel of flesh against flesh, and it intrigued her, sending a wave of heat up into her belly.

The door closed behind them and Sherin stopped, turning to say something through blackberry lips gone puffy and delectable. TiCara stepped up to her and, after a moment's hesitation, kissed her. She could feel Sherin tremble, then press closer, felt the first tentative fumblings of the rep's tongue against hers. It was as if she had never kissed anyone before.

Maybe she hadn't, at least not outside virtual reality. It wasn't common but TiCara had met others, like her old lover and mentor, Elia, who were more comfortable being intimate in VR than outside it. And yet, Sherin was kissing her back after her initial hesitation, awkward eagerness in the touch of her lips.

That touch jolted and aroused her. This job could be so much more than she had hoped for when she entered Vahn's office. Sherin wanted her, she could feel as much in the rep's quickened breathing and she meant to take full advantage of that on this trip. She had waited far too long for this chance.

TiCara could feel herself get slick with the thought and deepened the kiss, parting Sherin's teeth with her tongue and pulling her closer. Sherin went stiff for a moment, then molded her body to TiCara's, pressing tightly against her, wrapping her arms like iron cables around her waist and shoulders. TiCara gasped as one of Sherin's hands slid tentatively down her back to cup her ass through her uniform.

For a moment, she lost herself in their embrace, letting their bodies meld together until it felt like they were going to abandon all self-control and take each other there in front of Vahn's office door beneath the shining red lights of the secur cameras. But TiCara knew that she couldn't let herself go that far, not yet anyway. She had preparations to make, a job to do and a client who might not enjoy a free show outside his office. After a few pleasurable moments, she pulled back, sending out a single medusa to stroke the other woman's cheek.

Sherin shuddered and half-closed her eyes, as if TiCara had touched her with her own hand instead of her implant. TiCara had to force herself not to kiss her again, "We've got work to do, my starshine pretty. Fun must wait, sadly." Reluctantly TiCara stepped backward, the medusa lingering for an instant longer than necessary. Twenty machrons, the Kyrin equivalent of eighteen Earth hours, didn't give her much time to prep. She bit back a sigh.

Sherin's eyes were completely closed now and TiCara could see the breath catch in her throat. Then the corp rep training took over and a layer of ice spread over her features as she opened her eyes and looked away. "Of course. Follow me, please." Sherin straightened her top and turned on her heel to walk down the hall, only a quick, savage kick at a Vahn Corp Eye that came too close, conveying her frustration.

She missed but the gesture made TiCara smile just a little, though she could feel her own disappointment ache between her legs. She hated postponing her pleasures, especially the more unusual ones. But business needed to come first. That was how she'd made it this far.

She followed the other woman to her office where Sherin handed her a credchip. "Try not to blackhole his credit." Sherin almost smiled then seemed to think the better of it and looked stern instead. "I run the numbers for him. I'll know if you exceed what's needed."

"As if I would break one of my best clients. Silly starshine girl. Give me another kiss before I go?" TiCara stepped up to the rep's side but hesitated at her fierce glare. Instead, she settled for blowing the rep a kiss from her fingertips, hoping the archaic gesture would charm the other woman.

She couldn't be sure that she'd gotten her hoped for reaction, but she reveled in the blush that followed, darkening Sherin's skin from deep gold to dark brown in an instant. Then she backed away, chip in hand, her smile promising more to come. She could almost feel Sherin's gaze burning on her back as the door slid closed behind her.

Chapter 2

TiCara walked back down the corridor into the main space station, trying to use the walk to put Sherin out of her mind for the time being. She deliberately looked straight ahead, never up at the big clear dome over her head where the starfields blazed above Kyrin's surface. Too much time looking at the galaxies got to you, made you lose perspective, grounding; that's what they always told her at the Academy. All the things she couldn't afford to lose right now.

Her mind was already busy making a list of what her ship and crew would need for this trip. Basic supplies and fuel were automatically added, but including Vahn, Sherin and Vahn's bondarmin meant more planning, more food and fuel. She added several small luxuries and more processors for the nutrient dispensers to the growing list.

With the part of her mind not full of lists and supplies, she combed through her memories, trying to remember what she could about Electra 12. It wasn't much, just a few old spacer stories here, a snatch of bar gossip there. The bits and pieces swirled around, refusing to come together into something coherent. It was enough to make her shake her head in frustration.

She needed to talk to her contacts on Downside, spacers who could give her real intel about the asteroid, or at least enough to judge whether or not it was a myth and this trip a fool's errand. For that, she needed spacer talk, not the Nets. The Nets were corp-controlled, after all; any information on them could be accessed and manipulated by the Ears or other corps personnel.

Tru tell ran on the underground lines or in real-time. Just like the best sex. She thought of Sherin again and smiled. But then, this wasn't the time for that, either. She needed to go to the bars and see what she could find out. TiCara scowled at the thought, missing a younger, brasher self who might have chosen differently.

Her thoughts spun in a lazy circle until she remembered that before she went to Downside, she should call the *Astra* and have Erol, her Second, round up the crew and get the ship prepped for launch. Erol would also need to bribe the spaceport customs. Sirius shouldn't hear any details about this expedition, not if she wanted to pilot for them again soon.

Buying personal weapons was something she would take care of herself. A ship the size of the *Astra* usually didn't carry much, nothing beyond a small pulsar cannon or two, and lazers for the captain and crew. Corp subcontractors and smugglers depended on stealth and bribery to hide any contraband that they carried, not the firepower they could never carry enough of. Before this job TiCara thought it was a badge of honor that she hadn't needed any extra weapons.

But this trip wasn't going to be like her other jobs. Not the way that Vahn looked when he made it clear that he didn't want anyone to know about it. Someone, maybe multiple someones, must be very interested in him and where he might be going.

Not that her crew needed to know that, at least not yet. Just in case. She grimaced at the direction her thoughts were taking. Distrusting her own crew wasn't part of any job she thought she'd sign up for: this got more complicated every angle she checked. They were a good crew, loyal to her, but anyone might talk if the incent was right. Even her. She wrinkled her nose in distaste at that thought, even as she acknowledged its truth.

But she was going to need to tell them something about their passengers and their destination, enough to satisfy their curiosity and help them prepare. Just not tru tell until they were out of port comm range. *And then I can tell them that we're on a hunt for a 'stroid that doesn't exist. So very starshine. No mutiny risk there.* She managed not to roll her eyes.

And what happened once they got back? If it turned out that Electra really did exist, maybe Vahn's cred might have to be good enough to keep them silent for a while then, too. She suspected that the less any corp, let along his, knew about this trip, the better. As she considered that, she had to wonder how the asteroid, if it existed, kept its location secret? Did it have an asynchronous orbit around…whatever it orbited around? Did they memory wipe anyone who left?

TiCara's medusas coiled around her head, their movements erratic and nervous, reflecting her mood. She caught a glimpse of herself in the station's reflective metal walls and made a face. The medusa hard wiring into her brain had its downsides. What was the point of controlling her face and body if her implants gave her feelings away?

She strained to take in a deep, relaxing breath and quiet her mind until they went limp. A wary glance around suggested that no one else seemed to be paying attention to her, at least not enough to be troubling. But then, it was hard to tell for certain: groundies and spacers, the ones who weren't wired, often tried to ignore medusa pilots as much as they could. TiCara forced herself not to look for Eyes or up at the station cameras that she could see.

There was an unoccupied comm booth down the corridor and she strode over to it. Her fingers lingered on the entry pad before keying in the standard open code for Kyrin while she took a few seconds to run through scenarios in her head. Vahn would have to be a corp rep going to black market trade negotiations and Sherin his assistant. The bondarmin could continue to serve as a bodyguard. Or a nurse, or both, given that many bondarmini filled a range of functions. That was a story that would make sense to her crew, one that would encourage them to hold their tongues.

She sealed herself into the booth, clouding the walls so that no one could see her inside. Then she plugged her medusas into the console, letting the initial rush of the connection wash over her. Her implants would mix her brainwaves with internal signals, just as they did when she was piloting. It would make it harder for anyone to hack the call if someone was paying that much attention. Safer than using her hand-held to talk to the *Astra,* anyway.

She sent a brief message, letting Erol know that they had a client, a rep and his staff, who'd be riding with them on a confidential mission to one of the outer systems. She added a list of supplies that they would need, including the new ones that she'd just remembered. He and the crew would take care of the rest from there, creating passenger quarters from her cabin and the two cabins that had been converted to extra storage as well as prepping whatever else the ship needed.

She clicked off the connection, contemplating how much she had come to rely on her Second. It had been worth everything she'd spent to recruit him from one of her rivals. And he'd been happy to give up being a junior navigation officer on a corp ship to become Second on the *Astra* for a bigger share of the take and more independence. But much as she trusted him, she still wouldn't give him tru tell about Vahn and Electra, not yet. It wasn't just Vahn's request either, there was more, more than she was willing to admit to herself. She just wasn't sure what that something more was, not yet. She rubbed the side of her nose and frowned, trying to pinpoint what was bothering her.

That uneasiness was enough to make her hesitate before unplugging from the comm board for an instant longer than necessary, as she tried to center herself. If she didn't do something about the chaos in her head soon, she wouldn't be good for anything. TiCara sank down into the booth's cushioned chair and let her medusas warm up until she could feel her shoulders relax a little as she let her mind wander through some centering and breathing exercises.

As she released some of the tension, she became aware of other feelings. The medusa sockets had a sensuous quality that vibrated up the medusa coils into her skin. It was like sliding into a new lover, open and waiting for her, then feeling that lovely body closing snugly around her once she was inside. She thought of Sherin, naked and vulnerable, and her legs quivered as she started to get damp. She smiled as she caressed her thigh through her suit.

There was no time for this, none at all, if she was to seek out information and finish all that needed to be done before they left. But the more she thought about Sherin, the more she wanted that fulfillment, or something like it. Wanted it now. The fastenings on the crotch of her suit felt like they gave way and opened with just a thought.

Her hand slid inside her suit, slipping between her thighs. Her breath caught in her throat and she ground her crotch against the seat as her medusas switched modes, sending a sudden hot spike through her. She conjured Sherin's body in her imagination, silky skin pressed against hers. She used her tongue, her hands, her medusas on the beautiful rep, coaxing, teasing, caressing. The fantasy sent a white-hot spark through her, lighting her flesh on fire until she writhed, rubbing herself against the seam of her uniform.

Then she imagined Sherin flipping her over, burying her face between her legs. Sweat trickled down her scalp, ran under her jacket collar as the sensations built. Her fingertips sank deeper into the molten wetness between her legs. When she couldn't control herself anymore, she arched her back, locked her legs and came with a soft shout.

Catching her breath seemed to take forever after she pulled her medusas free. She gasped against the recycled stale air of the sealed booth until her heartbeat slowed. Only then did she remember to turn on the booth's air circulation function.

TiCara laughed at herself, the sound filling the little soundproof booth. Sex might be even better than she imagined if only she could convince Sherin to give in to her desires. And if anyone could do that, it was TiCara, Pilot-Captain of the *Astra*. She waggled her nonexistent eyebrows at her reflection in the booth's wall and studied her reflection for a moment. Her features suggested a mix of Old Earth races, like most spacers: straight nose, full lips, sharp cheekbones, light brown skin, narrow blue eyes. She wondered what Sherin saw when she looked at her. Her last couple of lovers told her that she was breathtaking, handsome even, like an old time vidstar.

Ridiculous flattery, of course, but if she could get Vahn's rep to see some of what they saw, she might enjoy Sherin's charms even sooner. That idea made her laugh again, this time a bit more drily. Sherin had been resisting her advances since they'd met and doing it more successfully than anyone else ever had. TiCara admired that about her, even though it left her hot and temporarily frustrated.

But once she was on the ship, fully exposed to TiCara's seductive wiles, well, then things might be different. *Would be different.* TiCara shook her head slightly, letting her medusas coil and wriggle free of the board, and her suit absorb her excess body fluid before she uncoiled herself from the booth seat. It was time to focus on more practical considerations. She checked the planetary time. The rep was something special, but if she didn't get her prep work done, there was no way to ensure that the journey would be calm enough to let her find out. She straightened out her uniform and wiped the sweat from her face.

Her thoughts switched to Electra and Vahn and what she needed next. But she kept getting distracted by everything she didn't know. What if the rock didn't exist? Or wasn't where Vahn thought it was? They could be drifting for lifetimes looking for a legend.

There was one obvious source to turn to, always provided that she wanted to ask. Elia had been flying ships when TiCara was still hiding in the port walls scavenging for her next meal. She herself had told TiCara that she had flown through most of known space. If anyone knew anything about the asteroid, it would be her.

But even with her former lover's boast ringing in her ears, TiCara hesitated. She hadn't seen her old teacher in more than a full revolution, going by Kyrin's annual calendar. It might be hard to find her, even harder getting good tell from her: Elia's ability to distinguish between legend, rumor and reality, had been blurring the last time they spoke.

And watching Elia get older reminded TiCara that she might face the same thing some day, if she lived long enough for Eternayouth to stop working for her. Elia had voluntarily stopped using the drug once she stopped teaching pilots, choosing to age naturally for reasons that TiCara couldn't understand. She shuddered just thinking about it; it would be Eternayouth for her until the corp techs figured out how to extend the functionality of medusas without it. Then and only then would she give it up.

Retirement without Eternayouth meant no more medusas, at least not as she was able to use them now. They stayed implanted and they still moved, useful as oddly placed fingers, but without their full sensory range. You needed Eternayouth for that. As for plugging into a ship and flying it the way she did now, forget it. She'd have to give all that up, giving up control to the onboard computer and nav system.

Thinking about that made her stomach hurt. Instinctively, she reached up and twisted her fingers between her implants, reassuring herself that they were still there.

She remembered the last time she'd seen Elia, remembered how the former pilot's hands lingered on her implants. She'd seen the longing looks, the barely muted desire for what the pilot had given up. In the end, it had been that sadness, even more than her retreats into fantasy and old boasts, that had driven TiCara away.

So what would Elia be doing now? Sitting around the bars telling old stories? She must have found some way to fill her time; the question was, what? And if TiCara found her, could she trust her enough to ask for tru tell about Electra? Elia might even be working for a corp again, for all TiCara knew. Cred was cred, after all, and even for a medusa pilot, corp retirement was no windfall.

She tried to imagine her former teacher working for the corps as anything other than a medusa pilot. The old Elia wouldn't have done it, had even been looking forward to leaving the corps behind. But now, who knew? "Old pilots turned teachers, smugglers or Ears," as the spacer saying went. At least if you survived long enough to be an old pilot. What else was there, once you stopped flying and Eternayouth stopped working or got left in your past?

Many groundies didn't want to work with medusa pilots. The sight of an old corp fighter pilot reminded them of all they'd lost in the Wars, or so many of them said. Retired pilots even hid their implants sometimes and pretended to be something else, out of necessity. TiCara grimaced. Stupid groundies and their stupid biases and spacegas stories. She shied away from thinking too hard about the shadow trades, the smuggling, the illegal VR vids, and other things former medusa pilots did to survive. There were too many possibilities. Elia could be involved in any or all of them by now.

Maybe there was another way, someone else she could talk to. Someone she had less history with. She opened her handheld and ran through her lists of contacts, but no one seemed like a better choice than her former mentor. Several were worse. TiCara swore quietly. Being indecisive was something new for her, and she didn't like it. Instinct and impulse, leavened with just a bit of forethought, had gotten her this far. Those traits would be enough for this job, too.

There were some possible advantages to seeking out Elia. A memory of writhing under Elia's attentions in the VR mods made her bite her lower lip as her skin flushed with heat. Even though she'd never been able to persuade her old lover to try sex outside virtual reality, they'd had a lot of fun together. She found herself reconsidering. Maybe she didn't want to ask anyone else, after all, even if there was no time for any fun. It might be good to see her former mentor again.

She made a face at her reflection and shoved all her doubts into the back of her brain. Enough of this. She would know what to do when she found Elia. Her instincts would tell her if the risks were worth sharing any tell about this mission. And, given how much time she'd already wasted, there would be no time to rekindle old feelings, nebula glowing or deep space dim.

TiCara got up with a sigh, clicked the booth door open and strode away from it, letting it seal behind her. She headed for the tubes that left the port to follow the old mining tunnels deeper into Kyrin, into Downside. That was the name the spacers gave their colony under Kyrin's surface. Vizhistory on the Nets said Downside was the spacer colony because Upside was too many creds and the tunnels were the best spacers could afford. But TiCara knew that wasn't all of it. She knew how badly spacers needed to get away from the endless sky for a while. Upside had the port and the big domes and the view, the never-never of the starfields. Downside had limits, boundaries, an actual ceiling.

TiCara craved those things as much as any spacer. The dark walls closed in around her as the gravitube dropped down two levels and she could feel her shoulders release tension she hadn't know they were still holding. She sighed with relief. This felt familiar, like the port on the planet she'd grown up on, before home became the *Astra* and the ports she regularly visited, like Kyrin.

When the tube door slid open, a dimly lit corridor stretched before her, the walkways that made up most of its floor moving slowly and inexorably along under the feet or other appendages of a dozen ship's crews and station personnel. The corridor was really only dark in comparison to the glow that lit Upside, but that was enough to ease the transition.

The walls around her sparkled from the reflection of the tubelights on the residue of the carcite and other minerals left over from Kyrin's past as a mining colony, as were the shafts themselves. The tunnels went almost everywhere on the planet, so much so that sometimes she wondered how Upside didn't collapse. Kyrin was an engineering marvel, fully deserving of its reputation for corporate ingenuity.

She took a deep breath, inhaling the scent of alien life that rose from the plants from twenty worlds growing in baskets and containers on the walls and ceilings, thriving under the artificial lights at the same time that they cleaned the air. Old Earth humanoids were the dominant life form on Kyrin so the port and its colonies catered to them, something she was grateful for. Wearing a full suit and tank planetside was no fun at all.

TiCara grinned a little to herself as she stepped out onto the walkway that led to the bars and hostels. This hadn't always felt like home. She remembered how different it had been when she first landed on Kyrin, how nervous she'd been, how alien it was. There had been no clients back then, no ship of her own. Even her medusas had been new.

One implant curved around her ear, its sensors reading her skin temperature and sending a soothing heat into the exposed skin of her neck. Now, she couldn't imagine living without them. Not after what she'd gone through to get them and all she'd learned to use them for. Her smile widened for an instant before it disappeared, before anyone else could see it and respond.

The walkways were crowded this time in the diurnal cycle but then Kyrin was a big enough port that they were never really deserted. She moved along purposefully, careful to glance sidelong at passersby without making full eye contact. The meeting of eyes was an invitation to sex, violence, a dozen other things, depending on how they felt about medusa pilots or any number of other factors. She knew better than to be drawn to that kind of distraction, not when she had an errand like the one she had set herself.

Ahead of her, she noticed a pair of Ears with a pack of Eyes scuttling at their heels. They were lounging on the platform at the intersection of two walkways, the man tall and thin, his head shaved and tattooed, the woman his twin, in all but the ink and the height. They looked her way and the woman said something too quiet to hear at that distance.

A chill went down her spine under her pilot's suit and her medusas stiffened, lying dormant now, like hair on the back of her neck. Did one of them recognize her? Her stomach turned at the memory of her time of "service" in the Ear dormitory on Lyriel. Two full revolutions around the Andromeda system's sun doing anything and everything that the Ears wanted to earn enough creds to enroll in pilot training. Old scars, inside and out, ached and stung as she tried to push the memories aside.

Part of her knew that those memories might be clouding her judgment now, making her see a threat when there was none. But noticing

Ears was second nature to her. She'd taught herself to identify and avoid them, even when they tried to conceal what they were. There was something in the way they carried themselves, the way they moved, like hunting cats, that made them stand out among regular spacers and other humans in the port cities.

These two weren't attempting to hide anything as far as she could see. But the Ears were always, without exception, trouble. They were assassins and thieves, as well as corp spies. Anything the megacorporations could afford, they did. And these two were definitely looking at her, watching her. Every instinct that helped keep her alive told her that she'd been noticed.

The woman got on the walkway behind TiCara after she passed them. She could follow TiCara easily from there and the pilot knew it. But why would they be interested in her at all? She was small fry, by corp standards. Vahn. It had to be about Vahn. Didn't it? Panic raced through her and she glanced around, looking for a hiding place from force of habit.

Word of today's meeting must have spread, but how? Belatedly, she remembered the Eyes in the corridor on the way to Vahn's office and wondered which corp was taking such an interest in his doings.

Then she wondered what she was going to do to rid herself of the unwelcome attention.

She clamped down on her panic, looking deliberately toward the first walkway exit as if it was the direction she always intended to take. As if she hadn't noticed that she had company. But it was very hard not to dart away from the main corridors and disappear. Hiding was something she knew how to do, even now; there were closed maintenance corridors that hadn't been used in revolutions, and she had ancient maps of most of them uploaded into her comm. Just in case.

But her flight would have told the Ears that they were on the right track. If they were following her so openly, maybe they weren't sure.

Maybe they weren't even following her. But if they were, right now, she was a hunch. If she ran, she was a certainty.

She took in a shaky breath. This might still be all right, at least if she didn't do something stupid. They wouldn't try to kill her, not here, not now. Too many Eyes and security, too many variables. Besides, while her death might prevent Vahn from taking her ship, he could find another easily. As for any other "services," her contracted time was ended. Anything past that was frowned up by corps agreement. They had other ways to control those who were in their debt.

So she just needed to continue doing exactly what she was doing, looking for a drink and old acquaintances. If she found Elia, she'd be careful not to give anything away, not where they could overhear anything. Then, all the Ears would learn by following her was that she liked to drink in spacer bars and had a few friends there, nothing more.

She let the thought of their frustration ease her fears as she slipped off the walkway and walked slowly into one of the bar corridors. The last time she'd seen Elia, it had been in one of these bars. The former pilot might still frequent it. She used to like her routine.

Bar signs gleamed above doorways as she looked around, remembering the last time that she'd been here. She drifted into one bar, then another, studying faces as if she was searching for friends or crewmates. When she moved back into the corridor, she noted that the Ear was still trailing her, and she nearly bolted. This had gone on too long; they were too interested in her. Now where could she go that the other wouldn't follow her?

She kept walking, looking at the signs until she saw one that she remembered: The Haven. It was the biggest and oldest of the spacer bars. And it had been one of Elia's early favorites, back when they first met.

She hesitated for a moment, considering what to do next: ditch her tail or continue inside to look for Elia. If she found her, they'd had their own simple code back when they were together. A few finger gestures and a word or two, just enough to set up a different meeting spot or time if neither wanted others to know what they planned. If she was here, TiCara hoped she would remember.

TiCara walked into The Haven and tried to calm her panic, to focus on what she needed and what Elia would ask in exchange for intel. Tru tell wouldn't be free, certainly not tru tell about a possible secret asteroid base for nano labs or whatever Electra's secret was said to be at the moment. She knew better than that. If their positions had been reversed, TiCara knew that she would have asked for whatever she wanted that the other pilot could provide.

Thinking about the price Elia normally enjoyed for tell made her breathe a tiny bit faster in something like anticipation. She wasn't sated, not yet and she let herself daydream, knowing how unlikely it was. It would be far better than just her and her medusas in a cold, sterile comm booth, if she could make time to enjoy it. Her implants caught her mood and caressed her neck, their little glowing ends programmed to know which nerve endings to touch to enhance sensation.

It was almost enough to make her forget the Ear at her heels. Almost. But she knew better. The space between her shoulders tightened until it felt as if her muscles were target-shaped, fear replacing desire in rapid succession.

The bar looked much the same as she remembered: a long dark tube of a room with tables, various things to sit on and tanks. Drinks and food circled around on the conveyor system that went from the bar to the tables and the booths. The lights were dim, the sounds muted. Even the patrons spoke quietly among themselves, as if afraid to disturb the calm of the place. Just the way her old mentor liked it.

TiCara stepped up to the order console and typed in the number of her favorite drink. She perched on a seat while the robot behind the bar mixed it, then set it on the conveyor belt to send it down to her. She picked it up and held it up to admire its rich ruby glow in the soft light. Debaran Kir was a glorious thing, if the vintage was right.

She turned away from the bar, sipping carefully and savoring the slight alcoholic tang of the drink as she looked around the room. There were a few familiar faces, human and alien, but no one that she needed to go out of her way to acknowledge beyond a head tilt and a small smile. Being wired set her apart, leaving her with more colleagues than friends. She liked it that way, most of the time.

She walked around the bar, checking the darker corners and booths. And there was Elia, just as TiCara hoped. Her stomach twisted a little in a nervous flutter when she saw the other woman. Elia's hair had begun to grow back around her medusas, though the pilot still kept it very short. It shone silver blonde above her wide-cheeked face and gray-blue eyes. There was a slight network of wrinkles around those eyes, visible even in The Haven's dim lights, but otherwise she looked much as she had the last time TiCara had seen her.

Her former mentor was sitting in a booth at the far end of the bar, beyond the crowd at the entrance and as far away from the methane tanks as she could get. Some things hadn't changed: Elia never could abide a whiff of methane.

But the pilot wasn't alone. TiCara looked at Elia's companion and froze, heart leaping into her throat. Then she turned away, trying to decide what to do next, hoping that they hadn't seen her. What was Elia doing with the other Ear from the walkway? He wasn't just any Ear either. TiCara was close enough to recognize the pattern of his skull tattoos. She shivered uncontrollably.

Her brain flooded with memories, all bad. Zig had been her most enthusiastic tormentor at the Ear dormitory, delighting in inventing imaginary infractions in order to inflict as much pain as he could. He had done everything in his power to extend her contract, then to force her break it, which would have placed her completely in his power. She felt like the girl she had been then: vulnerable, scared, hurt. Medusaless. Her hand dropped to the personal lazer in her belt and her fingers clutched the handle spasmodically.

But now she was attracting unwanted attention. The securbot at the door began to roll toward her, its warning light beginning to flash. She dropped her hand from her weapon and held her hands out to show that they were empty. Then she turned and set her drink down on the bar, fingers trembling just a little, before she regained control.

She could walk away as if she hadn't seen Elia. But then, the other Ear was still outside somewhere, waiting for her. And Zig had seen her. She realized that now, could see his head turn and feel his sidelong glance like a blow to her face. He was challenging her, waiting to see what she'd do next. She could almost feel him mocking her.

She dug her fingers into the plasticene of the bar to ground herself, slow her pulse, calm her panic. Both Ears would just follow her if she fled. She might be able to hide in the station walls, but what about her ship, her crew, her life? Her medusas dropped to her neck, sending out short bursts of soothing vibrations.

She grimaced at her drink, slowly gaining control over her initial panic. Her medusas drew back from her skin, hovering around her head, as her mood shifted from terrified to wary to white-hot furious. Her hand hovered once more near her belt as she imagined frying Zig where he sat. But there were too many witnesses and exile from Kyrin and being hunted by the Ears, as well as his current employer, was too high a price to pay for the thrill of killing him.

Besides, running wasn't going to get her anything she wanted. Instead, TiCara forced herself to turn and walk over to the table as if it made no difference to her that Elia was sitting with an Ear, any Ear. She pursed her lips at Elia in an all purpose greeting and hint of a promise of more to come. Elia smiled back, then jerked her head toward the Ear as TiCara sat down next to her. "'Lo, TiCara. Long time. Know Zig?"

Zig touched a hand to his forehead by way of acknowledgment. Something about the gesture conveyed both contempt and indifference. But he gave no indication that he recognized her and rose with a gesture that suggested she could take his seat.

TiCara's eyes narrowed and her grin widened, as if she couldn't sense the undercurrents in his reaction. Her brain spun. What was his game? And was it worth anything to her to play along?

Zig turned away from TiCara as if she was of no further interest to him. He stared at Elia until she dropped her gaze to the table before he spoke, "Get me what I want, pilot. And I'll get you what you want." Then he walked out of The Haven without looking at either of them again.

Chapter 3

TiCara watched Zig's black-clad form leave the bar before switching her seat to put the table between herself and Elia. She glanced around to make sure there was no one close enough to hear her before she turned back to Elia. "What was that? You working for the corps again? Or just the Ears?" Her lip curled when she said it, almost as if she was about to smile, like her words were something approaching a joke, but her hand beneath the table twitched, looking for a weapon.

Not that she would use it on her old lover, old friend and former teacher. Probably not. Unless she stood between her and Zig if the time finally came that she could kill him without repercussions. One of her medusas stung the delicate skin behind her ear and she jumped, pulled out of her fantasies. Elia was silently watching her across the table, still the same Elia, at least outwardly.

Only TiCara had changed. Or, at least, how she thought of their relationship and what they could be to each other had shifted. Sex, VR or otherwise, was no longer an option for trade. Not if Elia might be working with or for Zig. An ice cold wave caressed her skin, cooling any residual lust that lingered from her fantasies and she wondered for an instant if it was her imagination or her implants.

She leaned back, gently drumming her fingers on the table edge as if she was still waiting for Elia's answer. As if it would make a difference in how this tell would go. She leaned forward and tapped the table to pull up the virtual drink menu, selecting something without the Kyr's kick but with a meta booster. She would need to be alert for this.

She wondered if there was any way to ask Elia for tells on Electra without revealing her plans now. Her head spun, picking up, and then dropping ideas. Betrayal ached through to her bones, along with the fear that the Elia she knew might be gone forever. Even with the growing distance between them, she hadn't been ready for that, not really.

Once the corporations had you, they never let you go. It had been something that Elia used to tell her, back when she was in training. She'd been stupid to forget that lesson, even temporarily. Perhaps Elia had even forgotten it herself. TiCara's mood darkened as the silence stretched between them and she scowled, lost in her past. A spasm ran up her cheek at the memories and she covered it with her hand to hide it. This was more, much more, than she wanted to think about right now.

A new suspicion made her wonders if Zig had something on Elia or if she just wanted something from him. Shouting from another table broke through her thoughts and she shifted her shoulders, dragged a breath in, then slowly out. Elia was still watching her when she emerged from her thoughts, the silence still spreading over and between them like a blanket. The other woman's lips smiled, but her eyes were wary. Seen up close, her cheeks looked sunken and she looked like she might have been ill.

TiCara felt pity for her old lover edging out her anxiety and distrust. She hunted for the right words to say, the right gesture that would mend the breech. They could still be friends, couldn't they?

Suddenly, Elia grinned. "Missed you, TiCara. Like a blackhole in this port when you left. Nothing starshine for me, not even the carcite deposits." Her grin widened; carcite had been Kyrin's main export until the deposits ran out. The fragments still gleamed in the tunnel walls, a reminder of what had been. The old spacer joke made TiCara smile, despite her whirling emotions.

Suddenly Elia stood up, her body straight and elegant despite how ill she had appeared an instant before, and leaned over the table. She cupped TiCara's face in her hands and kissed her hard. The kiss startled TiCara and her lips parted under Elia's, more from habit than desire.

Elia's medusas fell forward and twined themselves in among hers in a movement that felt almost deliberate. But that was impossible. Elia no longer had that much control over her medusas, not without Eternayouth.

A shudder ran through TiCara. It shouldn't be this easy, this fast. There should be negotiation or tell, give and take. She shivered as a wave of memories of their time together washed over her, then as suddenly ebbed.

The flash of remembered passion coursed through her and then her body was her own again. She pulled her face from Elia's hands and backed out of reach. This didn't make sense, none of it did. Elia had never been enthusiastic about kissing her in meatspace when they had been together. She always hesitated, then withdrew rapidly afterward. This passionate embrace had already lasted longed than any they had had before, outside the mods. The realization was enough to make TiCara rein in any remaining eagerness.

It wasn't too late. She could still make an excuse and leave, even put credits into the bar for Elia's next drink, say she'd be back later. Or she could stay and let Elia think she was just here to see her again, gather some spacer tell before she had to leave.

Elia gestured upward with an odd twist of her fingers. It was a gesture from their old code. But TiCara didn't respond, not at first. They hadn't had a code for "Tell me if you're betraying me first." Perhaps they should have. Elia's fingers moved in another gesture, this one more impatient, demanding, insistent. She quirked a pale eyebrow, as if baffled by TiCara's reluctance.

"An Ear, Elia? Stop trying to distract me. Tell me what he wanted." TiCara leaned back against the booth. Her eyes narrowed as she studied Elia, moving beyond pity and lust. The other woman looked more than tired, more than lonely. Elia's gaze was almost hungry, feverish more than lustful. One of her hands trembled until she sat back down and hid it under the table.

"You forget so fast, Ti? You and me together, we were good. I want you to remember that." Elia's voice was a croon, a siren's call, beckoning TiCara closer. They stared at each other, and TiCara, despite everything, felt a familiar ache between her legs. But she tilted her head in the Systems standard gesture of refusal, crossed her arms across her breasts and waited in silence.

Elia waited her out for a long couple of breaths before she tossed her hands up in the air like she was surrendering. "Ears got no family, no friends, once they're Ears, Ti? Known Zig a long time, before you even, from back when he was just out of the crèche. He comes to me, asks nothing. Just tell between friends." She looked at TiCara earnestly, the expression sitting oddly on her features, like a mask.

"Ears always want something, Elia. You had no Ear friends when I knew you. Why now?"

"I knew you were afraid of them. Didn't tell you." Elia shrugged apologetically. "You didn't signal you'd be planetside now. Didn't expect to see you here," She paused, her eyes narrowing in suspicion. "What do you want, Ti?" Her tone got more formal, more corps standard, drifting away from the clipped syllables of spacer talk. TiCara wondered if she even realized it, if this was the way that she spoke to her Ear "friends."

TiCara wavered, trying to decide whether or not to leave before this went any further. Could she trust any tell that she got from the other woman? And if not, why was she still here? But if she left now, it would look like she was angry or jealous. Pilot-Captain TiCara could not afford to be either of those things, even if they were true.

Instead, she had to give Elia some tell she'd believe, in case there was a next time, a next meeting. "Got a job, El. Wondering about the nav through a couple of systems, what spacer tell was. Knew you'd tru tell me, not like the Nets." She twisted her lips up into what she hoped looked like a real smile and leaned forward, resting her elbows on the table.

"That it? For tru?" Elia glanced down at TiCara's breasts, then slowly back up, letting her eyes do her talking for her. She smiled suddenly and TiCara wondered, just a little, about the warmth in her expression. Elia had always kept her emotions locked up, buried. The older pilot had been too distant, too reserved for TiCara, and TiCara had been too difficult for her to control and they both knew it. It pulled them apart again and again. So why was Elia looking at her now like she'd forgotten all of that? Like she didn't remember how they'd parted the last time with hot words and hotter tempers?

She took a deep breath to steady her nerves. Give her a good ship and a clean, clear run any cycle. Games within games had never been something she liked. For a moment, she wished that things were the way she'd hoped they would be, that she had never seen Elia talking to an Ear, any Ear. That she hadn't known that Elia was lying to her now. That they could enjoy each other for old time's sake, if nothing more.

She missed Elia as she was, missed their simpler times together even if it had become just VR-fueled lust. Elia had been a companion, someone she thought she could trust and confide in under the right circumstances. Now, she matched Elia false smile for smile. "Leaving in a few machrons, love. Not this time." She pitched her voice downward and tried to sound regretful. It wasn't very difficult.

TiCara shifted back in her chair and reached for the console to buy Elia another drink. The other woman caught it off the conveyor when it came by and nodded as TiCara continued speaking, as if nothing had happened between them. "Sirius wants to send *Astra* to some 'stroids in the Gathwaite Belt, including some I can't find on the charts. Then over to the Aeon system to with a tech shipment. Heard any tell on those systems, El?" TiCara made her tone casual, as if she was just running down rumors.

Elia looked startled, leaving TiCara to wonder which story she was reacting to. Vahn hadn't given her the asteroid's coordinates yet, so she had picked the two systems that most spacer stories claimed held Electra. Did Elia's reaction mean that she'd guessed correctly? She couldn't read the other woman's face, not for certain, so she watched her medusas instead.

The implants retained some residual nerve connections even without Eternayouth to keep them at peak functionality. Now they coiled and swirled around Elia's neck, their movements random and slow. TiCara wondered if they reflected what was going on in Elia's head. Or if she was just projecting her own sense of wrongness onto their meaningless motions.

Elia tapped her fingers on the table. "You with me, Ti? Gathwaite System still has pirates. Asteroids are their main bases.

Ask for more creds if you're going there, Ti and run if you see any ships you don't know."

TiCara wondered if Vahn would pay more if she asked for it. But even if he did, his generosity wouldn't be enough to replace her ship or her life. Pirates were trouble. The *Astra* had outrun them before, just not with corps passengers on board, especially not one so high-placed. And that had been luck as much as skill. She found herself hoping that they were going to the Aeon System instead. Elia only gave tell about navigational anomalies there.

She made her face still and calm as she listened. The former pilot mentioned some ordinary nav dangers like odd meteorite formations before she got to the information that TiCara was hoping to hear. She began sharing tell about the asteroid Electra, without any prompting. It was clear that Electra 12 wasn't just a myth, at least not to Elia.

But Elia didn't seem to know much more than Vahn had already told TiCara. A few more details here and there about the asteroid's rumored ownership and history, some of which might prove useful. She added a couple of spacer tales about the nonhuman life forms that supposedly inhabited the place and TiCara let them all wash over her, dismissing them as unlikely. Then she moved on to the more mundane tales.

But there was one story about the asteroid's miraculous healing that stood out amongst the others. Elia mentioned a starship pilot who'd come to Electra and was healed of his/her/zir medusas on the asteroid. Just the idea made TiCara feel sick. Severe damage to medusas could kill a wired pilot: wiring was for life, or so she'd always been told. Besides, how could anyone stand to live without them, once they adapted to them?

She was shivering as she asked, "How could ze lose zir medusas and not die? Sounds like a VR story, Elia." *And what if it happens to me?* The thought overrode all her senses in a small wave of panic. She clenched her hands into fists in her lap where Elia couldn't see them, willing them to be still.

Elia shrugged. "Once wired, always wired, far as I know, Ti. But it's what's said."

TiCara inhaled sharply, then let it out with a sigh. She was over-reacting. It was just a story, nothing more. It had to be. Besides, if they found the asteroid at all, she'd be safe on the *Astra,* waiting for Vahn. She wasn't planning on leaving the ship, not if that might be what was waiting for her.

It was time to focus on safer topics, then be on her way. But she must have given Elia a clue that something was still bothering her because Elia brought up Zig again. "I know how you feel about the Ears," Elia said, her voice soft. "But they're not all like the ones you knew. Zig pays me in cred for gossip sometimes. Or we drink and talk about nothing. Not querying about you, TiCara. Just talk about ports and ships."

TiCara looked away and shut Elia out in an attempt to slow her heart's pounding race. Trying not to scream her thoughts out loud. Trying to concentrate on all that Elia wasn't saying. Ports and ships. *Ports like this one. Ships. Like the Astra.* He heart sped up, her breathing with it. She was going to break soon, if she didn't leave. She knew the signs now.

This had to stop: she had to regain control of her mind. With a ferocious effort, she used a meditation technique that she had learned on Aliandra, after she left the Ears. She concentrated only on her breathing, on the rhythm of her fingers on her knee under the table, until the urge to scream or vent her terror and rage slowly dissipated.

Elia was silent and motionless as TiCara got herself under control again, pushing away the despair that she still felt like this. Two Earth standard years as a bond slave to Ears to earn her medusas and her memories could still not be drowned in the past or in the bars or the

VR mods, not even seven revolutions later. She hated the way her pulse still raced when she looked back at Elia.

But Elia's expression was kindly and patient, just like it used to be when TiCara had attacks like this back when they'd been together. Then they had been more frequent, more severe. TiCara wished she still believed in Elia, but the time for that was passing. She struggled to find words, torn between competing impulses.

Finally, TiCara touched her hand to her heart to indicate that she trusted the other pilot. Elia did the same and they smiled at each other. And if TiCara's smile was less tru than it had been once, Elia gave no sign of noticing.

TiCara got up and pulled Elia to her feet. She gave Elia a light kiss on the lips. It felt like the right way to say farewell to what they had been to each other. Elia held her close a moment longer than she expected and whispered something that TiCara didn't quite hear. It sounded like an old spacer blessing, one that a previous generation of pilots used for a compatriot headed for dangers unknown.

Then Elia startled her by breaking off their embrace and looking at her for a long moment, as if she was memorizing her face. Her hand rested on TiCara's cheek and her eyes were sad. Then she pulled away and walked out, disappearing from The Haven without looking back.

TiCara watched her go and wondered what she should be afraid of, what she needed protection against. The corps and the Ears, always. If they wanted Vahn dead, they could sabotage her ship or have her killed anywhere, Downside or Upside or off planet. The corporations had their own laws and they weren't written for pilots on the dark side of legit trade.

But that was nothing new and she couldn't have attracted that much notice already, could she? And Elia didn't know about Vahn or this run. Or she shouldn't have known. Unless she and Zig shared tell about ports and ships and he knew more than he should.

TiCara pinged the console to let the cleaning bot know that they were done with their drink containers. She could only guess at how it to connect Zig and Elia's behavior and her tales about Electra to create certainty about what the former pilot knew and when. If she had more time to dig into it...but then she wouldn't have been down at The Haven looking for intel the fast and easy way.

The way she felt now made her want to go back a few hours. Do it all over again, this time listening to her fears and handling them better. She'd given too much away, made herself too vulnerable, panicked like the child she had been. But now there was nothing she could do about it except continue with her contract and hope that no more trouble came for her.

Her fears kept her wary as she left The Haven and she moved on to the other bars, drifting aimlessly down corridors and walkways in hopes of losing any remaining interest from the Ears. She drank, even gambled briefly with other spacers, just another spacer in port on R&R.

Then she slipped into a comm booth to call Erol again and have a look around her. There were Ears all over the walkways now, everywhere she looked, but maybe they weren't looking for her. Maybe there weren't even that many of them, and her fears were simply running away with her, cloning an Ear for each walkway. At least she couldn't see Zig or his companion, so that was something.

Erol must have heard that fear in her voice when she commed him. His voice sounded stilted, distant. After a moment, she realized that he was trying to sound reassuring, not something he was particularly skilled at. TiCara forced her nerves to still, her voice into its normal register, her accent into spacer clip. "I was at the bars for tell, saw a one from before the wires. Blackhole memories. My head's still low grav, sorry. *Astra* ready?"

Erol's voice lost its forced patience. "Aye, Captain. Ship-shape on supplies and crew.

Ji-min and Vijay set up quarters for the passengers. Vijay got the new chow dispenser in. Need give some tell to port, slip some creds their way, and we go when you're back and they're aboard."

TiCara grinned as she acknowledged him and commed off. The tightness in her middle eased its grip and she messaged Sherin next. The rep's beautiful face danced before her on the vid screen as she told her that everything was ready for them and asked about dietary requirements. Erol probably had that covered too, but she wanted Sherin to see her as thoughtful.

From Sherin's expression, it didn't seem wholly successful, but the rep sent her a food list before signing off abruptly. TiCara smiled at the comm screen anyway. Anything the rep was fighting this bad could be nova on this trip. For a single mad instant, she imagined indulging her fantasies again, but dismissed the thought with a sigh.

TiCara slipped out of the booth and into one of the spacer markets in a side tunnel. The markets were outside the rows of legal shops that faced each other across the station's main corridors and lacked their slick newness, housing themselves instead haphazardly in the old mine tunnels. She paused to let her eyes adjust to the dim light, her feet to the uneven floor.

From the corner of her eye, she could see Downsiders and spacers look her over. Most looked away when she stepped into the market, her stride settling into that predatory grace that had drawn her to medusa pilots in the first place. She glared boldly back at the few who didn't look away on their own and each one dropped their gaze.

She focused on looking for a certain stand among the many that crept their way down the tunnel. This was one of the oldest markets, a collection of makeshift stands and rusted metal pods that had been in place almost since Kyrin was founded, peddling refurbished and obsolete parts for old ships, exotic foods, used clothes and other items that the corps didn't care to sell themselves.

She found what she was looking for and stopped at a stand set off to one side of the main path. She greeted the woman seated behind the rusty table with a closed fist to her right shoulder, smuggler style. The peddler ran a thick hand over her tattooed scalp, the gesture eerily reminiscent of Zig for an instant, though her system and tribal tattoos were nothing that an Ear would adopt. She tilted her scarred face up to look TiCara over for a moment, then nodded an acknowledgement, but no recognition.

Wiring changed everything. TiCara thought about reminding her that they had met before, had hidden from station patrols together a time or two as children in the walls of a distant station, but decided against it. Instead, she spoke a phrase that made the woman stand, her eyes narrowing in appraisal. She gestured at TiCara, her fingers blindingly fast in a series of signals, and TiCara responded in kind. After they exchanged a final set of smuggler signs, the woman nodded. That was enough to gain TiCara entrance to a tent at the back of the stall.

There, credit exchanged hands and the pilot got two small lazers from a rack under a table. The seller even threw in a couple of old Earth-style throwing knives, all rolled up in a package that looked like a ship mechanic's kit. TiCara rested her hand on the package for a moment, trying to decide if she wanted to accept them. They weren't against planetary law, not exactly, but seeing TiCara with new weapons might excite curiosity if anyone saw them. And she'd had quite enough of that for the here and now.

But then, that might be as good a reason for extra weapons as any. She signed her thanks, then tucked a knife into the slots hidden inside the calf of one of her boots. The remaining one she hid in her blacksuit. Then, for the first time since she got her pilot's chip and her medusas, she pulled up her blacksuit's hood to cover them. The seller looked away, indicating that she had seen nothing, and TiCara left another cred chip on the table.

She left the market to walk further into Downside, looping back through its corridors and levels on a back way to the port. No point in making it easy for the Ears if they were still following her. The twitch between her shoulders said they hadn't given up on her yet.

CHAPTER 4

ELIA COULDN'T GET TiCARA OUT of her mind after she left The Haven. She tried hard to forget the look in TiCara's eyes when she saw Zig, tried instead to imagine how she would spend the shiny credits that Zig would pay her for the tell she was going to give him. Her last payment hadn't lasted as long as she thought it would. Nothing ever did.

She snorted softly. VR cost creds, room cost creds, nutrients cost creds. If she had still been taking Eternayouth, she'd have had to roll spacers at the bars to stay in creds. Or find a piloting gig and try to forget what it had been like to fly with medusas. DreamZone was cheaper and made her feel good, even better than Eternayouth had. Especially now that she had a regular supply. And Zig would make sure that she had her Dream, as long as she had what he wanted. She knew that.

Or she hoped that she knew that. Zig had also said he'd cut her off if she didn't have the tell he needed. He could be cruel and sometimes, she wondered why he was so willing to keep her supplied. But that always passed. Zig wouldn't cut her off. He was her friend and he knew that she needed to Dream. Besides, she had tell, nova tell, just the kind he craved.

She wondered if TiCara would ever understand that there were things more important than trust. The young pilot was such a crèche-infant in spite of all she'd seen and done. There were pleasures that you couldn't find at the end of a medusa, needs that had to be met that weren't all about physical sensation.

TiCara probably hadn't even realized how strongly she'd reacted when Electra 12 came up in the telling. She'd all but told Elia where she was going and what she feared most. Elia shook her head, letting her medusas swing idly for a moment. She could give Zig other tell, send him somewhere else. What if he wasn't telling her tru when he said he wouldn't hurt TiCara?

Elia grimaced at the thought. TiCara was no longer her mentee, no longer her lover, maybe not her friend any more. But she didn't want her to get hurt. Her feelings piled up like an asteroid belt collision, making her ache. She needed more Dream; that would help her hold them at bay, sort through them slowly and carefully until she knew which ones should be kept and which discarded.

Her hand rose in a habitual gesture and played with her medusas for a moment her body remember a shadow of what it was like to be alive and wired. More creds from Zig and his compadres meant more Dream. Maybe even a shot at Eternayouth. If she could manage *that*, well, everything would be starshine. She could have living medusas that responded to her thoughts again. Then she could go back to real piloting, leave this groundy life that she never wanted behind.

That thought made Elia smile as she entered her tiny sleep room off one of the habitation corridors. She flipped open her comm once the door sealed behind her. Zig's face loomed up, filling the tiny screen an instant later. "You got tell?"

"Tru tell: believe she's taking him to Electra 12, but no coordinates yet."

Zig's lips twisted in a snarl. "No location, no Dream. Told you that before."

Elia's hand trembled on the keypad. *He didn't mean it, he couldn't mean it, I need to Dream…*She inhaled sharply, "I've got another way, something she doesn't know about. Another inform."

"Use them, or it's no more Dreamyzone for you." Zig smiled suddenly and in a rare moment of full clarity, she realized how much he'd enjoy her withdrawal. He'd probably enjoy her overdose even more.

Elia shuddered as he clicked off. She closed her eyes, tried to imagine a life free of Zig. A life without DreamZone. Her body shuddered, each nerve ending sparking on its own in a mixture of dread and anticipation. She could be who TiCara thought she was. Or she could be…this.

There had to be a third way, something else she could do, but her head was too cloudy to think about it right now. A small pain shot its way up her arm and she put down the comm, tried to still the trembling in her hand. It would only get worse if she had to go through withdrawal, had to give up Dream completely. Options would have to wait. She needed to Dream so she could think and plan. Maybe Zig's corp would pay her for tell about what he was doing. Something told her that what he wanted to know was not authorized.

More pain, this one sharper, longer lasting. With a sob, she keyed a message into her comm, and after a moment spent staring at nothing, hit the send option.

CHAPTER 5

TiCARA GAVE A HUGE SIGH of relief once she reached the *Astra*. As she'd hoped, Erol was waiting for her, along with her crew, Ji-min and Vijay, and the ship seemed as ready to go as her Second had assured her that it would be. But anxiety was still driving her and she insisted on being shown all the preparations and supplies.

Normally, she had enough confidence in Erol that she didn't inspect the crew's work very thoroughly. He had proven himself already and her crewmembers were seasoned. But this trip was different, especially now: she had to be certain about everything. She told herself that it was the novelty of carrying rich passengers, the pressure to make everything perfect to impress Vahn.

For the next two machrons, she was all over the ship, inside and out. She checked the logs and verified the fuel stores when Ji-min was done with Engineering. Then she confirmed that the food, air and water supplies were adequate as Vijay prepped the ship's tiny greenbay with its plants and algae tanks.

Vijay was stoic about the additional supervision, answering her barrage of questions as he set the filters. In contrast, Ji-min was antsy, fidgeting, under her surveillance, even dropping an engine part that then had to be replaced from storage. TiCara met their anguished stare over the cracked casing and bit back an angry speech with a shaky breath.

This wasn't her; she was a better Captain than this, especially when she knew how badly Ji-min had been treated on their previous ship. She threw up her hands in a gesture of surrender and sucked in a deep breath. "It's all right, it's not you. Passengers, rich ones, got my nerves on the lazer's edge." *And then there's Zig*, though she left that part unspoken. She made an apologetic gesture over her heart, one that Ji-min would recognize from their home system.

Ji-min saluted and stood stiffly at military corp attention, something they hadn't done since their first couple of cycles on the *Astra*. Their face went completely blank and even their short-cropped black hair appeared to be standing rigidly on end, like medusas at attention. TiCara sighed and acknowledged the salute. "Permission to replace the part, Captain?" The engineer's voice was deep, their words clipped.

TiCara knew from experience that they could maintain this for machrons or more, once they settled into it. The corps trained their military engineers thoroughly, more than the medusa pilots themselves, and much of that training was harsh, even cruel. She took the hint and departed, with a muttered curse at her own carelessness in triggering her Engineer's anxiety, leaving Ji-min to find the replacement part in inventory.

As TiCara climbed the ladder to the tiny Bridge, Erol appeared at her heels. She climbed up and turned to face him as he finished climbing the ladder. "Don't you have preparations to make, Second?" The edge in her voice made her wince. She was doing this all wrong. Stupid job. Stupid Ears. Stupid Elia for thinking corp spies could ever be anyone's friends.

"Something you'd like to tell me about this trip, Captain? You've been on a comet tail since your first comm message." Erol towered over her, his dark-skinned and carefully shaved skull glowing a little under the Bridge lights. He seldom frowned, but this must be a special occasion, since TiCara realized he was glowering at her. And why shouldn't he? This job was his risk too, and she was second-guessing his responsibilities and alienating the crew.

That realization was enough to make her feel contrite, though not enough to give him tru tell. Not yet. After all, a shadow trade job was a shadow trade job, and as long as the creds were good, why wouldn't her Second trust her to set the terms as she saw fit? "These passengers, we need to impress them. Everything needs to be as close to diamond as we've got, no blackholes. Lot of creds at stake on this job. That's all." TiCara felt her medusas swarm around her head and neck like bees, not sure which impulse to react to and she forced them down and flat with an angry thought. "We do this, could be galaxy time after, maybe even leave the corp jobs behind. If we do right."

Erol gave her a cynical look. "One of them passengers female, Captain?" His eyelids drooped and his full lips twisted in an amused, knowing look as TiCara realized that she was more predictable than she realized. At least he had nothing to be jealous about. Ji-min and Vijay were casual lovers, but she had never been hot for any of her crew or they for her. Bad for discipline if things went sideways, a distraction if things were nova; that had been what Elia always said about ship-board romance.

And TiCara had always agreed with her. *But a passenger isn't the same as crew.* She nearly rolled her eyes at the direction her thoughts were taking. She *knew* better than this. Her hormones couldn't pilot this ship and she needed to remember that.

TiCara gave an elaborate shrug. "Maybe." Erol smirked and nodded, perhaps thinking of his own primary partner, Arnelle, back on Kraybourne, one of the planets on their usual run. "We got us a sekrit mission, Second, corp rep and all. Tru tell. Best go get the clean bots to sparkle the rooms up so the *Astra* looks diamond." She gave a self-mocking, dismissive wave to send him back down the ladder, and he went, laughing.

She watched him go, thinking about how hard it had been to trust him with her ship, her livelihood, at first. After all that she'd had sacrificed to pay for it, letting anyone else in had been very difficult. After all, everything she had gained could be so easily destroyed. One wrong step and she could lose it.

But, then, Erol had worked hard to win her trust as well; she had to give him credit for that. Saving her life on one of the outer systems two cycles back certainly hadn't hurt. Yet, she still wouldn't tell him who Vahn really was and where he was paying them to go. Not yet, not until they were out of port comm range. If the Ears could get to Elia, who knew how close they could get to others she trusted?

She grimaced at the direction her thoughts were moving and made an effort to shake them off. After this job, she wouldn't need to worry about Zig or losing the ship over debts. Vahn's credits would bring her more security, not less. She wouldn't accept any other outcome.

She stayed on the Bridge, watching the port through the windows, sensors and cameras while she did the ship's engine final prep. Not that there was much to see, apart from the usual activity of a big spaceport: spacer and groundy crews on the walkways, loaders working on new ships when they docked, all in a whirl of motion. It was almost impossible to pinpoint any single face in the shifting crowd.

She had decided to stop watching when she saw an Ear pass the *Astra*'s berth on a nearby walkway, bound for another dock. Her stomach twisted and she caught herself reaching for her lazer. With an effort, she drew her hand back. Maybe it was Zig, maybe it was some other Ear. Either way, she couldn't stop them from walking past her ship in spaceport dock. Much as she wanted to.

This particular Ear didn't look at or approach the *Astra* and she stopped shivering once he was out of sight. She started to go and look for him through one of the other outside cameras and caught herself… if she kept living in the past like this, she was going to be a bigger danger to herself and her crew than all the Ears in port. *Being alert was useful, being paranoid was a mind-killer,* one of her teachers on Aliandra said, more than once.

But her fears weren't hers to control, not today. What if it was more than a coincidence? What business did any Ear have down here? Maybe she should try and look Zig up, find out who he was working for now. Even an Ear had to have some kind of Net profile, unless ze was completely underground. But if Zig was tracking her or Vahn for one of the corps, searching for him on the Nets might attract unwanted attention. He probably had her search profiles flagged by now.

She swore softly. That ruled out the easiest way to find out background information on him, apart from asking a trusted source. She wasn't even tempted to message Elia now. Not if her old mentor claimed him as a "friend." The way Zig looked at Elia at The Haven was anything but friendly, but she hadn't seemed to notice. But perhaps that had been a performance for TiCara's benefit.

Her thoughts spun round like her head was in lowgrav until her whispered curses escalated fluently into several different spacer tongues. She made herself go outside for another quick inspection, checking the outside shell for trackers or anything else that might tell someone where they were going. This search was as fruitless as the last one, but it calmed her enough to finish the fuel checks and other necessary tasks.

When Sherin, Vahn and Sammo, Vahn's bondarmin, came on board a short time later, she was ready for them. Even if her stomach did a leisurely flip or two when she saw Sherin again. The *Astra* had a new pulse cannon and considerably more cushions than it had had on its last trip, as well as more different kinds of prepped cuisine than normal. Not to mention additional personal arms and a full medical treatment kit. She just hoped it would be enough.

Vahn got the best quarters on the ship, TiCara's own, as she pointed out as cheerfully as she could when she escorted him through the ship. He looked around at her room, relentless grays, blues and beiges of the ship's walls and ceiling broken by the splash of color from two brightly colored wall hangings. They had come from one of the Miyazaki system worlds, her first purchase to celebrate completing her corp indenture. Vahn's gaze rested appreciatively on them each in turn, giving her a small rush of pleasure.

She gave a quick glance around, verifying what she already knew. Her vids and clothes were all packed away and the hangings and the little dancing goddess on a high shelf were the only sign that anyone else normally bunked there. Nothing to tell anyone more about her than she wanted them to know.

He turned to her with a contented smile, "This is perfect, Captain. We will endeavor to stay out of your way." A single regal gesture to Sammo brought the latter across the threshold with an inflatable backrest in his large hands.

TiCara felt the walls close in as the big man filled more of the available space than seemed possible and she backed toward the doorway with a courteous bow. "Anything you need, Ser, my and I crew will do our best to provide."

"Anything, Captain?" Vahn shook his head as he sat down on her bed. "Such a rash promise. But we shall see. Thank you."

TiCara could see a ghost of a smile on his face as he lay down and smiled to herself as she left. She had a few other rash promises that she wanted to cash in on, too. The memory of Sherin's lips parted in a gasp in the corridor of Vahn Corp sent a pleasant warm wave of desire through her. But they needed to get away from Kyrin before she made any move.

To do that, she needed to get Electra's coordinates from the rep. Then she'd hope that they were tru and wouldn't send the *Astra* into a black hole. There had been tales about that too. She frowned at that paranoid fear and tried to dismiss it. Hopefully Vahn and his rep had vetted them first. The old man certainly wanted to live long enough to find the asteroid and he thought the tell he had was tru. That would have to be enough for all of them for now.

A quick check of the ship's secur cams on her comm and TiCara directed her path toward the Bridge. Sherin was there talking to Erol when TiCara climbed quietly up the narrow ladder. The pilot paused on the upper rungs to watch them for a moment; the rep was clearly more comfortable speaking with her Second than she was with her and the sight cheered TiCara immensely.

Indifference would have been jarring, harder to overcome. The rep's hair was down now, freed from its clip and flowing over her shoulders in a stylish ebony wave. Looking at it was almost enough to make TiCara miss her own hair, though not as much as it made her want to run her fingers through that silky mass.

Of course, she didn't stop with just looking at Sherin's hair. It would impossible not to notice the stunning symmetry of her face and the curves of her body, defying her blacksuit's efforts to curb them. There was something enticing about the way she stood, casually leaning against the edge of a console board as she spoke with Erol. She gestured gracefully with one long-fingered brown hand and Erol gave her a reluctant smile.

Then Sherin realized that she was being watched and her body shifted. When she looked over to meet TiCara's eyes, she turned corp rep cold in an instant, all expression shut down and her body going stiff and still. It made TiCara smother a laugh; the rep must be responding to her very strongly to be exerting this much control. She felt a warm haze of anticipation fill her at the thought. It might only take a little persuasion to seduce the other woman.

But they needed to get out past the asteroid belt and well on their way before she could put the ship on autopilot and find out. TiCara swung onto the Bridge floor, meeting Sherin's blank expression with one of her own. "Coordinates?" She made her tone disinterested, not letting her voice telegraph what she was feeling.

Sherin hesitated before producing a chip from an inner pocket and handing it over. "I'll want that back." She didn't meet TiCara's eyes again but she went on standing next to the pilot's chair, as if she was waiting for something.

All the groundies want to see how medusas work TiCara thought, stopping her hand before she made a dismissive gesture to clear the Bridge. This might prove useful later. *Well, let's see how she likes it.*

She sat upright in her chair and felt the hood settle down over her head and face. The visor and hood were clear so Sherin could watch as her medusa cables rose gently and fit themselves into the hood's sockets. Once plugged in, TiCara melded with the ship, preparing to maneuver as close to the speed of thought as the technology could get.

With the part of her brain not starting up the ship's functions and getting clearance to leave the port, she surprised a desperate look of longing or perhaps, repulsion, on Sherin's face before the rep realized she was watching and turned away. Maybe it hadn't been such a good idea to let her stay. But then, she had hoped the rep would prove more sophisticated.

It was hard to predict how groundies would react to medusa pilots. After the Wars, the pilots were the victors, the reason that your corp succeeded. They were viewed with awe and fear in all the spaceports.

Hostility or envy or repulsion were seldom expressed openly, except in the galaxy's backwaters. Now that the Wars were a fading memory, medusa pilots were less beloved or feared, at least from what she'd seen in the ports they had visited.

But then, she spent more time with spacers than groundies. Perhaps she had lost her ability to read them and their reactions were unchanged. She stifled a sigh. From where she sat, the rep looked neither intrigued nor aroused, the two responses that she'd been hoping for. Maybe she could startle Sherin out of whatever she was feeling. "This isn't all they're good for," she leered at the other woman.

Sherin turned on her heel and bolted for the gangway ladder to the lower level, tension clear in the set of her shoulders. TiCara caught the twitch of Erol's lips as he looked quickly away and restrained herself from smacking her head. She'd mishandled the rep once again, possibly beyond fixing, but there was no time to worry about that now. The *Astra* needed her, needed her focused.

It was time to do what she loved more than anything else. She looked first at the coordinates, verifying that the destination they were headed to was a sixty machron hour flight away, as Vahn had mentioned. Then she lost herself in the ship, extending herself through the network and circuitry until her body and the ship were one giant organism. She loved the power of that merging, letting it sweep through her mind with a rush. Her body felt alive with electrical pulses and signals, every nerve end sparking until she was nearly on fire with it.

It was also highly sensual, when everything went well. When she first plugged in, she was always aroused, on the brink of joining her ship in liftoff. While that would fade quickly, for the next few cycles, there would be no Sherin or Elia or even Zig on her mind, just her and the *Astra* and their glorious connection.

She maneuvered them out past Kyrin's security satellites and corps battle cruisers, then through the mob of smaller merchant and transport vessels that crowded close to the planet's surface. The *Astra* fed all the navigational images directly into her brain: asteroids, other ships, the planets and the moons of Kyrin's solar system. But beyond that, it showed her the stars and freedom, the boundless space of black velvet filled with distant lights.

For a wild moment, she wanted to just keep going, to vanish into the distant stars far beyond the corps and their Ears and Eyes. This was the freedom she dreamt of when she first got the *Astra*, the freedom she dreamt of with every job she took. The impulse filled her, then just as quickly ebbed away. There were too many things that she wanted from the corps to leave them all behind. Not yet, anyway.

She let out the breath she was holding and used Sherin's chip to enter the asteroid's coordinates into the nav system. After a moment, she recognized the Gathwaite System as the star map filled her visor. Pirates. She winced; pirates were as bad as Ears, maybe worse. The *Astra* would be outgunned: there was no question about that. Any pirate ship out there would be heavily armed. But at least that extra weight would make it harder for them to catch her ship, not at the speed that she knew *Astra* was capable of. She imagined herself patting the engine with a thought and nearly laughed out loud at the image.

Her mood turned more somber as she turned over their options; perhaps she should be looking for a way out of this job instead of fantasizing about surviving it. If the *Astra* were malfunctioning, she would be aware of it moments after she plugged in. And if that malfunction was severe enough to require docking at another port, compelling her passengers to find a new ship, that wasn't that unusual. It could even happen long before they got to Gathwaite.

TiCara imagined apologizing to Vahn and Sherin, then putting them on some trusted acquaintance's ship and sending them off on their quest for Electra. Then, she imagined all those lovely credits flowing out of her account. And Sherin walking away, likely never to return.

There was also her reputation to consider. While ship malfunctions could happen to anyone, her ship seldom had them. Whatever else this trip might bring, she couldn't deny that she was intrigued, and that she wanted to see if the asteroid existed.

That made her decision for her: lust and pride and fear roiled together in a powerful cocktail, one that was too much for even her implants to sooth. TiCara ran her fingers under her face shield, rubbing her cheeks. She was committed now. The *Astra* would just have to be fast enough, her pilot brave enough to deal with any pirates or other dangers that came their way.

Her thoughts turned back to Electra and the rumors that eddied and flowed around it. She found herself remembering Elia's story about the cured pilot with a shudder. If there was any possibility of being 'healed' of her medusas, she would have to be very careful. If there was anything to the story, of course. Spacer tales were notoriously tall.

She surprised herself by taking the chip out of the nav system and putting it aside for Erol to return to Sherin, now that the coordinates entered. At first, she had considered using it to lure Sherin to her temporary quarters to retrieve it. Now that notion seemed foolish, especially after seeing the other woman's reaction to her when she left the Bridge. TiCara acknowledged that she might have misread it, but if not, that look suggested that the rep was more squeamish than she had hoped.

Sherin had always been coldly professional when they'd met before, but TiCara had thought that she was sure that she recognized steaming hot desire under that icy veneer. Sherin probably had no idea how long TiCara had wanted her. TiCara closed her eyes, remembering the first time she saw Sherin sing at one of the bars. Her sultry voice combined with her beauty made her all that TiCara could think about when she was in port, at least for a while. But she was always surrounded by fans and TiCara had nothing to offer her, not back then.

But things were different now. Or at least that was what TiCara told herself. Sherin wanted her now, when she let her guard down. But if she was right about that, why was the rep playing games? Wanting a medusa pilot meant wanting the wires; everyone knew that.

There were few sexual taboos among spacers, apart from those around consent, and spacers were the dominant culture in most stations and ports. Corp personnel tended to follow their lead, with the exception of the conservatives who thought that modified humans like the medusa pilots were an abomination.

It was possible that Sherin shared their beliefs. The thought sent an icy chill through her.

TiCara went back through her memories, looking for clues that Sherin was repulsed by her. It was not all starshine. Even she had to admit that it was possible.

But maybe Sherin was just worried about getting involved with another one of Vahn's employees, even a temporary one, and fighting her attraction. That was something TiCara thought she could fix, given enough time, on this trip. The idea made her feel optimistic again and she hummed as she flew.

She was smiling again when Erol came to relieve her at the end of her shift. She loved the thrill of the chase, the power of seduction, winning a chance at nova sex. Those were skills that she had honed when she was working in the bars, trying to earn creds for her pilot's indenture and her medusas. She had loved stealing clients from the other bar workers, loved making them feel good enough that they came back to her again and again. She could do that again now, as long as Sherin reciprocated.

She stood up and stretched sinuously as her medusas slid loose from the pilot sockets. For an instant, she wondered, as she did sometimes at shift changes, if Erol wished that he was wired, too. How could you not want the rush of those moments when your brain and your ship were one?

Erol always said he didn't want them, but part of her wanted to delve further, to try and convince him. As it was, he would be flying the old way, using the instruments and navigation equipment to monitor the ship until they were ready to make the short jump to the next system on autopilot. Every time she saw him sit in the second chair, she wanted to talk him into getting wired. But not this time. She gave her Second a cheery wave as she moved toward the ladder.

Erol cleared his throat, his expression suggesting that he'd just eaten something unpleasant. But he didn't say anything, instead sitting down in the second pilot's chair and setting the controls, his movements fidgety and scattered. TiCara stopped and frowned, making an impatient gesture. "Out with it, Second. Tru tell me what's dragging a comet's tail through your head. I'm no mind reader."

"About our passengers, Captain…," he paused, his normally slow speech bogging down even further as he obviously hunted for words. His dark eyes looked out the porthole past her, like he didn't want to see her reaction. "I think they are not what they appear to be. Or at least the woman isn't."

TiCara tilted her head to one side and gave him a considering look, a slight chill spreading through her. What had Sherin done that she had missed? Erol had never given her reason to distrust his opinion. Maybe her lust was blinding her. "Tell me. What did you see?"

"When you were in the port, thought I saw her talking to an Ear. They were in the shadows, back near the storage tunnels so I'm speccing. Could be wrong, but I'm cert it was her or her clone, if she has one," he shrugged, the gesture reminiscent of one of the Old Earth vids he liked to watch. "Be careful, Captain."

TiCara frowned at him, then made a sideways jerk of her head by way of acknowledgment. The elation she had felt earlier at the possibility of seducing Sherin ebbed away, and a memory of Elia's face rose unbidden before her eyes. Maybe she was oblivious to a lot of things.

But they were away from Kyrin and if she wanted an excuse to leave the rep planetside, she would need Vahn's buy-in now. And a lot more than just her Second's hunch for evidence. So she would need to watch Sherin more closely, oh so much more closely, until she saw what she was up to, one way or another.

Perhaps the rep could be confined to quarters. Her quarters. A flash of heat replaced the chill and she bit back a laugh at her own expense. Especially when she paused to think about her current quarters, only recently converted from a storage unit. Hardly an ideal spot for seduction or romantic fantasies.

Then she added a shrug of her own. She needed to prove to herself that Sherin wasn't planning to betray them all to a fiery doom before anything more interesting could happen in fantasy or reality. For that, she needed more intel.

Erol turned back to the instruments with a nod. He would signal her if there was trouble, like he always did whenever anything went wrong. Like he just had.

TiCara reminded herself that she had passengers to check on, not just Sherin. She swept off the Bridge, heading to Vahn's quarters. Space travel was hard, especially on someone as fragile as he seemed to be. A personal visit would keep him sweetened up or so she hoped, and that couldn't hurt, no matter what happened.

Contemplating Vahn's health reminded her of Elia again. Regular injections of Eternayouth could go on until a human body began to reject them. How many doses became "too many" varied from spacer to spacer, depending on your metabolism. Elia had thought she was getting close to her limit, or at least that's what she told TiCara when she stopped taking the drug.

Now, she wondered. Maybe the former pilot had found something else and her body had started rejecting it? It hurt to wonder if she knew so little about her ex-lover that she couldn't be sure if she was taking a new drug, one that might be killing her. But there was nothing she could do right now, even if her suspicion was correct. She paused to collect her thoughts outside Vahn's room before she hit the buzzer.

When she went in, he looked even more ancient than he had on Kyrin, his hooded narrow eyes reminding her of a tortoise she had seen once in a clone zoo. The cabin smelled musty, like dust and old human, and she reminded herself to check the vents and circulation after she left.

For all his appearance of infirmity, Vahn gave her a shrewd look, like he was reading her thoughts. "Pilot-Captain TiCara, it is good to see you. Coming to check on an old man when your duties summon you elsewhere honors me. You are welcome and I appreciate your extra care." He smiled and bowed slightly without getting up. "Are we clear of Kyrin yet?"

She nodded and smiled back. "We're not out of the system yet, but we'll make the jump soon. There will be an alert to sling before we do that. Are you comfortable? Is there anything you need?"

"There is nothing that I need at present, Pilot-Captain," He smiled a polite dismissal. She realized, after a moment's hesitation, that he actually needed to sleep. It was fascinating. She never failed to reach for a stimul when she felt that way, given the opportunity. She slept only when her medusas told her she had to. They were better at monitoring her body than she was.

TiCara let the door slide shut behind her and began walking down the narrow corridor. After a few strides, she realized she was walking toward the room she'd given Sherin. She forced herself to stop and check the air filters on Vahn's quarters and verify the hallway air controls, getting both thoughts and medusas under control.

The filters seemed clean enough, though one of the monitors needed resetting. The mundane task slowed her down enough to think beyond impulse and to absorb what Erol had said about Sherin and the Ear. Perhaps the Ear was just an old friend of Sherin's, just like an Ear was an old friend of Elia's.

Or maybe that was one coincidence too many. A cold chill settled into her stomach. Suspicion overrode lust and she looked down the corridor toward the rep's quarters with narrowed eyes. The fact that the rep had private quarters on the *Astra* meant that anything she might be planning could already be in motion. There were no security cams in that room.

TiCara paused for a moment and checked for the throwing knives in her boots and plucked one from its sheath to slip up her sleeve. She had left her lazer in her quarters, something she'd have to change for this trip, but she didn't feel like going to fetch it, not yet. She was as secure as she could make herself for the moment. She shrugged. Now she would just have find the rep and let whatever game they were playing spin out to its conclusion.

CHAPTER 6

E ROL LOOKED OUT AT THE starfields and swore quietly to himself, once he knew TiCara was out of earshot. He'd left corp work because the choices got too hard. Or tru tell, they were making him too hard. Signing on with TiCara had begun with what he thought was a small lie, but now it was becoming a weight heavy enough to drag him down into much bigger ones.

No, not a lie: a betrayal. She thought he signed on with her because he was a junior corp pilot with no hope of advancement. She thought she had made him a better offer as a Second on the *Astra,* that he was taking a step up by signing on with her. And in a way, he was. But she had never asked many questions about his former position, his past or why a berth on her ship had looked so much better to him than what he had before.

Now, someone was reminding him of the choices he had made to get here and that reminder burned through him, searing through this new life he had built himself and razing it down to the foundations. He kicked the bottom of the comm board, aiming for a section where he could do no damage. The least he could do for TiCara was to keep her ship intact..

Of course, if he fulfilled this new betrayal that they demanded of him, a dented comm board would be the least of the Pilot-Captain's problems. Not that they let him in on all their plans, but he could guess. And what would be his fate or Arnelle's, once he told them where they were going and gave them the coordinates they wanted so badly? It didn't fill him with optimism, no matter what angle he checked.

He'd helped the Ears exert that kind of pressure before, back in his old life. He knew how it ended. A wave of nausea swept through him. He should have warned Arnelle before they left, should have told TiCara, should have done something! But it was too late, at least for now.

Even without that implicit threat hanging over him, he could only act once *he* found out where they were going. That thought twisted through him; he should have known by now. TiCara had trusted him before this trip, so why not now? He knew her well enough to know when she was withholding tell, knew well enough to recognize how rare that was. Like now.

It was easy enough to see what made this trip different from their usual run. He cataloged what he had seen of their passengers so far and his eyes narrowed. The old man was more than he seemed to be, clearly richer and more influential than TiCara had described him. He must have enjoined silence on TiCara, told her not to tell anyone. The emphasis on secrecy and speed before they left Kyrin made that much plain.

That TiCara had accepted that the restriction applied to her crew as well as to port personnel was different, new. It burned a little in Erol's mind, like a small betrayal that might be a symptom of something larger. The Pilot-Captain disliked rules, finding it more fun to bend them to the breaking point and see what she could get from the challenge than to follow them unthinkingly. It had been one of the reasons that he had signed on with her. So the corp diplomat or rep, whoever or whatever he really was, must have something that made it worthwhile for her to obey his rules.

Credits went without saying. She had never told him how much she still owed on the ship, but he could guess from the jobs they took and the risks she encouraged. That alone might be enough to get her to promise the galaxy, if the price Vahn paid was high enough, as long as the job didn't seem too dangerous. Or involve working for the Ears. That was a line that she would never cross.

Then his thoughts turned to the old man's assistant and paused there. She was nova beautiful, like a distant star. But TiCara was too smart to gamble her relationship with her crew on a lovely face and body.

Wasn't she?

Until now, he'd been sure that he knew the answer to that. Especially when the lovely woman in question had been seen speaking with an Ear right before leaving port. He wondered what secrets she had, what tru tell she possessed that would make an Ear want to listen to her. Or what lies she had told in her past that would make her open to betrayals of her own in her present.

He remembered when he, too, had spoken at length with the Ears, and gave them whatever tell they wanted. He also remembered the consequences for the people he betrayed. Those memories were like an unexpected trip out the airlock in a suit with a faulty seal. They remembered his earlier betrayals and they knew how to compel new ones.

The difference was that now they were offering to pay for it with credits in one hand, threats in the other. He worried more about the latter. If they had the information they said they had about his past, he might never pilot again, not even for the shadow trade. No one liked a traitor. TiCara, Ji-min, Vijay, his primary, all the friendships he had made in this new life of his, would vanish into the vacuum between systems if they knew him for what he had been. Was.

He knew it the same way that he knew that he could pilot his way through four of the populated corps systems by memory alone. The woman who called him before they left port hadn't even needed to spell out her threat. She had enough details on a few of his past crimes that he didn't question what else she knew. The consequences of discovery he could list for himself.

He raised long fingers to his face and closed his eyes, then rubbed them hard, frustration making him press down until small flashes of light danced inside his lids. There had to be a way out of this, but he couldn't see it, not yet. Maybe not ever. But there had to be something.

Erol stared out over the comm boards, letting the nav computer pilot the ship while he vanished into his own thoughts.

Chapter 7

SHERIN WASN'T IN HER QUARTERS, as far as TiCara could tell from the limited room sensors. She leaned hard against the old-fashioned button again, to make certain. When there was no response, she walked down the corridor and opened the hidden security consoles in one of the walls. Once she entered her code, the ship's secur cam footage displayed the *Astra*'s common areas on the small screen.

She trailed her finger over the pad, moving around the ship from the Bridge to the crews' quarters. Vahn was still in his quarters and her crew was at their stations or off camera, presumably sleeping or engaged in some other harmless activity. She checked the remaining cameras, two at a time on the *Astra*'s tiny secur screen, checking the common areas and corridors. Nothing out of the ordinary met her anxious gaze.

And she was anxious. Part of her wanted Erol to be wrong, wanted Sherin to be nothing more than she appeared to be. More than a part of her, if she was being honest. The rep intrigued, inflamed her, fascinated her. If Erol was right, she'd have to give up any hopes of being with the other woman, but she was going to hate making that choice.

She finally located Sherin, sitting alone in the small crew lounge that doubled as their mess hall. She found herself circling the screen with one caressing finger, wondering if the rep's skin felt as silky as she imagined that it would. Then she caught herself and yanked her finger back from the screen like she'd been burned.

If Erol was right, she was an idiot to get so infatuated with this woman. She closed and locked the security console back into the corridor wall with a sigh, her medusas clustering tight around her head and neck in an attempt at comfort. It was time to go get some answers before they had to get ready for the jump. Now, if only she was sure she knew what all the questions were. TiCara swore another silent vow that the *Astra* would never carry passengers again.

Even particularly luscious ones.

Especially luscious ones.

When she climbed the ladder up to the lounge, Sherin was standing and staring out the clear dome at the surrounding system. The distant stars were beginning to look blurry as the *Astra* built up to full speed to leave the Kyrin System. They'd be shifting to hyperdrive soon.

"The ship will be making the jump soon. You know how the slings work?" TiCara almost didn't realize that she spoken her thought aloud until Sherin jumped at the sound of her voice.

Once she stopped looking startled, TiCara thought that she looked sad, her kissable lips drooping a little at the corners. Her face had been tilted back to display her lovely profile, reminding TiCara of the tiny statue of an Old Earth goddess that she kept in her quarters, a memento of a past job. Sherin raised one hand to her head and stroked her scalp in an absent-minded gesture that struck TiCara as familiar, though she wasn't immediately sure why.

TiCara hesitated before stepping off the ladder, breath catching in her throat as she looked at the other woman. She was torn between wanting to make the rep smile, imagining what she might look like glowing in rare happiness, and destroying their small moment of rapport by confronting her with Erol's information and her own distrust.

At the same time, she also wondered what made the other woman look so sad. The thought of betraying her employer to another corp, perhaps? Revulsion at her attraction to a medusa pilot? There was no end of options, most of them not very appealing, at least to TiCara.

The moment of stillness didn't last long; Sherin realized that they were staring at each other and turned away to look back at the stars. There were tears welling in her dark brown eyes but she blinked them away, then ran her hand across her face with a fierce swipe. When she looked at TiCara again, her expression was blank and expressionless, like uncarved stone. "What was that, Captain?"

TiCara stepped forward and reached out for her, pity and sympathy driving the gesture as much as lust, making her forget her suspicions for a moment. She meant her touch to be comforting, but Sherin flinched away, her shoulders trembling. TiCara jerked her hand back, wounded. "Just wanted to give you tell about the jump, make sure you knew and got into a sling in time." They watched each other like wary combatants in a portside gaming ring.

Then, just as suddenly as she had recoiled, Sherin lunged forward, reached out and caught TiCara in her arms.

The pilot held her, shivering a little, as if Sherin's trembling was contagious. Then the rep gave a tiny sob into TiCara's shoulder. Surprised by a wave of tenderness she almost didn't recognize in herself, TiCara held her for a long moment, reining in her questions and suspicions. And trying to hold back her body's demands, which was much, much harder.

Sherin startled her further by pressing up against her, molding her body against hers until it was hard to concentrate. TiCara kept her hands still with an effort, trying not to take advantage of the other woman's vulnerability. Such self-control came with an effort, but then, she'd learned plenty of that from her time with Elia.

Instead of doing what she so desperately wanted to do and sliding her hands over the rep's suit, unfastening and caressing and baring her skin, she stroked Sherin's hair. It was a tentative, careful caress, forcing her fingers to do her mind's bidding, not her body's.

Sherin stunned her by placing a tentative kiss on the exposed skin of her neck, following it up with a gentle swipe of her tongue. She caught the lobe of TiCara's ear between her front teeth and nipped at the tender flesh. TiCara gasped at the unexpected contact, letting the sensations slide down her body and stroke their way between her thighs until it felt like Sherin's tongue and fingers were already where she wanted them most.

Unable to resist, she turned her face to Sherin's and kissed her, slipping her tongue between her parted lips. Sherin tasted like tears and honey, salty and sweet. TiCara wanted to savor that taste, that sensation. Drink in Sherin until she was sated, if she could ever be.

But then, there was that salty aftertaste. TiCara didn't often feel like she was doing something wrong. It was unfamiliar, unpleasant, and it interfered with all that she wanted to be feeling right now. Breaking off the kiss took everything she had. She tried to step back away from Sherin, but the rep only held her tighter.

So instead of pulling away, she twisted slightly and tilted Sherin's face toward hers with careful fingers. Sherin's eyes were closed tight now, no tears at the edges, as TiCara echoed the question that Sherin had asked when she came in, her brain automatically switching to spacer talk, "What's malfunctioned…sorry. I mean what's wrong?"

Instead of answering, Sherin locked her hands around her neck and pulled her into a fierce kiss, her tongue invading TiCara's mouth, shoving its way between her lips, probing and testing until TiCara gasped for air. It was like being devoured and she could feel herself edge perilously close to surrender. As if the rep knew exactly what she was feeling, Sherin slipped her leg between TiCara's and the pilot's hips rocked forward automatically, sending a wave of heat through her.

She should stop this; every instinct told her so. She should back away and find out why the rep had been crying and what else she was up to. The *Astra* could be in danger, and she and her crew along with it. But Sherin wouldn't give her tru tell, at least not right away, not until she won her trust. Maybe the best way to do that was to give the other woman what she clearly wanted.

Yes, that felt like a fine solution right now. She ran her hand down Sherin's back to the rounded curve of her buttocks and squeezed, pulling Sherin in closer until the rep moaned low in her throat. Her hips tilted forward against Sherin's thigh in response.

Besides, TiCara knew what it was like to have sex to forget, and that sometimes that was all that was needed or offered. And if she didn't take this chance, who knew how long it would be before she got another chance? Was she willing to walk away from a chance she'd been dreaming about for what felt like a dozen Old Earth years?

Perhaps she hadn't learned that much self-control, after all.

She bit back a grin as she reached up and unfastened the top of the rep's blacksuit. Sherin's skin was as silky as she had imagined and she gave an appreciative groan of her own in response. She could feel Sherin stiffen, just for a breath, then press back against her.

The rep began clumsily unfastening TiCara's blacksuit, shoving TiCara's hands away as she kissed her way down the pilot's collar-bone and exposed cleavage. She pealed back TiCara's suit like she was exposing a ripe fruit, her mouth urgent on TiCara's rapidly bared breasts. The pilot groaned again, the sound traveling up her throat and out between her lips until her entire body trembled with it.

Her own hands were just as frantic on the fastenings of the rep's suit, desperate to feel more of that silky, golden brown skin against her own. Suit fastenings had never seemed so very hard to undo. When at last she succeeded in baring Sherin's body to her waist, Sherin pressed her bare breasts against TiCara's as she leaned in for a long kiss.

With a soft groan, TiCara released Sherin's long black hair from the clasp that held it in place. She buried her hands in its ebony length, using it to pull Sherin's face up and back, arching her neck and shoulders. She bent down and used her tongue and mouth to caress the rep's neck and shoulders while her fingers got lost in Sherin's hair, reveling in her fantasies come to life.

As TiCara let Sherin's hair slide through her fingers like silken water, she touched the rep's skull, and nearly jerked away in astonishment. Sherin's scalp was rough and pocked, as if her hair hid heavy scarring. What could it be? Burns? The medic machines should have been able to heal an injury as basic as that.

But maybe she'd been too far from a machine when it happened. Or perhaps it was just one more mystery about Sherin she'd have to wait to solve. TiCara tried to remind herself that she had always liked a little mystery in her lovers and let her hand drop away from Sherin's head, trying to make her worries drop away the same way.

Besides, there were other things on her mind right now. Sherin went very still as TiCara lowered her medusas, letting them caress Sherin's neck and jaw with a dozen tiny electric kisses. The rep shuddered in her arms, huge dark eyes closed like she couldn't bear to watch but she didn't pull away. Her breasts heaved and her hands trembled against TiCara's skin, as if she was overcome by the sensations.

TiCara paused, fighting her lust for control. Should she stop? Could she? She wasn't sure. Then the thought fled as Sherin ground her hips against TiCara's, the motion reminding the pilot of her own urgent need. She extended a lone medusa to stroke its way down to Sherin's nipple, sending the smallest of shocks through the rep's sensitive skin.

Sherin wailed and jerked away, the noise suggesting loss as much as desire, at least to TiCara's startled ears. But before she could pull away, the rep's body shuddered against TiCara's, her thighs tightening around the pilot's legs. She ground her crotch on TiCara's hip and leg, her movements growing faster and more urgent.

TiCara bit back a smile as her implants fed the rep's sensations into her own brain. She knew that her implants were worth all that she'd gone through to get them, and more, but reminders were always… nice. She followed the medusas with her mouth, drawing her tongue slowly along the same path down Sherin's body until she pulled first one hardened nipple into her mouth, then turned her head to take in the other. She could feel Sherin's heartbeat race under her lips as she let several of her medusas trace their way over the rep's skin.

Sherin shivered, her muscles spasming, as TiCara dropped one hand down between her legs, forcing the blacksuit open below the rep's waist so she could caress her sex. She moaned, a sound that shook her from head to toe and TiCara grinned, sucking harder on her responsive flesh.

Then she maneuvered Sherin back onto the low table and stretched her out on it. The rep dropped backward onto the hard surface as if her body had no bones in it. Her eyes were still closed but TiCara was startled to see a new teardrop lingering at the edge of her long lashes. Once again, she wondered if she should stop, but she was burning with desire now, thighs slick with wanting. Her heart was beating so fast, it felt like it might explode from her chest.

Besides, hadn't Sherin given her every indication that the desire was mutual? Even now, the rep's hands were caressing her body. Then, Sherin raised her hand and gently touched one of TiCara's medusas, her fingers careful on its sensor as if she was curious about how it would feel or what it would do.

Dismissing her concerns, TiCara climbed up on the table to kiss the tear away as she balanced herself over the other woman's body. Sherin's hands turned to claws, fiercely dragging her blacksuit and boots off. Her hands were hot on TiCara's skin everywhere she touched. TiCara growled softly as Sherin's touch got rougher, pinching her nipples and breasts.

When she kissed TiCara again, her lips were hard, her arms like steel bands holding TiCara in place above her. Now it was TiCara's turn to gasp for breath. The rep opened her eyes for a moment, her expression unreadable as she rolled the pilot off her and twisted sideways so that TiCara lay on the table and she could strip TiCara's remaining clothing from her squirming body. TiCara groaned and laughed; this was so much better than her fantasies.

Sherin threw herself off the table onto the cushioned bench that ran behind it. Sitting up, she yanked TiCara around so that her face was between the pilot's thighs. After an initial moment of awkwardness, she began licking TiCara as if she had always known how to do it.

TiCara bucked at the touch of her tongue and moaned, "Inside me." She paused and hesitated at the desperation in her own voice. Her body screamed with need but did Sherin have to know how vulnerable she was? She stiffened, trying to control her nerve endings by sheer force of will. Her efforts failed miserably.

A chorus of moans tore themselves from her lips until she found herself begging, "Please." There were too many questions to be asked, too many answers missing. Her mind and her body warred with each other as Sherin sucked and licked with increasing eagerness, two of her fingers sliding inside TiCara's wetness below the circle of nerves on fire that was becoming the center of the pilot's universe.

Her body was responding to every swipe of Sherin's tongue, every twitch of her fingers. TiCara's legs tightened as her hips bucked against Sherin's mouth. It was as if she hadn't sex in entire revolutions. Her body was starving for more, far more than the medusa-driven fantasy sex of VR.

TiCara humped Sherin's mouth, hips rocking and driving upward as her nerve endings overrode her fears. Sherin's thumb found her clit and pressed down hard, barely moving, but the pressure alone was enough to make TiCara give herself up with a shout, her hips heaving under Sherin's mouth and hands.

The rep withdrew her fingers after a few moments, kissing the skin of her thighs while TiCara's shivers subsided. She reached for Sherin as the other woman suddenly drove all her fingers into her aching wetness, fastening her mouth to TiCara's clit in the same forward motion. The drive of her hand was relentless, pounding TiCara until the pilot came again with a shout that was nearly a scream.

Sherin leaned forward as TiCara's shudders finally slowed, resting her cheek on TiCara's thigh so that the pilot could feel her breathing, feel her heart race. She pulled her hand free leaving TiCara sated and empty, as the heat of the rep's touch began to fade.

They lay still, TiCara drinking in the lounge's slightly stale air in gulps. After a few moments, she caught her breath enough to reach out for Sherin. She tried to pull the rep onto the table with her, wanting nothing more than to feel Sherin's body open to her touch.

Sherin jerked away, shuddering. TiCara sat up slowly, letting her bafflement show. Had she done something wrong?

The other woman's eyes were wild, like those of a trapped animal. "You'd use those," she gestured at the medusas, "and I can't. Not now. I'm not ready." She stood up, fastening her blacksuit with sharp, jerky motions, not meeting TiCara's eyes as the pilot sat up slowly and reached out a hand toward her.

TiCara tried to find the words to persuade Sherin to stay but the other woman fled before she could say anything, running out of the lounge and leaving the pilot staring after her.

Chapter 8

TiCara couldn't see where Sherin went after she scrambled back into her suit and rocketed out into the corridor. Probably back to her quarters, but there were always other possibilities. And they were out of time. She needed to get into a sling of her own.

The pilot swore quietly to herself, catching her hand before she inadvertently yanked on her medusas. It wasn't their fault that everything that the rep did seemed to leave her a jumbled mess of conflicting emotions. Plus a good hard yank hurt wouldn't make her feel any better.

It wasn't as if Sherin's behavior instilled trust, even if she'd thoroughly enjoyed their encounter up until the rep's abrupt departure. TiCara grimaced, weighing her options on what to do next. Almost of their own accord, her fingers skimmed along the *Astra*'s wall, looking for a catch invisible to anyone who didn't know what to look for. A panel clicked open with a nearly inaudible whirr of gears.

Telling herself that she just wanted to make sure that Sherin was safe before she strapped in, she reached in and touched a button. The medusa sockets in the enclosed opening clicked open an instant later.

They were powered by a hidden set of actual gears, not like the wireless linkups in the comm booths.

Older tech was slower, but more reliable. Even the best of Ears would have trouble locating and using this particular back door into the ship's security system. Even if they did find it, if they weren't wired, they couldn't use the ship's computer and its electronic senses to augment their own the way she could.

Now to plug in and hope she wasn't dealing with the best of Ears, if that's what Sherin really was. For an instant, she closed her eyes, picturing Sherin's expression just before she fled. She looked terrified, confused, anything except calculating. TiCara clenched her fists in frustration. Scaring Sherin off had never been her intention. She just wanted the other woman where she could keep an eye on her, as well as both hands, her mouth and anything else that the rep might enjoy.

And if she was honest with herself, she wanted this entire trip to be nothing more than a foolish chase after an impossible dream that would end with them safely back at dock, Sherin in her bed, Vahn's credits on her chip and the old man looking for a real solution. It was so little to ask, and yet it seemed so unlikely right now.

Her medusas ignored her doubts, snaking down from her head to insert themselves into the waiting sockets. The tiny ship schematic screen rose up without any conscious prompting on her part, which was good since her mind was not on threats to the ship, internal or external. That was the point of this particular back door: if the main cameras didn't work or she couldn't use them, this backup would tell her most of what she needed to know about the state of the *Astra*.

It would be more useful if she paid attention to it, though. With an effort, she forced herself to focus, to let the computer feed her mind from its own sensors. At first, she received a blur of images that triggered all sorts of sensations in her. Making sense of them took longer than she liked. If Sherin was working for the Ears, she could be up to anything while TiCara wrestled with the computer. It wasn't as if sabotaging a jump was that difficult.

She shuddered at that particular thought and kept searching. After a few moments of showing her circuit schematics and a minor issue with the food processors, the ship complied with her desire to see the key life support sensors. That alone wouldn't tell her where Sherin was, but it would tell her where the ship's oxygen was being used, as well as how much was being consumed. She could figure out who was doing all that breathing on her own.

Sherin's quarters were empty. The last threads of the lingering clouds of desire in TiCara's mind vanished, replaced with a rush of adrenaline and anger. It felt alien and unpleasant, but then so did fear and uncertainty and she knew those emotions quite well, especially when it came to the Ears. Even the meditation techniques she'd learned on Aliandra weren't enough to help her master her fears.

She caressed her medusas for comfort, for grounding, and felt the tide of emotions subside. Anger could be useful, if she used it right, or so they told her on Aliandra. She frowned at the console, then maneuvered her way further into the feed: Engineering, the Bridge, all the places where a rogue rep could do significant harm to the ship. Still nothing. Vijay was likely in his quarters, Ji-min was at their station and Erol was on the Bridge, or so it appeared. Vahn's quarters only showed signs of two people.

Then she tried the storage bays, as well as the hidden compartments where smuggled goods could rest beneath floor panels or in walls, insulated from port customs scanners. She didn't deceive herself into thinking that she was the first to use such things. If Sherin were more than she appeared to be, she could find the more obvious hiding places easily enough if she searched hard enough.

Though why she thought the rep might be looking for either a place to hide or smuggled goods, she couldn't say. Perhaps because it was something she herself might do, if she found herself on a strange ship in a similar situation. Go to ground somewhere that felt safe, figure out what to do next. Just like she had done when she was a child, after her crèche was destroyed.

She took a deep breath, centering herself, reining in the urge to the direction that her thoughts were going and forcing them to return to the present. Guessing was futile. Wanting to know where the rep was, that was rational. Guessing why the rep was doing whatever she was doing without more information was just that: guessing.

Other than a blip in one of the aft bay cameras, where an anomaly of some sort caught her attention briefly, she saw nothing she didn't expect to see. Making a note to check that bay soon, she looked back at Vahn's quarters again. The rep was there now, based on the sensor information that showed three people in the room.

TiCara almost disconnected the link with a sigh of relief. She didn't need to spy on Vahn, after all. But she found herself turning on the security camera in her quarters with a thought and watching it anyway. There was nothing wrong with certainty. Or something like it.

Sherin was giving Vahn something in a cup. She bent forward, long black hair hanging loose and hiding her face from the camera. TiCara would have given anything to see her expression. Anything. She rolled the feeling around for a moment then grimaced as she let go of it and the edge of obsession it carried with it. She was just curious, that was all. Nothing more, nothing deeper than that.

Vahn gave his employee a skeptical look and waved the cup away. There was something sly in his expression, as if he knew how she was spending her off duty hours.

Or as if he didn't trust her. TiCara rubbed her chin and frowned. What if he had brought the rep on this trip so that he could keep an eye on her? In that case, TiCara wondered if he'd had her tracked. A guttural phrase in port common lingua danced past her lips. If she hadn't been wired in, she might have moved her head, tilting it in a nod of admiration. Why hadn't she thought of that?

As it was, her lips curled in a small smile. If that was what he had done, then the old man had had his fun tonight. Next time, if there was a next time, she'd make sure to remove everything the rep was wearing and toss it out in the corridor. They didn't need an audience to make it any hotter between them. Unless, of course, that Vahn's interests were less prurient than that.

Even with all that uncertainty, a flush ran up her thighs at the thought of continuing what they had started. She watched Sherin and Vahn for a few more seconds. If she had more time in port, she'd have set up her security system for sound as well as viewing, but cargo didn't talk, as a rule, so she'd never gotten around to it. She wondered if Vahn's creds would stretch to that kind of upgrade for the next trip.

Then she wondered if she should go and wait for Sherin to leave Vahn's room. Given how the rep had left her, it was hard to tell whether she'd be welcomed or spurned. She hovered over the controls, hated uncertainty filling her once again.

Her eyelids drooped a little and the ship sent her the tiny chiming alarm that told her that the stimulants were wearing off. She gave the timekeeper on the screen a startled glance before realizing that the ship's sensors were right. She would need to sleep just like a groundy and do it soon. With any luck, she could sleep right through the jump. TiCara sighed with frustration. If the corps could create an interstellar drive, why not a substitute for sleep? She shouldn't need it any more.

But then, madness was not an appealing option, and she'd heard all the horror stories when she was in training about the medusa pilots who gave up sleep and food for more time linked in. Her fingers flickered over the controls of the security panel, triggering the secur cameras along the route that she thought Sherin would probably take from Vahn's quarters. There were already alarms on Engineering and the Bridge; she would have to hope that they were enough.

With a thought, her medusas disconnected with an audible click. The panel closed smoothly as she withdrew from it and turned toward her temporary quarters, obedient to her body's needs once more. It seemed like only seconds later that she was lying in her sleeping cube, letting its sensors read her from head to foot. A gentle heat spread from her shoulders down her back as the memfoam sensors responded to what they thought she needed most. They vibrated slowly, loosening her muscles

She played gently with a medusa that coiled down past her shoulder. It wrapped itself around her fingertip in a caressing motion, the touch soothing her even more than the mattress. That was one of the quieter pleasures that came with being wired. After the first group of test medusa pilots crashed into the nearest planets, the next thing the engineers had done was to program the medusas to sooth and calm until the pilots could unwind, eventually fall asleep.

They said it was the shock of being wired in directly to their ships that drove them to it, but TiCara suspected that wasn't really the reason. It was the exhilaration, not the unexpectedness of that connection. Who could bear to sleep when the universe was theirs? When they could keep flying and forget all about their slowly failing human bodies?

She remembered the first time she had plugged her medusas into a training computer as the jump sling automatically wrapped itself over the bed in response to the ship's alarm. There had been a flash of heat, of light, followed by a flood of information. Her body had convulsed as her brain tried to process all of it at once. She barely remembered flailing and babbling until Elia's second had injected her with something that made her limp and relaxed.

After that, it had been all about riding the waves of input, like learning through a sleep module. She remembered thinking that she never wanted to sleep again, not when there was something so much better that she could be doing. But the implants and the ships were programmed to stop that from happening. Begrudgingly, she found herself agreeing with the updated design.

TiCara felt her medusas plug themselves into the *Astra*'s sleep settings on the console near her head. They could be overridden if there was an emergency but otherwise, she was going to be asleep for the next six cycles.

Her last waking thought was to ask the computer to search its archives for more information on Sherin Khan. They were too far out for live Net access but the computer would have backed up and stored station data while they were still in port. Maybe she could learn a little more about where the rep had been before and what she'd done, maybe even why she had responded the way that she had.

If nothing else, she would have sweet dreams about the other woman so it would be jump time well spent. Sleep took over with that thought.

CHAPTER 9

TiCara woke up to the insistent chime of an alarm. She reached out and smacked her clock hard. It was voice-controlled, so her gesture was unnecessary but the noise had worked its disturbing way into her last dream, the one about being hooked into a VR module with Sherin, just as the machine suddenly began to malfunction.

TiCara grimaced with annoyance. That dream had been getting interesting, right up until the time that the machine broke down in a sparking, beeping mess. Then she realized that the noise had been coming from the comm connection on her handheld, not the clock on the shelf. She reached over and picked it up, squinting at it as the room got gradually brighter around her, its sensors responding to her movement.

Her handheld's screen displayed the code for Vahn's comm, and she frowned at it before flipping on the audio with a sigh. "Yes, Ser?" She sat up, leaving the video turned off. He could live without seeing her newly woken and naked. "Is anything wrong?"

At the sound of her voice, the *Astra*'s wall niche opened to display her blacksuit, cleaned and ready. A new set of undergarments, synthesized from organic proteins by the ship's computers, appeared next to it. She stood up and hit the button for the portable sonic shower.

"Pilot-Captain, I would like to see you in my quarters, when you have a moment."

TiCara grimaced. Didn't he ever sleep? No wonder he looked so ancient and tired. That thought wasn't reflected in her voice when she answered him, though. "Yes Ser. I will be there soon." She wondered what the old man wanted. Then she wondered if Sherin would be with him when she got there as she showered and dressed. She wondered which alternative she should be hoping for as she stepped into the corridor, letting the door slide shut behind her with a quiet beep.

A quick tap on the nearest nutrient console dispensed a container of a beverage that smelled like a warm spiced tea from Earth, with a full meal's protein and vitamin content added to it. She gulped half of it down, then paused to savor the spicy sweet taste as it lingered on her tongue. Then she drank the rest of it slowly, enjoying the flavor. Vijay had outdone himself this trip. This tasted even better than the previous mixes. She smiled and keyed in a quick complimentary message to him on her handheld.

She disposed of the container in the recycler and started for Vahn's quarters, Sherin filling her thoughts once again. Maybe she should have overridden her medusas, taken another stimul, gone after the other woman to talk instead of sleeping. Her failure to do that might have ruined everything. Frustration filled her again and with it, a sharp sense of annoyance.

What did the rep really want from her? Or she from Sherin? It wasn't as if she hadn't thought about the sex enough, but it was always less complicated in her fantasies, and, if she were being tru, she hadn't thought past it. What was she supposed to do now? Sherin had begun to touch a place inside her, a place that she thought was numb. And she wasn't sure that she liked that feeling.

She clenched her fist and punched one of the walls as she passed it, turning her hand sideways so that the blow didn't catch her knuckles. The impact was still enough to make her pause outside Vahn's room and shake out her fingers, frowning at her own foolishness. The last thing she should be doing was hurting herself; frustrated or not, she'd need her hands for whatever came next. She shook her medusas out, letting them soothe the crankiness of her mood, and composed herself before she hit the entry request button.

Vahn was sitting up when his bondarmin let her enter, looking far less exhausted than when she'd seen him last. She resented him for that, almost as much as for the abruptness of his summons, before dismissing her annoyance as pointless. There was no sign of Sherin and she wasn't sure whether to be relieved or unhappy.

She bowed respectfully. "What can I do for you, Ser?"

"I find myself concerned that others may be interested in our journey, interested enough to be tracking us now. Did anyone contact you or your crew before we left Kyrin, perhaps asking about Electra 12? Or me?" He steepled his fingers together and studied her over them, an antique card player's gesture.

TiCara tilted her head to one side and studied him in turn. What was he really after? And why now? If she had betrayed him to another corporation, she would hardly tell him about it. And if he needed reassurance this early in the trip, then he should have taken one of his own trusted ships and used one of his own corp's pilots.

She opted to break the silence before it could become too oppressive, letting her resentment show just a bit in her tone as she answered, "The *Astra* is a good ship, Ser. And my crew is loyal. As per your request, even if they were not, they do not know our destination yet. They have had no opportunity to tell the Ears or anyone else. Do you have any reason to believe otherwise?" She bit her lip as the last phrase rolled out. That sounded angry, not cool and confident. Not reassuring.

Vahn smiled in response, the kindly expression failing to reach his eyes. Those remained deep space cold. But his voice was mild and calm when he answered with a placating gesture, "Of course, Pilot-Captain. Your loyalty is unquestioned and I'm certain it is true of your crew as well. I merely wonder about accidents, slips of the tongue, to use an Old Earth expression. You have checked the ship for tracking devices yourself?"

TiCara started to insist that her ship was clean, that she had checked it thoroughly before they left Kyrin, every compartment and storage bay. It was tru tell, as far as it went. Except that she hadn't checked the ship with a full sweep since Vahn's party came on board. Not since Sherin boarded and she saw that glitch on the bay's display while she was looking for the rep. But he didn't need to know about that yet and she recovered quickly. "Yes, Ser. All has been confirmed clear." She bowed, her expression a formal mask.

"Thank you. I can rest more easily now," Vahn relaxed back into the cushions on the bed with a sigh of his own. This time, his eyes looked warmer when he smiled. He accepted a container of something from his bondarmin and asked the man about his medication, before complimenting TiCara on her preparations and the quality of the *Astra*'s nutrient meals.

A polite dismissal followed and TiCara found herself out in the hallway with the door sliding shut behind her. She grimaced, her face turned away from the door and the external camera feed. This was exactly as she had imagined a trip with passengers would be: far more trouble than it was worth.

She walked quietly away down the corridor, as if everything was as it should be. She didn't increase her speed until she was around the corner from Vahn's room, and then she nearly flew in the ship's lowgrav, bound for Engineering and its more complex security scanners.

CHAPTER 10

VAHN WATCHED THE DOOR CLOSE behind her, then gestured to his bondarmin. "She is lying, perhaps without meaning to. Go. Check the bays and the smuggling holds. I want to be certain."

The large man nodded, and slipped out the door, his movements panther-quick and equally silent. A schematic of the ship rose in front of his left eye, circling as he turned his head. He followed it down into the depths of the ship's storage.

The image hovered, its lines a shining blue as it led him on through all the main bays. He checked each bay, seeking and finding as many of the smuggling holds as he could locate. Some were so cleverly hidden that it took him longer than he liked to find them. He had been a corporate ship inspector before he trained in medical tech; Vahn had hired him for both skills. These should have been much easier for him to locate.

He began to feel a grudging respect for TiCara, medusa-freak that she was. These were some of the best-designed smuggling caches he'd ever seen. In fact, he suspected that he was still missing a few. His doubt rested in his belly like a stone. He didn't miss things. Or, at least, he never had before, as far as he knew. Life as Vahn's bondarmin must be making him soft, careless.

He growled at his twisted reflection in the shiny metal side of a shipping container, and that was when he saw what he'd been looking for. The tracker was a good one, new and sophisticated enough to look as if it was supposed to be attached to the container, had always been there. It might be a sealing latch. Or a climate control sensor.

But he knew better. He had seen tech like this before. It came off easily when he pulled on it, tugging its tiny magnetic base free from the metal it clung to. The tiny greenish light told him that the device was active and it blinked out when he deactivated it. For a moment, he thought about smashing it. That was what Vahn would want him to do to be certain that it couldn't be reactivated.

He looked it over carefully, then reached into it and snapped one of the wires with his broad, flat fingers. That should be enough to disable it permanently. He put it back where he found it, tucking the broken wire up under the casing so that a casual observer couldn't see that it was no longer transmitting. A smile warmed his face as he walked away. Let them wonder who had found it and why they'd left it there. Carelessness should cause doubt.

He continued to check the other bays, but found nothing else. It was time to give his report. He clicked on the band at his wrist and the schematic disappeared. He climbed slowly upward, once even seeing TiCara turn down a corridor ahead of him. Any thought of telling her about the tracker vanished as soon as it appeared: the Captain didn't seem foolish enough to have placed a tracker on her own ship, but then, she hadn't seemed foolish enough to have missed one either.

Vahn could tell her if he wanted to. He shrugged as he walked down the corridor to his employer's quarters. The old man was not going to be happy about this.

Chapter 11

TiCara paused outside the hidden alcove in the tiny Engineering room that concealed the master security console, suddenly strangely reluctant to plug in her medusas and do yet another ship's scan. She probably wouldn't find anything this time either. She should just go and get a status from Erol, then get ready for her next shift.

Her lips twisted into a wry smile as she caught the direction her thoughts were going. She knew better than to sabotage herself for a pretty face. Or even a beautiful voice. Unbidden, she remembered Sherin's singing, the rich tones echoing off the distant metal walls of one of the spacer bars. She rubbed a hand across her forehead, her movements jerky and abrupt. Her medusas swirled, trying to deal with the tide of emotions that she was feeling. She forced herself to reach for the catch to turn off the alcove's shielding.

Before she could open the sensor controls, Erol slid down the ladder from the passageway above and dropped to the floor behind her with as heavy a thud as he could manage in the ship's lowgrav. She spun around, startled, and unconsciously dropped into a fighting stance.

He was scowling and holding a small metal object in one large hand. Even from a meter away, TiCara could see that his knuckles were white with tension.

She straightened cautiously before she spoke, trepidation making her voice thick and deep, "What is it? What's that?" *Please, no...*her thoughts spun in a prayer to something, though about what she wasn't sure. Even before he opened his hand, her medusas were writhing around her head, reflecting her thoughts as she frantically calculated everything that could have gone wrong, had gone wrong, might yet go wrong.

"Tracker, Captain," Erol spoke just as she recognized the thing for what it was. She reached for it, instinctively, as if holding it in her hand would make it more real. How could she have missed this when she checked the ship over before they left? Unless it had been placed after they launched? She wondered what else she might have missed and a sick dread filled her.

"It was disabled when I found it," Erol continued, flipping it over so she could see the broken wires, before dropping it into her outstretched hand. He crossed his arms and glared at the wall just past her shoulder. His mouth was set in a rigid line and she suspected from his frown that he was working through his own list of suspects.

"Where?" TiCara turned the thing over in her hands, keeping the touch of her fingers light, as if it might poison her if she wasn't careful. She wondered where Ji-min and Vijay were, then moved on to wondering the same thing about Vahn's bondarmin and Vahn himself. Not that it was any use. Sherin's face filled her mind, nudging the other ones out, no matter how hard she tried to avoid the thought.

"It was in the aft cargo bay, clipped onto a crate. It was just fortune's grace that I saw it on the scanner. It must have been destroyed or malfunctioned before I could get it."

TiCara snorted a little. She never trusted to fortune any more than she trusted to luck if she could help it. Someone had managed to plant a tracker on her ship and they avoided her vigilance to do it. Then someone else had found it and disabled it. Or destroyed it after it had done what it was supposed to do. The wires hadn't parted on their own, from what she could see; they had been cut or broken by external pressure. How did they find it? Or did they already know it was there?

The feeling of dread switched to a fiery, barely contained rage. She would find out who planted this on her ship. And nothing like this would happen again.

She spun on her heel and turned to the security console, putting the tracker down while she keyed in the codes to open it with a jerky motion, then wrenching open the cover on the sensor sockets. Her medusas were plugged in almost before she got it turned on, pulling up the cameras and the sensors in the aft bay as fast as she could think about it.

But nothing stirred now under the pale green running lights, no movement disturbed the cargo crates. She reset the ship's computer timestamp with an override code to see who had been there a few machrons earlier. Still nothing. With a disgusted noise, she reset it again: still nothing.

Erol stirred restlessly next to her, his emotions expending themselves in fidgeting. She ignored him with an effort, resetting the clock back to shortly after they left Kyrin. When she finally found what she was looking for, it happened so fast that she might have missed it if she had blinked. There was a haze over the camera's lens for an instant, perhaps for three humanoid breaths, obscuring the view just long enough for someone to get from the door to the crate and out again.

Someone knew the best angle for a shadow trade crew to view their hold. Someone knowledgeable. TiCara found herself thinking of Zig. She hoped she was right, hoped that he come aboard somehow and planted it. *Anybody but Sherin*. It was as close to a prayer as she had voiced since she was a child. She froze the obstructed screen, and stepped sideways so that Erol could see what she was looking at.

He swore, then squinted at the screen, "Looks like Haze. They sell it as a spray in the shadow markets in Kyrin and the other ports, say to use it on the Eyes to blind them. I thought it was just sales speak but it must be tru tell after all. At least it works on something, since it sure don't work on most Eyes." He grimaced and stepped away from the screen. He paced until TiCara finished setting up a scan that would check for more blocked and obscured cameras elsewhere on the ship.

Then she moved the clock forward to a machron before Erol found the tracker. Vahn's bondarmin appeared briefly, checking the bay. She saw him reach over and pick up the tracker, and turn so his shoulders blocked her view of his hands. Then, he disappeared from view.

One mystery solved. If he hadn't disconnected the tracker, she couldn't imagine who else would have. Which meant that Vahn now knew that the ship had been tracked, that her captain had failed to make it secure, and that her crew might be compromised. She froze the screen on the bondarmin and frowned at Erol.

"One mystery solved. But I doubt he planted it." His tone was firm, convincing. It made sense: why plant it, then pretend to find it if you didn't know you were being watched?

TiCara's medusas clicked free of the console and she rubbed her scalp hard. She scowled down at the screen, then back up at her Second "So who did?"

Erol rubbed one hand over his shaved head and looked at his feet. "Got the old man, the bondarmin, the crew, you, me. And the rep. Unless there's someone else hiding on board."

TiCara gave that a moment of consideration. "No," she said, at last. "I checked the whole life support system the last time I plugged in. Can hide from the crew, but can't hide breathing from the *Astra*. Where'd we source the crate?"

Erol shrugged and named one of their usual shadow trade partners. It might have been them, but it was unlikely that they would endanger a profitable trade relationship by placing the tracker. They both silently dismissed that possibility, at least for the moment. TiCara found herself thinking about Zig again. What if he had compelled someone else to plant it?

"Not the crew, unless someone got to them."

TiCara glanced at him. "Everybody's got a price. It's just that some are higher than others."

Erol looked away, his shoulders caught in an uncomfortable hunch. "No reason for the old man or you to do it," he said at last. "Ji-min would have had them load the crates, Vijay might have checked the bay. But I think it's the rep, Pilot-Captain."

It was TiCara's turn to look away, body tensed as if she had received a blow. Or expected a new one. He had to be wrong, he had to! But she asked anyway. "Why her?"

"The Ear. Who else would want to know where the old man is going, where you're going. The wire-fried Ears, they want to know everything." His eyes glinted with an sudden rage and he bared his teeth at the console wall as if his mind traveled far away from the *Astra*. TiCara gave him a startled look, wondering what the Ears had done to him. He spoke so little of his past; now she wondered if they had more in common than she had realized.

He plucked the tracker out of her hand before she could react. She hadn't realized that she had picked it up again. "This is corp-tech." He flipped it open and wrenched the cover back.

They both stared down at the little device, the symmetry of its mechanical interior making it clear that it was no shadow trade knockoff. "I talked to an Ear in Kyrin, too," she said at last. "But I didn't plant a tracker on my own ship." Her voice shook a little, looking for doubt, for denial.

But her Second was implacable. "You're not going to let a starshine-pretty like that one spin a nebula past you, are you, Captain?"

TiCara scowled and fidgeted with the edge of the shielding. She couldn't make herself look at Erol, seeing instead Sherin's face super-imposed on every surface she glared at. She wanted to believe that Erol was wrong, and the longer she didn't look at him, the longer she could go on hoping.

Then he cleared his throat, shattering her fantasies, and her shoulders sagged. She scowled at him and muttered, "I'll talk to her."

"Is that best, Captain? I could—" He cut himself off at her gesture and stood, tense and poised, waiting for whatever she was going to say next.

Something about his tone felt wrong, as if he had some kind of personal need to encourage her distrust of the rep. TiCara sensed something out of place, but didn't recognize its source. It couldn't be Erol; he been loyal to her since he came on board. She had to be imagining the wrongness. He was right: it had to be one of the crew, the bondarmin or Sherin. And only one of them had been seen talking to an Ear right before they left port.

But even if he was right, what was she going to do with the other woman? The *Astra* was too small to have prison quarters. Of course, if her Second was right and they could convince Vahn of it, there might be another possibility. "If you're right, we need somewhere safe to put her while we're moving. Then we'll need to convince her employer that she planted the tracker so we can drop her off somewhere planet or stationside. Check the computer for the locking codes for her room?"

Erol nodded. "I'll get it set up." He nodded and climbed up the ladder to the next level.

TiCara watched him go, then sealed up the security console. Even her medusas couldn't sooth the sinking pit in her stomach, though they made a valiant effort and sent a soothing wave of heat through the tense muscles of her neck. Once she accused the rep of corp espionage and locked her up, that was it. She'd never find out if the other woman still sang, or what she was upset about in the crew lounge, or what she tasted like. All of those things struck her as equally painful.

It was the *Astra*'s hum around her that decided things: this was her ship, her home, her everything. Whatever she had to do to keep it, she would do. She picked up the tracker from the console where Erol had left it and tucked it into her suit. The small object sent a cold chill through her, made her remember who she was and how she'd gotten here. No one was going to take that away from her, not even the most beautiful woman she'd ever met.

TiCara left Engineering, headed for Sherin's quarters. This time, the rep was where she expected to find her when she checked the cameras. TiCara imagined that she could feel her breathing through the room's door before she even tapped on the chime to let the other woman know that she was outside. She made herself override her hesitation and doubts and hit the chime hard.

The sound was enough to make her wince. She needed to be more subtle than this, make sure that Erol was right, before she did anything that she couldn't take back. Closing her eyes, she wrapped herself in shreds of doubt and hope.

Then the door slid open and Sherin stood just inside, as if she'd been waiting for her. The sight of her made TiCara's pulse race, her breath catch. They stared at each other, each one seemingly waiting for the other to make the next move.

Then TiCara stepped forward and Sherin stepped back, letting her in. The gesture reminded TiCara of a dance, like the one she'd been doing with the rep when they met back on Kyrin. And now she was about to make them take a huge step away, perhaps off into the never-never of the starfields. The knowledge sat in her stomach like a lump of meteorite.

Sherin's face was a mask, unreadable and blank as one of the *Astra*'s walls. TiCara wondered what she was thinking, what she could say to break through that shell. She forced herself to speak first, instead of giving into impulse and reaching out to let her hands and her medusas speak for her. "I need tru tell, rep." She walked further into the room, pulling the disabled tracker out of her suit but holding it in her closed hand as she let the door's sensor close it behind her.

TiCara met Sherin's impassive stare with one of her own, looking for a signal for what she should do or say next. She tried to imagine that she was facing a stranger and she planned her next words carefully. But there was something in Sherin's eyes that changed her, that yanked a different response from her than the one she'd planned. "I looked for you afterwards, but I couldn't find you."

Sherin dropped her gaze and turned away, her fingers running through her hair and over her scalp in that same nervous gesture that TiCara had seen earlier. It reminded her of the scarring on the other woman's head and she blurted out, "What happened to you? To your head?" Unthinkingly, she gestured with the tracker.

Sherin's eyes went wide, then she shot a fierce glare at TiCara before looking away. She glanced down at the bed, then back up at TiCara, her face stone once more. "Ship fire. I didn't get out in time. Was that all you wanted to know, Captain?"

It was as if they were back on Kyrin and they hadn't been anything more to each other than they were before they left the port. TiCara ached and burned, letting words bubble up to her lips, then swallowing them back down again, judging each to be too desperate, too angry, too revealing. Finally, she settled for a gesture and raised her arm between them and opened her hand to display the tracker.

She watched Sherin's every movement, every breath, looking for signs of betrayal. Or innocence. Part of her still hoped that the other woman would react by looking shocked, protesting that she didn't know what the device was.

Sherin said nothing, did nothing beyond taking a quick breath and frowning, her expression suggesting dismay and resignation more than surprise. She crossed her arms and tilted her head to one side, considering first the tracker, then TiCara. "Not my pretty, Captain. Why did you think it was?"

It wasn't enough. TiCara saw her own disbelief reflected in an instant of hurt on the rep's face. The fleeting wounded look on her face was almost enough to distract the pilot, but not quite. "Crew says you met with an Ear in port. Did the Ear give you this? How much cred did you take to put it on my ship?" She could hear the fury in her voice, welling up from every centimeter of her body.

Sherin flinched, then scowled. "You think your crew will tru tell you more than me? Vahn sends me to negotiate with Ears as well as shadow trade pilots. Or did you think yourself so nova that you're the only one I talk to for him?" If TiCara was ice, Sherin was blazing hot, a barely contained wildfire. TiCara could feel the heat from nearly a meter away.

It made her gut twist with want, need, desire so desperate that she would have taken the other woman then and there if Sherin had given her any sign that she wanted her, despite everything that had happen. She triggered a shock from one of her medusas, letting the momentary pain distract her from what she wanted and pull her back to what she needed to do. "So the Ear didn't give you this?" She motioned at Sherin with the tracker, letting her tone convey her disbelief. "What did you get from him then?" When she imagined Sherin talking to Zig, betraying her to Zig, all desire fled, leaving nothing but anger behind.

"Would you believe anything that I told you now was tru tell? You've already decided that I put this thing on the ship, that I'm working for the Ears." Sherin dropped down onto the bed, making the shelf that supported the mattress creak with the sudden impact. She gestured around at the tiny space and added, "Do you want to look for more? Maybe I put those things everywhere I went on your precious ship." She bared her teeth in a savage grimace.

TiCara's wounded feelings crystallized into a ball of pure pain somewhere in the middle of her chest and she said the most hurtful thing that occurred to her, "So sex with me was just like spraying Haze on the camera? You should turn Ear yourself, not just spy for them. I hear it's worth more creds."

Sherin's face blanched and her full lips thinned into a straight line. She seemed to choke on her words and she swallowed hard. Then she suddenly buried her face in her hands, her elbows on her knees. It looked to TiCara as if she was crying and involuntarily, she reached out to caress her shoulder, only to hesitate, one hand frozen in mid-air.

Instead, she asked again, "Did the Ear in Kyrin give you anything? If this isn't yours, give me tru tell so I can decide what to believe." When Sherin didn't respond, she started to pace around the room. It was all she could do not tear through her belongings, looking for more trackers or any other sign that the rep was working for the Ears.

Sherin's handheld was sitting on the small shelf next to the bed and TiCara craned her head, trying to see the screen. When she glanced around, Sherin was still bent over, face in her hands, but now she appeared to be regaining control. TiCara nudged the handheld over, glancing at the list of messages. It was Zig's name that she was expecting, or fearing to see, but it was Elia's name that leapt out at her. She backed away from it as if she'd been stung.

But Elia wasn't an Ear and she wouldn't track the *Astra*. Her certainty faded nearly the moment it appeared. Would she? She thought back to every moment, every gesture of her encounter with her former lover on Kyrin. She remembered her sense that something was wrong, that Elia had changed, and her heart ached. The former pilot had to be involved in this somehow.

TiCara emerged from her thoughts swearing, a stream of port curses pouring from her lips. Somehow, the older pilot must have realized that they were going to Electra from something she had let slip. Any tru coordinates for the asteroid would be worth serious cred to an ambitious Ear. That had to be why she'd paid or persuaded Sherin to plant the tracker on the ship. Or perhaps, someone else, if Sherin was telling the truth. But that was unlikely, given the rep's behavior. Sherin and Elia were obviously partners in something.

She turned back to the other woman. Sherin lifted her face from her hands and TiCara could see her tear-streaked cheeks. Her eyes were still full of unshed tears. "What more do you want from me?" Her voice trembled. "I have nothing left. Nothing without..." She gestured at TiCara's face as her voice trailed off and she turned away.

Nothing without...what? Me? TiCara couldn't believe it. Nothing Sherin had said or done so far suggested that she felt that much of a connection, that much passion. The rep was playing games with her. That's what all this was: one big game, with dire consequences for TiCara and her crew. And she was going to tell the rep that, tell her and expose her for what she was and leave her in a port on the way back from Electra. Her voice came out as a snarl, "You--"

Her handheld pinged loudly. Erol's emergency code was an urgent summons, cutting off what she'd been about to say, demanding all of her attention. She stared at it for a moment, then back at Sherin. The rep looked at her handheld too, some emotion that TiCara couldn't read twisting her expression. "I'll deal with you later," TiCara snarled, then turned on her heel and left the room, her medusas swirling in a cloud around her.

CHAPTER 12

S HERIN WATCHED THE DOOR CLOSE behind the pilot and cursed herself for not going after her. She remembered TiCara watching her sing in the bars, her face lit with an adoring glow. No one else looked at her quite the same way, as if they heard her the way that she wanted to be heard. Then she'd gotten wired and went away and Sherin hadn't seen her again for several revolutions.

By then, Sherin had become a pilot herself. Until Electra. Until she'd been left with nothing, no medusas, no identity. It had been worse even than that, since what was left made her doubt everything she had before getting wired. She hadn't sung since then.

She scrubbed her face angrily. She was being foolish. She had a new life now, a new mission. And that should be enough to give her hope. They said that she could get them back, that she could be all that she was before. Better, even.

But...she couldn't help but think about TiCara and Vahn. The one wanted her, broken as she was and the other had trusted her enough to make her his personal representative. She wasn't giving either of them anything comparable in return, and that hurt. Her birth crèche had always prized honor and honesty above all else and had raised her with those virtues in mind. While she had grown up and moved away from its influence, those early lessons still held sway.

And the way TiCara looked at her gave her chills, made her want to open herself up to the pilot like she hadn't been able to do with to a lover since everything changed. The pilot was different. She could see the vulnerability under all her bravado, see that she was holding in some deep hurt that Sherin wanted to ease. It had something to do with the Ears, that much was clear.

Thinking of the Ears made Sherin tug sharply on a lock of her hair as she wound it around her finger. She wished that she never gone near them now, never accepted what Zig offered. But Elia had vouched for him, said he was her friend. At the time, that seemed enough.

Black holes take them both! The older pilot had seemed so sympathetic and friendly when they first met. She was the only one who Sherin had been able to talk to about what had happened. They met many times at the port bars, sharing stories about their lives. It was only natural that their talk would turn to past loves and Elia mentioned TiCara. That had been enough to keep Sherin coming back, wanting to hear more. Elia became more of a friend and a confidante each time they met. And now that friendship was going to drive her to destroy every hope she had of a new love, a new life.

Sherin punched the mattress under her and tried to think about what to do next. If she was still wired...but then, she wouldn't be in the mess she was in now if that was true. The fight drained out of her with that thought. She collapsed flat and threw her arm over her face. There had to be something, some way out of this that didn't leave her life a complete wreck in its wake. That tracker wasn't hers, even if she did know what it was. So who had planted it there?

Her brain spun with emotions and memories and she couldn't focus on any of them. Finally, she settled for remembering the way

TiCara's body felt under hers. The memory of silky tan skin against hers and the pilot's soft moans were enough to have her unfastening her suit and undergarments a moment later. Maybe if she was satisfied, at least for the moment, she'd figure out what to do next.

She bared her breasts and ran her fingers lightly over one, then the other, stroking and tugging her nipples into solid points. In her imagination, it was TiCara's hands, TiCara's mouth, sucking, nibbling. The thought sent a bolt of pure lightning through her and she felt her thighs tense, wanting more.

That feeling sent one of her hands down between her thighs, while the other continued to caress her full breasts. She slipped her fingers into her aching wetness, wishing desperately that she had a toy or VR mods to use along with them. Imagining TiCara touching her was fun, but a VR TiCara would be close to being with the real thing.

Just without medusas.

She tried to picture the pilot without her implants and failed: she'd noticed her once she was wired, not before. They looked like part of the pilot now and even in her fantasies, Sherin couldn't take them away from her. Instead, she tried to imagine the other woman using them on her, setting her flesh on fire with their touch. Caressing her in ways that she couldn't yet bear outside her imagination.

Her other hand wandered instinctively over her body, searching for the most sensitive places to touch. She caressed herself, teasing her body to life in search of a quick release. Her head was full of TiCara and the way she smelled and tasted and what would have happened if she hadn't run away from the lounge.

Every nerve ending tingled as her sensations concentrated around the nerve endings beneath her thumb. She gasped and uttered a moan of her own, then another. Her legs locked as her hips rocked against her hands and she nearly fell off the bed when she came.

Sherin lay there gasping for a few minutes and laughed at the craziness of the situation that she found herself in. The sound startled her; she couldn't remember the last time she'd laughed at anything, not like this anyway. That thought nearly made her cry. She wanted to laugh because she was happy, not because everything was so utterly hopeless. The old Sherin, before she was wired, she used to laugh a lot. Sherin missed that person right now, missed her with all her heart.

Besides, she wanted to laugh with TiCara. Right now, that seemed impossible. Sherin sighed and groaned. Now she had to try and find a way out of this mess. She got up, took a shower, then lay back on the bunk, her eyes closed as she tried to think.

CHAPTER 13

Z IG WATCHED THE *ASTRA* ON the main monitor of his ship and gave the image a savage grin. That little fool of a pilot had no idea that they were chasing her and that she was going to lead him to everything he'd ever wanted. If he did this right, he could blackmail Vahn and probably even force the techs on Electra to pay him to keep their secrets. If they failed to comply…or even if they did, he could convince the other corps that he could sell them everything there was to know about the asteroid and its labs.

He was going to do this right. Not like the times before. His employer had been very clear about what kinds of results would be acceptable, and he planned on delivering what they wanted. They just didn't know what else he planned to gain from this trip.

He thought about what he had hidden in the aft cargo bay of his ship and hid a smile. Two top-grade military robots would be all the guarantee that he needed to capture it all: the coordinates, the tell, the credits and the pilot of the ship that they were pursuing. The rush of pleasure he felt was enough to justify pursuing the *Astra* instead of trusting to the tracker alone. Hardware failed and traitors had second thoughts so he and Yva would have to be their own fail-safe.

TiCara had been his before, her body his to use as he pleased. He had almost acquired enough creds to buy her indenture and extend it when it completed and she fled the Ear dormitories without a backward glance. This time, there would be creds in plenty and he could use them to buy out all her debt. She'd be his until she paid all of it off and he'd ensure that would be quite challenging. He felt a spasm between his legs as he hardened at the thought.

Even better than owning TiCara, he'd be one of the most powerful men in the known galaxies. At least for a little while. Once he sold the information, he would have to find another way to gain power. Even blackmail had its limits. He was realistic enough to understand that. But he meant to make the most of it while he could.

"Zig, we are too close." The voice of his companion Ear startled him back into the present, dashing meteorite ice on his fantasies. He had almost forgotten that she was there. Yva leaned forward, the lights glinting off the bare skin of her shaved head. She frowned at the nav computer screen and tapped the controls with one long finger. The gesture slowed them down, putting more distance between them and the *Astra.*

He had always hated Yva, hated that she commanded more respect and influence from their instructors and their employers. He loathed her cool competent ruthlessness that had succeeded when he had failed on their only previous mission together. For a wild moment, Zig thought about overruling her, about moving in even closer to the other ship to make sure that they couldn't escape. If only he could have gotten another partner, one easier to control!

Resentment surged as he thought about how carefully he had groomed and selected another Ear, a more malleable one, only to have his recommendation dismissed and his employer insist on Yva. She was there to monitor him as much as to complete the job, he knew as much by the way she watched him.

But she was right about their speed, at least this time, and he forced himself to sit still and look at their ship's maintenance screens instead. "They won't notice us," he tried to make his words sound believable, but they sounded hollow even to him.

Yva tilted her head to one side and studied him as if he was an interesting alien life form. "I'm here for the assignment, foolish Zig. Not for you. Find the asteroid, get the coordinates for our employer, transmit them and return to the station, nothing else. I don't know what more you want. The pilot? Didn't you get enough of that silly wired bonebag in the dorms? She wasn't even an eager bedmate and had few other uses even then." She snorted, the sound disturbingly loud on the quiet Bridge.

Zig looked at her and imagined what she'd look like with her neck broken. Yva must have seen something in his face because her blaster was in her hand, barrel pressed against his neck before he could draw breath. "Foolish boy," she crooned, "I'll fry you before you make a move. And our employers will hang your flayed skin in the entrance to headquarters as a warning to those who don't obey orders." She gave him a sharp-toothed grin, all points and angles.

He pulled away from the blaster's edge and tried to shoot her a grin of his own in response to show her that he wasn't afraid. She moved the blaster closer, pressing it into his neck, and glaring at him until he bowed his head in acknowledgment, tempering his rage and resentment with fear.

She was right about the consequences of getting caught: when he killed her, if their corp found out, the penalty would be death. So he'd have to be very careful about it.

A sharp beep from the computer screen yanked their attention from each other. Zig growled as he keyed in the code to see the status failure that had set off the alarm. "Tracker's disabled. How in all the black holes..."

Yva glanced over his shoulder. "Maybe the wirehead freak has gotten smarter. You hid it, yes?"

Zig glared at her. "*I* didn't hide it. She'd never let me get close enough. I had...a confederate on the ship do it for me." A movement on the screen caught his eye. Was the *Astra* moving faster, increasing the distance between them? "Are they running? We've got to catch up!" He elbowed Yva away from the controls and began keying in the command for the acceleration, his fingers frantic. Their ship shot forward in response.

Yva snarled. "You always were dense as a dwarf star where she was concerned! If they see us, they'll run and hide and then we'll get nothing, not without the tracker." She shoved him back into his seat and hit the controls to slow them down again.

Had the *Astra* seen them? A moment later, the other ship jumped for a nearby system at full speed. There was a blur as they were left behind. No question about whether or not they knew they were being pursued now.

They both froze, stunned. But Yva recovered first, grabbing the controls. "I'm taking command," she spat. "Enough of this."

Zig seethed and reached for his own blaster, only to draw back his hand. Much as he hated to admit it, her reflexes were a fraction better than his. She would get them caught up to the *Astra* again, if anyone could. They were heading for Gathwaite from their last coordinates. Electra had to be there, somewhere.

Once they got to Electra, Yva would become expendable. He knew far more about nanotech than she did. If he could land on the asteroid, the techs would talk to him and he would get what he needed. Selling what tech he could steal or bargain for might even be worth more in the long term than the mere coordinates.

And Yva, well, Yva would get what was coming to her then. He let his imagination run away with him while she plotted a new course in the *Astra*'s wake.

Chapter 14

TiCara pulled out her handheld the moment the door to Sherin's room whooshed closed behind her. She raced for the nearest ladder that would get her back up to the *Astra*'s Bridge fast enough to deal whatever was going on. "What is it?"

Erol's voice boomed in her ears. "Ji-min just spotted a corp ship behind us. It keeps slowing down, then getting close again. Like it's chasing us and doesn't care if we know it's there."

TiCara's breath hissed through her teeth. Had the same corp planted the tracker on the ship? But if they had, why follow them? Her medusas lay suspiciously quiet against her ears and neck. She already knew the answer then, or suspected it and they had no need to sooth or calm. Tracking and following them, assuming it was the same culprit, suggested a personal interest.

Her stomach turned as the memory of Zig as she had seen him last filled her head. Zig and Elia. He must be following them now, following them on Elia's tell. That had to be it. Why he was following them instead of relying on the tracker didn't matter, at least not as much as getting away.

Erol slid out of the pilot's chair when she swung up onto the Bridge. He backed away as she darted into the chair and sent her medusas into the computer's plugins with a single coordinated motion. He moved over into the gunner's chair that they almost never used. The *Astra* had more firepower than it had carried on previous trips, but TiCara knew that it wouldn't be enough to do more than startle a corp ship, maybe damage it a little.

But they might be able to get away if the other ship's pilot was surprised enough to back out of range while they jumped. Erol opened the navigational computer above his chair and began prepping the pulse cannon. He caught TiCara's eye and she could tell that they were both thinking the same thing: too many shots and they'd be out of power and dead in space, nothing left to jump with.

It would be better to jump now, if they could. She checked to see if they had enough fuel to jump at all and confirmed that they did. The *Astra*'s navigational computation was slightly more reassuring; they could make it to the Gathwaite System on a jump, but they'd have to find a place to refuel before they left, or sooner, depending on what was waiting for them. Now to hope that Electra wasn't a myth and that Vahn's connections were good enough to ensure them a warm welcome. It was a lot of shaky intel to hang a job on.

TiCara winced at the direction that her thoughts were taking. At least the *Astra* had something that the corp ship chasing them probably didn't: her. She sucked in a deep, shuddering breath and centered her thoughts on the coordinates that she had gotten from Vahn. Then she kicked the ship's acceleration up, all the way to top speed, just under jump trajectory.

Belatedly, she remembered their passengers a few moments before taking them to full speed into the jump. A vision of Vahn and Sherin flattened to the floor of their respective quarters shot across her mind. She briefly forced herself out of the ship and nudged Erol, who was fastening the webbing on his chair to prepare for the ship's acceleration. His eyes were closed but they flew open at TiCara's touch. "Passengers," she muttered.

He nodded guiltily as if he had forgotten them too and tapped the comm. TiCara sank back into the ship. The rush of circuitry flowed over and through her like a wave. The electrical connections sparked as her synapses touched them, adjusting them here, redirecting them there. The *Astra* sang at her touch, fluid and responsive as it always was when she and the ship were one.

She thought about the ship following them and an instant later had a view from the *Astra*'s tail. Their pursuer dwindled into the distance, caught by surprise, or so she hoped. TiCara grinned at the sight. But it wasn't going to be enough. Any corp ship that was space-worthy had more power at its command than her shadow-trade engines. They could catch up eventually, if they had some idea of where the *Astra* was headed. And if it was indeed Zig, he had a very good idea.

Now to hope that it wasn't Zig and that the other pilot knew nothing about their destination. TiCara let her consciousness merge with the navigational system, comparing coordinates and nearby systems as fast as she could think. She could see the Gathwaite System, as well the Aeon planets and their surroundings, spread out in front of her mind's eyes against the splendor of the starfields.

Part of her couldn't help but pause to admire them and the galaxy around them. Plugging into the ship was the ultimate in sensory overload, visual and sensual. A comet licked the edge of her consciousness, its distant tail blazing bright against the velvet black of the space between the stars.

She turned the ship toward it, hoping to use its wake to hide in until they could jump to the Gathwaite asteroid belts. Let the corp pilot behind her try to find them then. All she needed was space to maneuver and they could outfly almost any of the corp crews. Even

Zig. She laughed silently, feeling the vibration spread out through her implants.

Practice enabled her to spare a few thoughts for the status of the crew and her passengers and she dipped into the ship's sensors to check their status. Vahn and his bondarmin were in Vahn's quarters, presumably already in their slings, from their readings. It would take some time for the *Astra*'s gravitation spin field to reestablish itself when they got to the other end of the jump so hopefully they would remember to stay put until then.

She kept looking. Sherin was in her room, right where TiCara had left her. Just looking at her readings, she felt a jangle of mixed emotions. If things were different...if the rep could plug in, she could share the ship with her while the two of them merged their minds. Adrift from their fears and anger, she and Sherin could explore each other's minds without limits or boundaries, get to know each other without lies.

Wait, why was she fantasizing about Sherin having medusas? Why would...a wave of sensation from the Astra swept over her and she lost track of her thoughts and what she'd been imagining. But she couldn't stop herself from wondering what Sherin was doing now and whether or not she regretted her betrayal. Or if she was still planning on trying to contact Elia or Zig.

TiCara's medusas sent a quick chiming alarm to her synapses at her sudden rage at that thought and she pulled her thoughts away. It was a bad idea to get this emotional while she was plugged in. She knew that, knew what happened when pilots got distracted. It was generally ended in a wrecked ship and a dead crew.

TiCara thought something like an apology at her ship and checked on the crew next. She found exactly what she expected: Ji-min and Vijay were in the slings just outside the *Astra*'s tiny greenbay, waiting for the jump and ship's gravity to return. Probably napping, judging from their quiet readings.

Erol was right next to her, of course, and she started to move past him without checking his vitals. But something made her pause. His readings were odd, off in a way she didn't expect. He was using more air than he should be and seemed agitated. TiCara wondered if he was sick, but surely Vijay's medical sensors would have picked up on that. He ran them every time they slept, dealing with the more mundane and milder illnesses during their down time with a med feed. She made a mental note to have Erol report to their tiny medical computer once they had shaken off their pursuers.

Another check on the aft monitors and sensors to check on the corp ship again, now far behind them. But still too close. She located the comet and with a thought, she aimed the *Astra* for the far side of its tail. Then she sealed the view screens and sent a warning pinging through the ship, telling everyone on board to stay slinged while they jumped.

Debris blew against the *Astra*'s hull, showering and pitting its wings and shell with particles. Part of TiCara winced, thinking about the damage to her ship, while the rest of her reveled in dancing them away from pursuit. For the next few moments, she focused on moving them to the far side of the comet and plotting a path that would keep it between them and their pursuers. With enough of Erol's good fortune, the comet would travel close enough to the asteroid belts that TiCara could take them from one hiding place to another with a short jump that would save fuel.

She smiled at the *Astra*'s nav board and concentrated on keeping up with the comet.

Chapter 15

SOME TIME AFTER THE *ASTRA*'s jump, Vahn began to recover, at least enough to wonder what had happened to prompt the ship's sudden acceleration. Were they running from something or towards something? The *Astra* Second's communication that they were avoiding debris was reasonable, unless one considered their destination.

And the hidden tracker that was no longer hidden. Were there others, not yet discovered? It was not a concern to be dismissed lightly.

Vahn suspected that they were being pursued as well, but by whom? The possibilities were legion: business rivals, corp associates, his own clan. He sighed wearily; to have lived long enough to have acquired so many enemies was a heavy burden. Would they were all as honorable in their dealings as he.

He stretched a little and let his breathing settle, centering himself.

His enemies would rue their actions once he reached Electra. The technicians there would correct his wretched body's reaction to Eternayouth. He had their assurances of that, and he trusted that he had gotten tru tell from them, once enough credits exchanged accounts. An image of himself before he began to age rose in his mind and he longed for it, as he might a lover.

But they weren't near Electra yet and there were dangers in plenty to face. The first priority was the matter of the tracker. Once he knew who had planted it, he would know better which foe might be close enough to him to pose a genuine threat. All he needed to investigate further was ship's gravity restored and his stomach to cease trying to crawl up his throat.

He spared a glance at his bondarmin. The man sat still in his chair, eyes closed and breathing careful. He appeared to be meditating rather than sleeping. It was a sensible choice and Vahn spared him an approving thought.

He had not hired the man from anyone connected to his corp or his clan. Each of those was too close to him in their own ways, too likely to betray him, and he wanted this trip kept secret. He would lose all credibility if the techs could do nothing and he had to crawl back to Kyrin the same old and broken man who had left. Better to die off planet than to go through that again.

Instead, he had hired a bondarmin from a subcontractor he was not connected to by blood or commerce to protect and nurse him, and a shadow trade pilot who owed him no loyalty beyond the credits he could pay her to transport them. Once this job was done, she would find another contract and move on, forgetting this trip in the ones that followed. He trusted to her pragmatism even more than to her greed. He spent a few moments contemplating what he knew of each, his bondarmin and the woman piloting her ship through the systems, weighing each vice and virtue against each other.

Sammo, the bondarmin, was cold and calculating. He was also looking for a way to return to his distant home. There had been an incident involving two dead men in a portside dock that had caused him to seek employment elsewhere. But there had been a crèche and a group marriage on that planet as well, and a longing to return that was nearly palpable when Vahn met him.

Vahn had promised him that he would settle matters with the authorities on his homeworld, that he could go back home once his job was complete. Nothing in Vahn's experience suggested that this kind of promise would not buy absolute loyalty from such a man.

The pilot was less easy to read, apart from her need for credits. He hired her for several jobs before he thought he had taken her measure. In the end, it had been TiCara's clear desire to be free of the corps and the Ears that decided him. To her, creds were freedom, and that freedom was nearly everything. Her loyalty could be bought as long as that sale brought with it the possibility of such a future and required nothing outside of her rather limited moral code.

As for his own corporate rep, he had thought that he knew what motivated her as well. The problem was that he didn't hold the key to that motivation and he wasn't sure who did. Bringing her on this journey had been a calculated risk, not merely an opportunity to have a pretty face at his side. He was honest enough to admit that might have been enough for him once, before his health began to fail. But he had seen the way that she and the pilot looked at each other, so he thought that perhaps TiCara's presence would be enough to ensure Sherin's loyalty.

But now it seemed that he had been wrong. Maybe it was time that he and Sammo spoke to his rep about trackers and Ears.

He wasn't certain that she was responsible for this betrayal, but he needed to find out. Already, the idea that it was Sherin gnawed at him, disturbing his thoughts. He cleared his throat to capture Sammo's attention. "I think that we need to visit our esteemed rep, when next this tub rights itself. I have questions for her and I would like you to accompany me."

Sammo opened his eyes halfway and nodded, as if speaking while the ship was still accelerating was too much for him. Perhaps it was. Vahn noticed that the man's face had a greenish tinge that did not bode well for subsequent jumps. He made a grimace of sympathy before he closed his eyes to wait.

It wasn't long. The *Astra*'s walls shuddered around them as the ship slowed down and its internally rotating engines kicked back on. Vahn made himself a silent promise that after this trip, he would travel on starships big and luxurious enough to maintain consistent gravity at full speed. After this trip, he would do many things the way that he preferred to do them.

He let Sammo help him up and tried to ignore the creaks and pops of his joints. There would be no forgiveness for anyone who tried to sabotage this trip. Nothing was going to keep him in this failing shell of a body. That thought was enough to keep him moving with grim determination.

Fortunately, it wasn't far to Sherin's quarters. Sammo raised questioning eyebrows when they reached her door, then hit the door buzzer when he saw his employer's head jerk of affirmation. Vahn let his face slide into a bland corp expression, pleasant and unchallenging. In contrast, when Sherin opened the door, she looked panicked and there were drying tears left unheeded tracks down her cheeks.

She scrubbed at her face as she asked, "What is it, Ser? You could have commed me and I would have come to you." Sherin looked from Vahn to Sammo, then back again. Something that she saw there was enough to make her close up, make her posture stiffen and her expression turn blank.

Vahn smiled, letting a tinge of reassurance warm his face. "I needed to speak to you and did not want to wait. At least no longer than it took for the esteemed Pilot-Captain slow down enough to restore the gravity after our unexpected jump. Do you know why she decided that jump was necessary?"

At the mention of TiCara, Sherin looked away and gestured them inside her tiny room. Vahn took the only chair and she sat on the bed, while Sammo was left standing behind their employer. Were it not for the tension in the room, Vahn thought, it would have made for a most relaxed tableau.

"I have not spoken to her...for some time. Our tell was interrupted by an urgent comm and she left. She did not tell me why." Sherin's face was still devoid of expression, but her shoulders were now hunched, as if to avoid a blow, and her hands rested rigidly on her knees.

"That suggests unexpected bad news. Perhaps engine malfunction. Or an external threat. Sammo found a tracker in one of the bays and we believe it to have placed at the behest of one of my rivals."

Sherin flinched slightly, a shadow crossing her face for the flicker of a breath, before it vanished and she raised one eyebrow. Tilting her head, she gave her employer a concerned look. "Was there any indication of who might have placed it, Ser?"

It was exactly the question he would have expected from his trusted rep, when she had occupied that role. But he had seen that flinch as well. Guilt or previous accusation? Sammo had left the disabled tracker in the bay, after all. Any of the crew or the captain could have found it. But why accuse his rep instead of his bondarmin? Or each other?

Guilt, then, was the obvious answer. Whoever her accusers were, they must have seen something he had not. A cold rage boiled up in Vahn. How dare she do this to him, after he had hired her, despite her damaged state? He had paid her very well and treated her with honor, entrusting her with his daily affairs, his arrangements, even with hiding the decline of his health. He had given her purpose when she had none. What had they offered her that could outweigh what he had given her?

"Which Ear gave it to you?" His voice sounded like a growl to his own hearing.

Sherin stared back at him, wide-eyed and startled. "No, Ser! I did not bring a tracker on board. I...I told the Pilot-Captain that too, but I don't think she believed me." A tear trickled down her cheek and she scrubbed it away, the motion of her hand rapid and furious. "I did not betray you, Ser Vahn. You must believe me."

"Why did the Pilot-Captain not believe you? She must be wiser than I to have become so quickly suspicious." Vahn could feel Sammo shift into a defensive posture behind him and a distant part of his mind reminded him to add more credits to the man's account. He would earn more than his agreed upon fee on this journey.

Sherin dropped her face into both hands, a cascade of ebony hair shielding her expression for a few seconds. When she looked back up, it was obvious that she was beginning to regain control. "I am sorry that you have received bad tell, Ser." The glance she threw at Sammo was a flame of pure hatred. "I spoke to an Ear before we left Kyrin, but it was regarding another matter, not about you or your concerns, Ser. TiCara has an unreasoning distrust of all Ears and accused me of planting the tracker because one of the crew saw us sharing tell."

Vahn suppressed another flash of anger. Why had the pilot confronted the rep instead of telling him? It should have come to him first to discipline his own employees. "Which Ear was it?"

Sherin looked at her hands. "It was the one called Zig, Ser. I know him from...before. He is a friend of my mentor, former Pilot-Captain Elia LJ786." She made a vague gesture at her head by way of conveying the "before" and "after" that she referred to. "We spoke of navigation and he wanted to know more about Pilot-Captain TiCara and whether I had seen her in port. I told him I did not know her and had heard tell only that she was a good pilot. That was all the tell we exchanged." She looked up at Vahn, dark eyes pleading now.

This time, Vahn found himself looking away. Could he believe her? It was the word "navigation" that had him worried. If the tracker was meant to reveal Electra's location, and the techs learned that it was his own employee who had betrayed them, they would be within their charter to refuse to help him. Killing him would be almost secondary to that.

Zig, he knew of only by reputation. Not an Ear that he would hire to represent his interests, based on the little tell that he had heard. He wondered why another corp would, until it came to him that the Ear might be working on his own, might have gone rogue in this matter without his employer's knowledge. But there was nothing he could do about that now. The tracker had been purposefully planted, suggesting Ear involvement, whether directly or through an agent on board the ship.

Sherin coughed and murmured, "I didn't give him the coordinates, not the tru ones. I couldn't do that to you. Or her." Vahn refrained from asking which "her" the rep meant, and bit back an angry retort. It was clear which of them was more important from the tone of Sherin's voice.

"But you don't know what they offered, what they said they could do on Electra." She ran her fingers through her hair and over her scalp in a nervous, jerky gesture. Her voice shook with emotion. "I went there before, back when I was a medusa pilot, with a different employer. They were working on new tech in their labs. I was there because I was curious, wanting to see what the tech would do. Then, something went wrong, and the nanobots were released. I lost consciousness and when I was resuscitated, they…my medusas were gone." Her voice broke.

Vahn frowned, filling in the gaps in what she was telling him. Her tale matched much of what he had already heard. "They, your shadow employers, offered to have them restored if you betrayed me? And you expect me to believe that you refused to do this?"

She glared up at him now, angry at his obvious contempt. "Do you know what it cost me to deny this, Ser? To be whole again, to be able to fly as one with a ship, even a small one like this?" She gestured around at the walls of the *Astra,* her face filled with desperate longing for an instant, before shifting back to outrage. "But I couldn't. You would have never forgiven me. And she--she would not want me, not if I did that. Now, neither of you believes that I'm giving you tru tell and I'm losing it all anyway. Again." She slumped on the bed as if the fight had drained out of her.

Vahn felt a small twinge of compassion. True, she had nothing but motivation for betrayal, and he had no reason to believe her tell. But she was lovely in her vulnerability and despite knowing better, he was drawn to her and found himself wanting to accept her explanation. With an effort, he stilled his emotions and asked another question. "How long have you known the Pilot-Captain that she should have such a hold on you?"

Sherin's voice was dull and listless, but got more animated as she got lost in her memories. "She used to come to hear me when I sang in the bars. Her face, the way she watched me, she was really hearing me, not like most of the others. I was the most amazing thing that she'd ever heard. I could see that in her face. And she wanted me, wanted me so badly I could taste it even on stage. But we never spoke, not back then. Too afraid." She smiled a little, as if she was laughing at herself.

Sherin paused to draw a shaky breath, before continuing, "Watching her with the other medusa pilots, that was made me want to get wired. They were all so strong, so full of possibilities. I wanted that, almost as much as I wanted her, so I got wired myself. Then I went to Electra and was…cured. After that, you hired me. And you began hiring her."

"At your recommendation," Vahn pointed out.

She nodded. "She's a good pilot, reliable, just what you wanted. But I wanted to be near her, to see if she still saw me the way that she had. She was different too. And she was still wired. I couldn't bear to get too close to them or her, too close to everything I'd lost. Who would want me without them?" Her voice broke again and she started crying.

Vahn tilted his head to look up at Sammo. His bondarmin made a small motion with his hand, one that suggested locking and sealing a door. It was clear from the set of his mouth that he thought that Sherin was trying to manipulate her employer. Vahn looked away, studying the wall for a moment and weighing his suspicions and fears against each other.

She could not be allowed to contact the Ear again, not while they were still in flight nor any time thereafter until their mission was complete. Her handheld was sitting on a shelf nearby and he reached toward it, only to discover that he would have to stand to pick it up. Instead, Sammo reached past him and dropped it into his out-stretched hand. Sherin looked up at the sound, but said nothing. She was silent as Sammo checked the rest of the room for other handhelds or communicators.

Then he helped Vahn stand. Vahn looked down at her. "You know that I can't let you out until we reach the asteroid. It would be a nova risk, and I do not have another such risk in me, not now. Sammo will make sure that you have food. The ship will provide everything else that you need." He turned and walked from the room, his bondarmin at his heels.

Behind him, his former representative was silent, her gaze fixed on them as the door slid closed behind them, cutting her off. Sammo yanked the panel off the door lock and crossed one of the wires with another. Not enough to do permanent damage: they could still free her. But she would stay in her room and Vahn could worry less about what she might be doing for the rest of their trip.

"Let us find out what the good Pilot-Captain is evading and whether or not she succeeded." He gestured and Sammo led the way back to their quarters.

Chapter 16

TiCara strained her senses and every sensor and view screen that the *Astra* had trying to see if the corp ship had followed them into the comet's tail. It might even be shadowing them on the other side of it, where the sensors couldn't pick up. As the moments, then a machron, then two passed, the strain began to tell and her concentration wandered. Erol's fidgeting distracted her, that alone being enough to realize that she was tiring. Even being wired could not keep her body on red alert indefinitely.

She wrenched her attention to the navigation sensors and the coordinates that Vahn had provided. How much longer did she need to do this? Were they still out there? She took precious moments to orient where they were against the comet's current trajectory to determine where they were headed.

Something looked wrong with the Electra coordinates at first glance, but when she checked again, the anomaly had vanished. She must be imagining things. Navigation showed her much of what she expected: they were close to the outer Gathwaite planets. Between them and the far side of the system where Electra was supposed to be located, there were 3 planets, their moons, an asteroid belt and a lot of moving objects, including pirates, if the tell was true.

As TiCara tried to remember what else she knew about the system, the pirates were so close to the top of the list of her fears, that they almost went without mention. Gathwaite was a system with minimal corporate control, but she had trouble reconciling its reputation in the spacer bars with the stories about Electra. If the system was lawless, who controlled the asteroid? Who guarded it? She couldn't imagine a sophisticated lab setup or its equivalent surviving without corp protection.

That contradiction by itself was enough to revive her doubts about the lab's existence.

She nudged the *Astra*'s information cortex, trying to tap deeper into it at the same time that she flew the ship, but her medusas responded with a sharp warning. She was going to overload herself very soon if she kept it up. TiCara tried to shrug that off, but was unsuccessful. Her implants began blocking her access to nonessential functionality.

TiCara surfaced long enough to glance at Erol. "Look up Gathwaite after we settle. Need more tell. I'm going to hop us into the 'stroid belt, hide us there." Before he could answer, she was back under, lost in the tide of information about the ship and its status.

When she thought she had a solid enough sighting on the edge of the asteroid belt through all the comet debris, she sent out a warning to all aboard, then nudged the *Astra* into the belt. It was a just a short hop, not even a jump really, but she felt it jar painfully through her overextended body until she ground her teeth together to stay conscious. She pulled them out of the jump shivering and swearing at the pain in her head, surprised and annoyed at how poorly she was handling something that should have been relatively simple.

But then she wasn't as focused as she should have been and she'd been on edge since before this trip started. That thought drove her to pull up the sensors for Sherin's room. Readings were high, suggesting strong emotions and a lot of movement. But nothing more than that, nothing to tell her whether to rep was anxious or injured.

Or to tell her if Sherin was thinking about her and what they might have had. TiCara groaned and quietly promised herself a long trip to a VR spa when next she was planetside. If the best her meat-space interactions had to offer was Elia and Sherin, she was better off in virtual reality. She shook her head and opened her mouth, moving her jaw from side to side to ease her rapidly growing headache.

Some of her medusas detached themselves from the ship and were brushing her jaw and her neck in a wave of warm vibrations. She relaxed into their touch as well as she could while she checked the rest of the sensors on the ship. At least she still couldn't see the corp ship on the aft sensors or in any of the other views. Maybe they had lost them.

She let her consciousness roll over into the weapons system, checking its status as well. Erol had everything they had armed and ready. They might be able to shoot before running, if the corp ship or pirates found them. That might be enough to let them escape. But better to not be found at all. She let herself roll back out of the *Astra* with that thought.

Erol was frowning at the consoles when she was able to turn her head to look at him. She nearly frowned herself. She wanted to drift in the gentle comfort that being plugged in gave her, wanted to drift in her fantasies once more before she had to leave them behind for awhile, perhaps for good.

Instead, she made herself ask, "What is it?" She hoped that he hadn't found their pursuers, not again. She wasn't ready to fly like that again, not right now.

Erol jumped in his seat as if he had forgotten that she was there. He didn't meet her eyes as he spoke. "I thought the coordinates changed from the first time I looked at them, but that can't be. Probably space dust clouding my head." He shook his head. "Sending you everything I could find on Gathwaite, Captain."

A feed rode from his console to her medusas, filling her in on everything that her ship had stored on the system. It wasn't much more than she remembered: the files some mining, some agriculture, pirates, asteroid belts and a few other unimportant details. The corps in the system had heavily armed ships and the miners and farmers had some kind of protective guild to protect themselves from the pirates. And probably were the pirates, when times were lean. It didn't mention Electra or nanotech or anything else of any use. "Shady tell. Guess we'll just be going in and find out," she grimaced and rubbed her head.

Something was definitely wrong with her Second. He was still fidgeting, but he also wasn't meeting her eyes when she glanced at him. When she stopped to think about it, he'd been behaving oddly this entire trip. Not that she blamed him. Between the passengers, the tracker and the corp ship, emotions had been running high and it was already more than she thought she had bargained for.

But that wasn't really true, at least not for her. She knew what she'd bargained for on this trip. Sherin's face rose in her mind, and the rest of her beautiful self wasn't far behind. TiCara swallowed a lump in her throat at the idea that she was never going to touch or taste the other woman again. There had to be another way, some solution that would make it possible for them to be together. But she wasn't seeing it, not now.

Erol cleared his throat and TiCara emerged from her thoughts to squint at Gathwaite 's sun through the viewer. It was nothing special, just a yellow star slightly smaller than the one that Old Earth orbited around. Its size meant that it was freezing on the outer planets and the asteroid belt. Good thing they weren't planning on being planet-side much.

Her Second tapped the console with his fingers to get her attention and she gave him a grimace of apology. She must be drifting pretty badly to tune out so much. Erol wrinkled his nose at her and hesitated, lips parted but still not saying anything. TiCara made an impatient gesture and Erol closed his eyes for a moment. Then he opened them, cleared his throat again and said, "Look, Captain...TiCara, I have tell I need give you."

TiCara frowned. This couldn't be good. He was only formal when things were very serious. Her handheld buzzed sharply: Vahn's code flashed on the screen when she looked at it. Probably wondering why they had been moving so fast. That much speed would have been hard on the old man. She would need to check in with him soon or lose what she retained of his confidence.

But she clicked the option to postpone in favor of hearing whatever it was that Erol was about to say. Anything that came with this much hesitation couldn't be good. She wondered if he had found a berth on another ship and was choosing now to tell her.

He glanced at her handheld, then back up at her in time to catch her impatient head jerk of assent. Then he went back to looking at the screens. "Before we left Kyrin, I...heard tell from someone I had not spoken to in a long time." Erol paused and frowned, as if he was lost in some unpleasant memories.

TiCara fought the urge to howl with impatience. She needed to rest and there were passengers to attend to before she could do that, but she clamped down on her frustration as well as she could. There might be a very good reason for all this reticence. An image of the tracker popped into her head unexpectedly, and once she started thinking about it, she couldn't stop. The sooner her Second set her mind at ease, the better.

He was still staring at the screen in front of him and frowning, but his expression had shifted. He stiffened and leaned forward, "Captain, you might want to plug back in. I'm not sure but I think we've got more company."

TiCara swore and clicked back in, letting her senses extend through all of the ship's scanners. Before the comet, there had been one ship out there that was too close for comfort. Now, there were four.

Navigation informed her that they were just inside the edge of the outer asteroid belt. So the ships were either mining security, flying in remarkably close formation. Or they were pirates. Given the way this job had gone so far, it wasn't too difficult to determine which ones these probably were. "Need to run for the asteroids and find a big rock with craters," she told Erol.

She slipped back into the ship's computer as he swore in turn and hit the alarm to notify the passengers of another unexpected acceleration. It wouldn't be as bad as the last one because the *Astra* was too far into the belt for even a short jump, but they might not appreciate the distinction. But there'd be time to explain that later. If they made it.

TiCara whipped the ship through evasive maneuvers, twisting and spinning around the nearest asteroids, and dodging between two that were about to collide. Behind them, the pirates began firing, their shots clearly intended to disable, though she doubted that they could aim that effectively, given what she was making the ship do. Which meant she might get her ship destroyed trying to save it.

Time to find a hiding spot before that happened. She looped around the next asteroid, and flinched as the *Astra* shuddered and a loud klaxon alarm sounded through the Bridge. They'd been hit on one of the wings. She could feel the *Astra* list sharply starboard and she compensated with a sharp shift in the engine and thrusters.

A visual map of the known asteroids popped up in front of her with a thought. She scanned it in a blink, then three, spinning and turning the map as she did the same with the ship. *C'mon, give me something*, she thought with desperate impatience.

There! There was a flat space just big enough to accommodate her ship several asteroids away. As long as nothing hit them on the way there, they'd be okay for the moment. The *Astra* lurched forward in a corkscrew pattern between and around several asteroids before she brought it in to land in a cloud of dust on the space from the schematic.

The ship shuddered to a halt and there was a sharp bang as momentum forced the nose into the nearest rock. TiCara thought abject apologies at her ship, and belatedly, at her crew and her passengers. It had been a bad landing, made worse by the hit they had taken. Now all they could hope for was that the ship only had problems they could fix. And that they could stay hidden long enough to patch it.

Of course, as long as she was making a list, she could add hoping that none of the other asteroids hit them in the mean time. TiCara groaned and rubbed her hands over her face as she unplugged. Being linked into the *Astra* after the ship was hit was like feeling the wound herself. She needed to disconnect to think, as much as for the comfort of her body.

Erol was unbuckling from his safety harness and unfastening hers when she finished blinking her way all the way back into her aching body. Whatever he had been going to say was apparently forgotten in the surge of emergencies and the insistent clamor of the ship's alarms. She answered her handheld as Erol slipped down the ladder, off to check on the rest of the ship.

"Ser, are you all right? My apologies, but we were being pursued by pirates. I'm coming down to speak with you after I assess the damage. Are your employees in your quarters?" She was torn between hoping that Sherin was there and hoping she wasn't. The tracker was still on her mind and she wanted to talk to the rep about it again, without an audience.

"Captain, we are bruised but otherwise intact. My rep is confined to her quarters but Sammo is here with me. Please come to us as soon as you have verified the status of the ship. My thanks." Vahn clicked off.

TiCara scowled at her handheld as she tugged off her safety harness. That was odd. Why was Sherin confined to her quarters? But then, this wasn't really the time to try to learn mind reading. She'd find out soon enough.

Before she went to go and check on the ship, some instinct made her check the Electra coordinates again. This time she was sure of what she was seeing: they had shifted slightly since she first entered them after leaving Kyrin. It wasn't a huge shift, a matter of a few degrees, but it was enough to ensure that she might have missed the location altogether if she wasn't aware of the change.

She stamped the pins and needles from her legs when she stood, her mind spinning at the significance of this. Had Sherin given her tampered coordinates? Had Vahn been deceived when he bought them? She answered Erol's call in a daze, acknowledging that the rest of the crew was unharmed but that the starboard engine had been hit. They were looking at it, but he sounded as if his optimism had been left behind in Kyrin.

TiCara dropped down the ladder to the lower corridor, and told Erol that she'd join them soon. She clicked off her handheld and hesitated. Every instinct screamed at her to go confront Vahn first, find out what the shifting coordinates meant.

She knew that had to wait, but it was going to be difficult to deal with her passengers and her ship in the exhausted state she was in. Reluctantly, she signaled her medusas to reset her mood to alert and controlled. Slowly, their touch turned ice cold on her neck and scalp, cooling her tangled emotions along with her skin until she shivered at the contrast.

The *Astra* needed to come first, regardless of what else she wanted to do. Then Vahn. She headed for the damaged part of the ship first, promising herself that she would deal with each problem one at a time. If worst came to worst, and they were stranded on this asteroid for long, they might need to enable that tracker again. Rescue by the Ears might be better than dying from lack of oxygen.

Unless that Ear was Zig. She lost her footing and slipped down the last few rungs of the ladder she was on at that thought. But there would be time to worry about last resorts later. All residual fantasies fled as she worked her way through the ship, assessing the damage as she went.

The crew let her know what they'd found as soon as she reached them. The pirates had hit them hard: they'd lost an engine as well as all the sensors on that side of the ship. The *Astra*'s metal skin was torn, exposing her delicate electronics to the vacuum outside as well as the dust of their hard landing. Ji-min nearly wept as they gave her that final bit of bad news.

TiCara found her hands clenching and unclenching in an effort to not punch the walls and howl in despair. As usual, it was Vijay who was most optimistic. "We still have life support and the greenbay is intact, Captain. Nothing to worry about for some time." He didn't specify how long that would be and none of them asked. But he added, "We also still have that synth skin from the time we disguised the ship to look like a small freighter. Can we use that to cover the electronics until Ji-min can clean and fix the tear?"

TiCara nearly hugged him, stopping only when she remembered how uncomfortable that would make both of them. Instead, she settled for an approving grin and used his old corp ship rank. "Starshine, pure starshine, Lieutenant. That could work. What do you think, Engineer?" She turned to Ji-min and was relieved to see the other's face light up.

"Yes, Captain, it might. We'll try it and see what it does. It'll be much easier than trying that work in a suit." In moments, they had devised a plan of attack that sent Erol and Vijay outside in suits with the synth skin cover while Ji-min went to work on the engine from inside the ship. Once outside, they could also check for the pirates and set up the external sensors to supplement the damaged ones.

TiCara lingered long enough to get them started, long enough that she began to sway from exhaustion. But instead of going to her cabin where her medusas were insistently encouraging her to go, she went to Vahn's quarters. En route, she calmed her medusas temporarily with a protein shake from a nutrient dispenser. It wouldn't substitute for sleep for long, but it would have to do for the moment.

She was still drinking it when she buzzed the door to Vahn's quarters. Sammo raised his dark eyebrows at her when the door slid open, but he stepped aside. TiCara grimaced. She was in no mood for more formality, and gave Vahn only a small bow by way of greeting. "I apologize for the roughness of our landing, Ser. The ship has sustained damage and my crew is ascertaining what we will need to do to fix it. As for the pirates who shot at us, we have not seen them yet, but they may return soon. We need to be ready."

"And the first acceleration that we experienced?"

"There was a corp ship behind us. It got too close and I took us through part of a comet's tail to hide the ship before we jumped. Should blackhole our location for them."

"That was excellent thinking, Pilot-Captain. Your apologies for the roughness of the journey are unnecessary. I understand that both the speed and the evasion were needed. Does your crew have an ETA on when the ship may be ready to fly again?"

"They hope to have one soon, Ser. I will let you know when they tell me." TiCara wondered if there was something more, something the old man couldn't bring himself to voice yet. It could be nothing good. She noticed that he hadn't mentioned Sherin and decided it was past time to ask. "Why is your rep confined to her quarters, Ser? And on who's authority?"

Vahn's face tightened, a cold rage welling up in his expression just long enough for her to see it. What had Sherin done to trigger that? "We locked my former employee, Sherin Khan, into her quarters. My apologies that it was done without notifying you, Captain, but you had other concerns. We believe that she planted the tracker on the ship and that she approached my rivals to betray me. But then, I believe you also had suspicions of your own."

TiCara swallowed hard. True, she thought Sherin guilty too, but it was different hearing that same accusation from Vahn: the words sounded colder, more hard-edged and cruel. The way he described it was like something an Ear would do. Was there a Sherin that she hadn't see yet? Was Sherin ever what she had seemed to be?

For the first time, TiCara doubted her own ability to see through any Ear's disguise. Had she been horribly wrong about the rep? "Yes, Ser, I was suspicious. I spoke to her but was called away to assess the threat of the corp ship. Our discussion was...inconclusive. I did not know that you also had reason to distrust her."

"At first, I did not. But when Sammo showed me the tracker and I spoke to her, I understood what my rivals had offered her. She was unable to convince me that she could deny such a price."

TiCara's forehead wrinkled in astonishment. What was he talking about? She thought back on her conversation with Sherin, about the rep's nervous rubbing at her head and her reaction to medusas. A horrible suspicion began to form in her mind. But she had to know the truth. She forced the words out, "And that was?"

"They offered to restore her medusas, Pilot-Captain. She was on Electra on a previous trip and some rogue nanotech cured of her implants. Surely you can imagine what a loss they must have been? I knew of this when I hired her, but had not heard that anyone claimed to be able to restore the tech." Vahn looked grimly disappointed now, as if a favorite child had failed him. "I had originally hoped that she could tell me more of the asteroid, perhaps guide me here to negotiate with the techs, but her short term memory had been wiped of those details. She remembered only what had happened to her and little else."

TiCara caught at the shelf next to her to steady her swaying body. She only just managed to keep her jaw from dropping open. When Elia had told her that tale back on Kyrin, she had thought it a myth, just more spacer fantasy. Like Electra itself. But if the story was true, the asteroid must be what Vahn said it was: both real and a large nanotech lab. And not all of that tech well controlled, from this story.

"I see from your reaction, Captain, that you did not know about this. I was unsure as to whether or not it was something Sherin Khan had told you. I know that you are, or were...close."

TiCara bit back a hysterical giggle. Instead, she focused on the results of Vahn's revelations. "So you dismissed her from your employment and locked her in her quarters. Did you search for any more communicators or trackers?" Sammo nodded in response.

She was a tangled mass of emotions: horrified pity and relief, desire and disappointment, love and loathing. What she needed more than anything was to rest and think. "Very well. Ser, I must rest and then go assist my crew. I will update you in a half cycle as to the condition of the ship and when we might depart. My Life Support Officer tells me that the food dispensers and air flow should all be undamaged. We are able to keep all critical services running."

She stopped herself from telling them how long they could maintain that state. If Vijay was wrong, all of their concerns about trackers and Ears, betrayal and loss, might mean much less in the near future than they did right now. TiCara bowed formally and left Vahn sitting amid his cushions.

It was only when the door closed behind her that she realized that she had forgotten to ask him about the coordinates. Of course, if they couldn't get the ship spaceworthy, the coordinates weren't going to help much. Lost in her thoughts, TiCara stumbled and caught herself on the wall. She added one more question to her list to follow up on later as she walked slowly toward her quarters and long-delayed sleep.

Chapter 17

TiCara's brain whirled with thoughts about the coordinates, the state of the ship, Sherin, Sherin's past, pirates and Ears. It was all too much for her for her to handle right now and for a change, she knew it. For the good of her ship and her crew, she needed to sleep. The situation would be no less painful and difficult after she woke up.

Still, her thoughts hung on her until she felt as if she was wearing a blacksuit made of rock. She tried to imagine what she would have done had she been in Sherin's place. Her stomach turned at the image of losing her medusas. That reaction was enough to direct her steps to another meal console for another protein drink. She drank her meal quickly in the quiet of the deserted crew lounge and debated on whether or not to ping Erol's handheld and ask for a status.

But she knew he would call her if they found out anything new. TiCara rubbed one hand wearily over her face, then dropped the drink container back into the dispenser to be sterilized for reuse. By the time she reached her quarters, she was thinking so hard about all of it that she almost didn't realize that she wasn't alone.

Sherin was sitting on the corridor floor outside her room, her head resting on her knees. She had a mediwrap on one hand, from wrist to fingers, and TiCara could see a bloodstain on it. "What...happened? How did you get here? Vahn told me he locked you in your room."

The other woman tilted her head to one side and looked at TiCara sidelong. "Your locks are old tech, Pilot-Captain; you need an upgrade. I took the panel off on the inside, then broke through the fused wires. A few cuts and bruises and I was out. I was going to come looking for you but I guessed that you were busy from the way you were flying and crashing. I waited here instead of going to the Bridge."

TiCara opened her door, then leaned up against the wall next to it. "I should just put you back in your quarters. But I'm nearly black-holed now. Too much wired time doesn't leave me a lot of reserves. You can come in or you can go on sitting out here. Either way, I'll want tru tell from you later. After I rest, assuming you don't plan to kill me in my sleep."

Sherin looked momentarily shocked and her voice was uncertain as she continued, "You had tru tell from me before. But I've got more now. I can show you that it wasn't me." Sherin waved a handheld at her as she scrambled awkwardly to her feet. TiCara could see that she was trying not to use her bandaged hand, and against her better judgment, leaned down and helped her stand up.

Touching Sherin brought back her earlier feelings and a wave of longing filled her. She didn't want to let the other woman go. It didn't matter what she'd done or what she was going to say. Before she realized what she was doing, she had wrapped her arms around Sherin and the rep was leaning into her shoulder with a heavy sigh. Together they stumbled their way across the threshold into TiCara's room.

Sherin turned her face up to TiCara's and kissed her, her lips gentle, but with enough pressure to part the pilot's lips. TiCara felt Sherin's tongue in her mouth an instant later and welcomed it in, deepening their kiss. She restrained her medusas with an errant thought, but she knew that she was too close to the edge to control them for long. And that wasn't what Sherin wanted.

TiCara pulled away carefully and dropped onto the bed. She held Sherin's uninjured hand in hers and pulled the other woman down to sit next to her. With infinite care, she unwrapped Sherin's injured hand and looked it over. The wound was deeper than the rep had implied and it was still bleeding.

She reached over and pulled out the med kit that Vijay had placed in all the crew and passenger quarters and sterilized the wound before putting a clean bandage on it. Then she held Sherin's hand up to her mouth and kissed her fingers.

A gentle wheeze interrupted her reverie. Sherin was leaning back against the wall, her eyes closed, sound asleep. TiCara's lips quirked in a smile, and she stood up and shed her blacksuit. When she was naked, she lay down beside Sherin, pulling the other woman around to lay next to her. Sherin woke up enough to undress with TiCara's help, then they fell asleep in each other's arms.

A chime from TiCara's handheld woke them a few cycles later and TiCara reached for it, groggily. Erol's code flashed across the screen and she turned it on. "Yes, Second?" She could feel Sherin stir against her and she let her free hand slid down the other woman's shoulder, enjoying the silky warmth of her skin.

Erol's voice boomed out of the speaker. "Captain, we've got the synth skin in place and Ji-min's set up the cleaners. We should know within a cycle if we can fix all the damage. Still no sign of the pirates or the corp ship. They must be waiting for us out there."

"Very good, Second. I'll come and check on your progress in a cycle. Go get some sleep if you're done." TiCara noted that the ship's computer had sent her a nonurgent message but clicked it off without reading it and turned to Sherin. Everything else could wait a little longer. She stroked Sherin's hair gently. "Now tell me what you wanted to tell me before we fell asleep."

Sherin rolled over and reached for her suit. Belatedly, TiCara realized that they hadn't put their suits in the ship's clean closet. She wrinkled her nose as Sherin pulled a chip holder out of her suit. It reminded her that she hadn't also asked Vahn about the coordinates. "That chip you gave me, the one with the nav location for Electra—are you sure those coordinates were good?"

Sherin looked up, dark eyes wide and startled. "Yes. Vahn's contact vouched for them. Why?"

"They don't look tru. They've shifted, like someone put a worm in the code." TiCara studied Sherin in the cabin's dim light. She could see nothing to tell her that the other woman was lying, so maybe she had been given the chip in good faith.

Had Vahn thought the same thing? Maybe he had paid for decoy coordinates as well as the real thing, and was holding the real ones in reserve. She had heard about such things from other pilots.

But there would be time to ask Vahn about that once the *Astra* was ready to fly again. They weren't leaving the asteroid with coordinates that she had no reason to trust. It crossed her mind that given how little this client seemed to trust her, she should have trusted her own crew more. She sighed, feeling the weight of quiet frustration settle into her bones.

Sherin interrupted her thoughts by holding up her handheld and displaying a string of communication messages. "Vahn took my main comm unit, but I had this one in with my gear as a backup. These are the messages I exchanged with Elia and Zig. All of them." She held it out, her expression focused and her mouth set in a determined line.

Reluctantly, TiCara reached out and took it from her. While she started to read the string of messages, Sherin pulled on her undergarments and vanished out the door. TiCara cursed herself for letting her guard down; the rep shouldn't be roaming the ship until she proved her innocence. Erol was right; it was too easy for her to be careless with this woman. She picked up her own comm and checked the monitor to verify that Sherin was going no further than the food dispenser.

Then she forced herself to ignore the roiling of her nerves and look at the rep's handheld. The first few messages were the ones that TiCara had already seen. Reading them now, she was willing to convince herself of how little Sherin had explicitly agreed to do for Elia and Zig. It didn't put all her doubts to rest, but it did help ease the sharp ache of betrayal that had been gnawing at her, just a little.

As if she knew what TiCara was thinking, the door slid open to reveal Sherin holding a tray. She set it down on the shelf next to the bed and sat down an arms length from TiCara before holding out a container of something warm and sweet smelling.

"What is that? I don't recognize it. Something from your home world?" TiCara opened up a second container and sniffed at the hot, spicy stew it contained. Her stomach rumbled its approval. "Or home station? I'm ravenous and it smells amazing." It embarrassed her that she didn't know where Sherin had come from originally and hadn't asked before.

Sherin smiled. "I'm from New Chindai, near Kyrin, but this is something from my favorite eatery on Aliandra. It's a blend of grains and nutrients with the spices that Vijay included in the dispensary." She ate enthusiastically as TiCara watched, distracted from her own food by a desperate desire to touch her. Sherin looked back at her when she was finished and licked her lips happily. "Try it."

TiCara twisted inside, torn between desperate longing and distrust. She ate her stew, savoring its rich flavor, then turned her attention back to the messages on Sherin's handheld. Elia mentioned a friend, one who could broker a profitable deal for Electra's coordinates, and it took very little for TiCara to picture Zig. Other messages were more obscure: what did "other measures will be taken" mean? Was that why the other ship had been following them?

There was more about how Sherin should cooperate and get the coordinates for them, how doing this would help her get her medusas back. How her life would return to the way it had been before she lost them. TiCara looked up. "Why didn't you tell me what had happened to you on Electra?"

Sherin's face went gray, her eyes distant. "I tried. But even on Aliandra, it was so hard to talk about it. I walked into those labs as a medusa pilot. Then two or three machrons later, I was on the floor screaming in pain. I passed out and when I woke up again, they were gone. Then they wiped our memories so all I could remember afterward was waking up, none of the counseling or how I got us back to port or anything." Her expression twisted and she buried her face in her arms and sobbed, the sound echoing heartbreakingly against the *Astra*'s walls.

TiCara reached out but paused, her hand hovering between them as her feelings rocketed back and forth. She should take Sherin in her arms and dry her tears with kisses. She should be a captain first and finish reading the messages before demanding answers. The conflict warred through her until she was sure that her own medusas would never be able to sort it all out without a full reset. TiCara sighed and settled for resting her hand lightly on Sherin's shoulder. "I'm sorry," she said finally, wincing at how inadequate that sounded. "What happened after that? How did Elia find you?"

Sherin sniffled and looked up, tears still running down her cheeks. When she spoke, her voice was still choked. "When I got back from Aliandra, I tried to go back to the bars. But it was too hard to sing and I couldn't get a berth on another ship. The story went viral and I didn't want to talk about it, couldn't talk about it. My former crewmates avoided me, I had nothing and no one. But Elia met me at one of the bars and she coaxed the story out of me. She is a good listener."

TiCara gave her an astonished look. She remembered Elia as a commanding presence, one more accustomed to speaking than listening. Even as she had seen her last, there was a ghost of that Elia still looking out of her eyes, the one that wanted to be in charge and in control. She must have wanted something from Sherin, wanted it very badly, to work so hard to win her confidence.

Sherin rubbed her cheeks. "She introduced me to the Ear, Zig. Said he was a friend of hers. We would talk...about what happened, how I felt afterward. One of the agents that they knew put my name forward to Vahn to become his rep and he hired me. I thought it would all be so much better after that!" She gestured upward in the general direction of Vahn's cabin and swallowed another sob. "But I didn't give them the tell that they wanted."

"Sherin, what did they mean by 'other measures?' It's in one of the last messages they sent you."

"That's what I wanted to tell you: there's someone else involved. I didn't plant that tracker, but someone else did and I think that they're still on the ship." Sherin had stopped crying now and her eyes went wide and pleading. "You've got to believe me. This is tru tell. I talked to Zig before we left, and Elia before that, but I didn't give them tell, not about Electra, and not about you."

TiCara took her hand off Sherin's shoulder at the sound of Zig's name. It was impossible for her to believe that Sherin wouldn't tell the Ear anything that he wanted to know. A memory of pain and humiliation swept over her and she could feel herself start to tremble. She closed her eyes and fought for control, gasping for air with each breath like she'd been airlocked.

She could feel Sherin draw closer and reach for her. Then she found herself being held against the rep's shoulder. Sherin stroked her hands gently over her shoulders and back, carefully avoiding her flailing medusa while TiCara struggled for control, finding just enough to restrain her implants from spilling over on to Sherin's exposed skin.

Sherin leaned in and kissed her cheek "TiCara? Are you here? Breath with me." She sat back and began chanting in a complex pattern that a distant part of TiCara's brain recognized as being similar to one that she had herself had learned on Aliandra. Slowly, she sat up and began to follow the pattern, embracing its familiarity as she chanted along with Sherin. Slowly their voices entwined and TiCara could feel her breathing match their rhythm.

She took a last deep breath. "Thank you. I'm back now. Were you on Aliandra after you...after you lost your medusas?"

Sherin nodded. "The masters helped me recover, enough to work for Vahn at least. But I miss being wired so much. I look at yours and I remember what it was like when I was whole. I imagine what it would be like to be with you, with both of us wired...and I want that. This--" Sherin gestured at her head and her body, "is so limited." She looked away from TiCara and stared at the wall.

"But you didn't trade the chance to get them back for the real coordinates for Electra?" The question was out of TiCara's mouth before she had a chance to hesitate, to change it into something less cutting. Now it was out, writhing between them, and she couldn't take it back.

Sherin pulled away and stood up, distress visibly twisting her features. "I thought you were starting to believe me. Doesn't this mean anything to you?" She gestured at the handheld, her hand shaking.

TiCara's breath caught in her throat. No matter what Sherin said or did, it didn't take anything away from how lovely she was. She desperately wanted to believe her tell because of how much she wanted the other woman and she knew it. This was weakness, foolhardy, potentially fatal weakness. She clamped down on her emotions and her medusas at the same time.

"Do I need to put my blacksuit on again for you to hear me?" Sherin was standing over her now, hands on her hips. "Can't you see me for more than the way I look?" She was close enough that TiCara could smell her, close enough that TiCara could tell how much the other woman wanted her too. But from the set of her shoulders and the look in her eye, this was as close as TiCara was getting to what she wanted unless she organized her thoughts and spoke carefully.

TiCara sighed deeply and looked away. Sherin was right and she was owed an apology. She closed her eyes and emptied her mind before she spoke, "I apologize. Now, if you are giving me tru tell and this other asset of theirs planted the tracker, how could I find them?"

"You have secur cams on this ship, yes? Sensors?" Sherin jerked her head at the *Astra's* walls. "You can watch them and listen, too, when you're wired. Someone will signal from this ship to let them know we're moving again." She gave TiCara a fierce look. "And it won't be me."

"But by then it may be too late. We don't have enough weaponry to win against the pirates or that corp ship. If they can find us, we're blackholed."

Sherin's mouth pursed in an expression of astonishment and her eyes widened. She must have assumed that the pulse cannon would be enough or that the *Astra* had other weapons hidden elsewhere. TiCara wished that she were right, if only because they would have had more options.

TiCara's handheld buzzed, interrupting their discussion, and she reached out and pulled it off the shelf with an apologetic gesture. "I have to answer. It's about the repairs." She saw Sherin's jerky nod of acknowledgment from the corner of her eye. "Second, status?"

"The synth skin is staying on, Captain, and Ji-min has made progress on the repairs. We should be ready for liftoff in a few cycles. Vijay is coming on shift now and he'll continue with the cleanup and repairs."

"Nova work, both of you. Tell Ji-min to get some sleep. You, too. I'll be down there soon to help Vijay and inspect the ship."

"Aye, Captain."

TiCara put down her handheld and got up, with an over the shoulder glance at Sherin. "So...you want me to spy on my crew for you to prove your tell and, perhaps, also spy on your former employer and his bondarmin." She rubbed her hand over her face, medusas dancing with the gesture. She wanted to believe that Sherin was innocent, that her crew was innocent. That left Sammo as the most likely suspect. But she had no plan for how to prove that.

Sherin studied her without speaking until TiCara turned away and stepped into the sonic shower. The two women eyed each other with more caution than lust across the small room, each waiting for the other to make a move. Finally, TiCara held out her hands. After a moment of hesitation, Sherin shed the clothes she was wearing and stepped into the shower with her.

The waves traveled over their skin, vibrating their nerve endings like a massage. TiCara pulled Sherin in close and kissed her slowly. They pressed up against each other, merging their bodies into one. One creature with two hands, two mouths, two tongues and ten fingers, all bent on exploring and savoring everything it could reach.

TiCara trembled at first from the strain of controlling her medusas, to keep them from exploring Sherin's silky flesh along with her mouth and hands. She wasn't sure she could bear to see the other woman pull away like she had earlier, not now. No matter what. Finally, she forced her implants to lie flat and quiescent over her skull and down her neck, and by unspoken agreement, neither woman touched them.

Still, with Sherin's soft moans of pleasure filling her ears, TiCara wished that she could show her how much more she could do with her medusas. It made meatspace sex so much more satisfying. But Sherin wasn't ready and the restraint and control made her try harder to please the other woman without using the implants she had come to depend on.

But the insistent chime of the timer on her handheld intruded, breaking the mood until they were left standing apart and looking at each other awkwardly. "I'll come back as soon as I can," TiCara said finally.

By then, she had begun pulling on her suit and slipped her handheld back in its pouch. She stopped and looked at Sherin before she walked to the door, then reached out to stroke her cheek. "I'll set the secur cams and the sensors to look for any transmission signals that shouldn't be there." She gave the other woman her best effort at a reassuring smile and they kissed in what TiCara hoped was a temporary farewell.

A moment later, the door slid shut behind TiCara as she strode down the corridor. She switched levels before she set up the security triggers that Sherin had asked for, including a secur cam near her own quarters. She needed to be sure of Sherin and she needed to do it soon. Before the other woman seized her heart and refused to give it back.

Once that happened, TiCara would be completely torn between love and employment, love and the loyalty she owed her ship and crew. *Surety was a thing easily bought with more security*, she thought as she set up the triggers and monitors. Or at least, she hoped so.

She clicked the console shut and checked her handheld for status updates. Ji-min had sent her a message when they went off shift, letting her know the current state of the cleanup and repairs. By the time she got to Vijay, she would know what was still needed. She read through them and noted that the message that she had ignored in favor of sleep was the computer's file on Sherin. She hesitated over it for a minute, then decided that it could wait for the moment.

Which just left Vahn to deal with. And she should have a status update for him shortly, if all went as well as Ji-min thought it would. They would also be discussing the coordinates, tampered and otherwise. Sherin's face rose unbidden in her mind and she flinched. She had never suspected the other woman of that hack, only Vahn or whoever sold him the coordinates.

But perhaps she was wrong to be so trusting. Sherin used to be a pilot and that meant that she had the technical skills to change the programming on the chip if she wanted to. She wondered if Vahn had come to the same conclusion. He had her imprisoned, so he had to have something solid to go on. Coordinate tampering, along with the tracker, would be a lot of hard evidence against Sherin. All she had to counter that was a hope that the other woman was not as guilty as she looked.

CHAPTER 18

TiCara was contemplating Zig and Elia almost as much as she was thinking about Sherin by the time she reached the damaged part of the ship. Her distraction meant that it took her a moment to realize what she was looking at, but once she did, she gave a low whistle of admiration. Ji-min and Erol had done nova work with the skin and the cleaning. Much of the scorching and the dust from the landing were cleaned and there were far fewer singed connections to wound her eyes.

Vijay was already hard at work, safety mask covering his face as he used an old-fashioned soldering iron to weld the connections back together. It made TiCara smile to watch him work; he always said that the old tech was more reliable than the nanobots that the rest of the crew would have deployed.

But even he couldn't deny that that bots were faster and got deeper into the circuitry. She put a facemask of her own, opened up a sealed container of cleaning bots and sent them scurrying over one of the dust-contaminated areas that still needed to be cleaned. Then she began stripping away burnt wires to clear the way for Vijay to work.

As she worked, she added the pirates and the corp ship back into the jumble of worries in her head. It was, she reflected, getting very crowded in there.

To ground herself, she explored the mass of burnt wires with her medusas, letting their sensitive touch tell her which connections could be salvaged and which would need to be replaced. She let the ship tell her what it needed, where the worst of the damage remained. It was both a relief and a burden to let that information go through her hard wiring. At least they were definitely getting closer to the end of the critical fixes.

As if on cue, her handheld buzzed with Vahn's code. She clicked it on, reflecting that it was uncanny how he always knew to call when there was a change in status. If she didn't know better, she'd think the old man was wired himself. "Ser, I was about to contact you myself. The major repairs are nearing completion. We believe that we'll have the ship ready to fly in a few cycles."

"Good news, Captain-Pilot. But I am concerned about the amount of time that it is taking us to reach Electra, as I am also concerned with our pursuers. Will your ship be able to elude the latter once these repairs are complete?"

She could practically hear his anxiety thrumming through the speaker. For the first time, she wondered how long he had to live, given his condition. But maybe he just longed to recapture his old virility. Either way, TiCara wasn't sure what to tell him. She'd need to verify her sensor results with Ji-min and Erol first to determine how stable the repairs would be. Then she'd need a plan for what to do if they would only last for the short term.

"Ser, I will need to verify the state of the repairs with my crew. As for the timing of them, I can tell you that we are working to repair the damage as quickly as we can." Some bit of malice made her add,

"Perhaps Sherin Khan could assist us, since she's had medusa ship training."

She regretted the comment once it was out of her mouth. If Vahn sent Sammo to check Sherin's quarters, he would realize that she had escaped. Vahn's voice crackled back almost immediately. "Please notify me if things become as dire as that, Pilot-Captain. On another critical subject, I would imagine that on a ship this size, life support functions are limited when all the engines are not fully operational, is this not so?"

TiCara wrinkled her nose and acknowledged Vijay's nod and shrug. Well, if he wasn't worried yet, it was too soon for her to be. "We should be within that window, Ser. I will verify the state of the repairs and formulate a plan to reach our destination. Rest assured that I will have a new status for you soon." She clicked off at his assent.

"I'll give tell just like him by the time we get where we're going," she remarked sarcastically to Vijay as she surveyed the state of the engine that he was working on. "His style is growing on me."

"Where is it that we are going, Captain? I heard Ser Vahn speak of Electra. That Electra the legendary asteroid?" Vijay tilted his facemask up on his forehead to see her response.

TiCara swallowed a curse. With all that had happened, she had never told Ji-min and Vijay the truth about this trip. Or Erol, for that matter, though she suspected he already knew. That she had forgotten that worried her. At this rate, she wouldn't need a memory wipe to forget anything.

"Yes," she answered simply. "Ser Vahn asked me to keep it confidential until we were en route. Then his bondarmin found a tracker in one of the cargo bays and he's accused Sherin of planting it. There's a corp ship on our tail and pirates hunting us in the asteroids and we've got to get past them both." Once she laid it out like that, she realized that it sounded far worse than it had when she kept it under her medusas.

Vijay seemed to visibly swallow most of his questions, though his dark eyes went wide at the end. "What will we find waiting for us on Electra, Captain? If we get there?"

They were good questions. TiCara thought of Sherin's fingers rubbing her scalp and shuddered, wishing she had a better answer. "Ser Vahn wishes to visit a nanotech lab there to be cured of his illness." She hesitated to tell even one of her crew information that her client had not approved. It felt as if she was violating his confidentiality, rightly or wrongly.

"Did his rep plant the tracker? Erol told Ji-min she was confined to quarters." Vijay was looking at the engine again, as though the answer to this question was less important to him.

TiCara directed the cleaning bots over to a new section and considered how to answer that. She found herself watching Vijay more closely, wondering if he could have planted the tracker himself and was hoping to deflect blame, before dismissing that scenario. Vijay was one of the few beings on board the *Astra* who wasn't behaving oddly. "Vahn believes," she said at last, "that whoever planted it was in contact with a rival corp's Ears." She waited for a reaction, an anomaly, anything out of the ordinary from her crewman.

Vijay gave her an unreadable look. "He believes? But you do not? Creds are a hard motivator and the Ears are another. Many have been caught between the two." He shrugged. "I believe that this part of the engine damage is fixed, Pilot-Captain. Will you verify?" He gestured at her medusas and stepped aside.

TiCara leaned forward and let her implants trail over the engine, then sink into the wiring, their sensors working to pick up the remaining damage. "Other side's hit hard. We need to get that, too." She stepped back to see how they could best reach the seared connections that she'd just found. They were too close to the wall; they'd need to use the repair bots after all. "Many? But not, for example, you?"

Vijay leaned against the wall and gave her a dark-eyed blank look. "I did not plant the tracker, Captain. But anyone who tells you they are above that kind of betrayal has not yet been offered their price. Sometimes, it is something that one cannot resist. Love or violence can be as strong as creds." His expression grew distant and TiCara could see pain at the back of it. Whatever he was remembering, he had been hoping to forget it, and she felt guilty for bringing those memories back.

"My thanks for your truth." TiCara nodded and returned to directing the repair bots, reining in her curiosity. She knew from the rare occasions that they had spoken like this before that she could not delve too deeply with him, not without making him shut down. As long as he did his job, she thought, he could tell her or not tell her whatever he chose.

"Trouble, Captain?" Erol's voice made her jump. She'd forgotten how little her Second slept during a crisis.

"Not exactly. Or maybe not yet. Depends on what happens when we try to lift off." TiCara grimaced and gestured with her handheld. "Why are you awake already, Second? I need my crew ready and rested for what we need to do next."

"Which is? I'm sorry, Captain. I couldn't sleep, not even with the *Astra*'s help." Erol looked hollow-eyed and worn out.

TiCara wondered if he'd eaten, or if he was foregoing that as well as sleep. "Go eat, Second, if you haven't already. We'll need to run the bots through that section we can't reach. After that, we'll need a plan and I need all of you alert to discuss our options. The pirates will be waiting for us." *And we'll have to hope that we can outrun them or trick them.* It wasn't a thought that she needed to speak aloud, not yet.

"With permission, Captain," Vijay's voice cut through her thoughts. "The synth skin can be made to look like something other than metal and we still have some left."

"Enough to cover the rest of the ship?" Erol sounded eager and that alone was enough to make TiCara smile. Perhaps he was just worried about their current situation and nothing more.

"No," Vijay tilted his head to add emphasis, "but maybe enough to make it harder to see."

TiCara realized what he was thinking before he said it. "A rock among rocks or an asteroid among asteroids," she mused. "Nova. We'll have to go back outside to apply it though."

By the time Ji-min joined them, disguising the *Astra* was underway, with Vijay and Erol applying the last of the skin to the ship's outside surface while TiCara supervised the repair bots. While they worked, TiCara asked her engineer about both the state of the ship and about the tracker.

Ji-min's reaction was, unsurprisingly, more intense than Vijay's. When TiCara implied that they might have brought it on board, they shut down, barely responding. It took TiCara some time to understand that her engineer was deeply wounded. Explaining Vahn's fears and her own did little to smooth things over. TiCara bit back a sigh, wishing that she was better at handling her crew.

Finally, she settled for a simple apology and the assurance that she was asking everyone the same questions, before switching the subject back to the ship and the repairs. She asked questions in such detail that it made it clear that she still respected the engineer's opinion and their work. After several rounds of questioning, Ji-min began to respond, though still in military cadence. "Pilot-Captain, the repairs should hold if the bots can get into that section and clean it up." They gestured at a section of wall. "They won't hold at jump speed, Pilot-Captain.

But should hold up for standard acceleration." They stood stiffly, eyes directed over TiCara's shoulder.

The latter sighed. But she had brought this upon herself and she knew it. Subtlety was a virtue that she always promised herself she'd learn. Eventually. "For how long, Engineer?" Ji-min spouted a complicated formula that TiCara only partially understood and she held up a hand to stem the tide of technical information.

"We are going to an asteroid called Electra 12. It's on the other side of this system. There are pirates and a corp ship out there, waiting for us to run, plus a bunch of fast moving rocks between us and the nearest planets. Vijay and Erol are disguising the *Astra* as an asteroid in hope of buying us more time. The ship is damaged and our fuel is limited. These are your variables, Engineer. How long?"

Ji-min gave her one horrified stare before snapping back to attention. "No idea, Pilot-Captain. A few cycles, some machrons, all the way back to Kyrin on the slow road: could be all, could be none, begging your pardon, Pilot-Captain." Their face shut down again as they withdrew into the military shell that they wore when uncomfortable and stressed.

This time, TiCara was more than willing to let them wear it. It saved them both from further dissection of her tracker accusation. For now, she would take their word for it and hope that her apologies and refocusing them on the ship repairs would hold them together and keep them going.

It didn't help to know that she was about to have another awkward conversation, but at least this time, she knew she was right about her suspicions. She left Ji-min hard at work and this time, she didn't stop to bow to Vahn at the door when she entered his room. "Ser Trinh Vahn, you have chosen to distrust me so far as to give me scrambled coordinates instead of tru ones. On what you have claimed as your clan honor, are we in the same system as the asteroid Electra 12?"

Vahn blinked slowly at her while his bondarmin hovered between them in a defensive posture, not quite standing in front of the old man. TiCara growled at him and waved him aside, and with an uneasy glance at his employer, he stepped back two paces so she could face Vahn. "I am sorry, Pilot-Captain, that you have discovered my small subterfuge and that it has angered your." He studied her face a moment, then stood unsteadily, leaning against the side of his bed and gave her a formal bow of apology. "It was, perhaps, an unnecessary precaution." He gestured to Sammo.

The bondarmin turned, clearly reluctant to stop watching TiCara directly, and reached into a pouch on one of the shelves. He pulled out a chip and handed it to Vahn. The old man extended his hand to TiCara. "On my honor and that of my clan, these coordinates are tru."

TiCara stepped forward and took the chip from his hand. "They'd best be starshine, Ser, or we'll all end up adrift in the never-never until the pirates get us." With that, she turned on her heel and left, heading for the Bridge. Once there, she plugged the chip into the nav computer and confirmed what she could see there against every starmap she could find.

She sat back with a sigh. Now, she would just have to trust the old man. And her crew. It would all have to be enough to get them there. TiCara promised herself that she'd never trust this much to her luck again and closed her eyes to wait for word from Erol and Ji-min that the *Astra*'s disguise was complete.

Chapter 19

THE COMET HAD SPUN PAST before Zig and Yva had a chance to notice the pirates. By then, it was too late to worry about where TiCara's ship had gone. Fire from the pirate ships hit their shields, searing away part of their ship's tail before they could react. But once in motion, they were a formidable team. Zig accelerated quickly while Yva headed to the pulsar cannon array to return fire with their other crewmembers.

At least they had several cannons, and a bay big enough to house multiple crewmembers firing at the same time. Zig sighed with something like relief as he felt the slight jolts that indicated cannon fire. Any pirates that got close enough to them would meet a fiery end; he trusted Yva to see to that.

Of more importance was the fact that he had lied to her and things were not going to be nova when she figured that out. He didn't have permission from their corp to take this ship into the Gathwaite System, certainly not to engage in a firefight with pirates. But that could be dealt with when they got back. Or when *he* got back. He sent the ship through a sudden sharp loop through several asteroids, unconsciously mimicking the path that TiCara had taken earlier.

Cheated of one prize for the moment, the pirates were taking more risks to try and capture a second one, buzzing the ship and firing on nearby asteroids so that the impact showered Zig's ship with debris. Answering fire ripped through one pirate ship and Zig grinned as he spun them around for another pass. The pirates scattered and their firing became more erratic.

Zig dodged his ship between and around a few more asteroids. He wondered where TiCara's ship had gone to ground. She would have outflown these amateurs in her sleep, but if she were hit, she might be hiding out. A lazy admiration tinged his thoughts. Yva was wrong; the wired pilot could be an eager bedmate with many uses. Provided she was sufficiently inspired.

Another pirate strike against the shields reminded him that they weren't out of danger yet and that there were more important things to worry about. He moved them further out, and felt his ship shudder again as Yva returned fire. The motion was enough to jar his thoughts as much as his body, sending his thoughts into a spiral of doubts and fears.

He had planned better than this, had even set up fail-safes if something went wrong. After all, he knew better than to trust to a DreamZone-addled ex-pilot's attempts at leverage. True, the corporate rep might yet come through, but he didn't really expect it. He imagined that there were other ways to come up with enough credits to have her medusas restored, if that was what she really wanted. It wasn't going to be enough on its own to compel her cooperation.

But that left his backup, the one that he was sure that Elia didn't know about. Why hadn't he heard from him? If he didn't get an update soon, he'd be compelled to deploy his own...leverage. He gave a twisted smile. His agent on Kraybourne would act efficiently once he sent her word.

But then what? He didn't have anything else to force his contact to give him what he wanted once his agent carried out his orders. Fear was useful until it didn't exist any more. That notion was enough to turn his thoughts back to the pilot herself. If he was compelled to admit it to himself, what did he have to force TiCara to submit to him if owning her debts wasn't enough? True, he could destroy her ship and collect the insurance he had taken out on the debt. He imagined her broken and vulnerable, with no one to turn to except him.

The vision sent a pulsing sensation into his groin as he pictured possessing her once more, this time without a contract to protect her. Still, it didn't arouse him as much as it once had, particularly when he considered how easily she could kill him in a vulnerable moment. There would be no indenture to protect him either. Arousal fled at that second thought.

But the picture of the credits he would get from selling Electra's coordinates was more enduring. Now, that was enough to arouse his whole body and his mind in the bargain. With that, he could possess any medusa pilot he wanted. He could even make his own; there were plenty of desperate wannabes out there looking to get wired.

Reflexively, he rolled his ship over and slipped it sideways between two asteroids as Yva and her crew hit a second pirate ship. He had gained them some space and cover, moving into a space just outside the belt and hovering behind one of the bigger asteroids. They could wait here for the remaining pirates, and pick them off as they emerged. They could also wait for the *Astra*, at least long enough to see it if emerged on this side of the belt.

Then either his contacts would reach them with the coordinates, or the other ship would guide them to Electra. He weighed his options. Once he knew the coordinates, perhaps the pilot and her crew would be far more expendable than he had originally thought. If the *Astra* was destroyed and her crew along with it, he wouldn't even have to pay his contact or Elia. Fewer complications all around…as long as he could give up TiCara.

Her face popped up in his head and he savored the memory of pain and rage in her eyes, the feel of her body under his hands, the thrill of bending her defiance to his will. She'd had more spirit in her than any of the other indentures. But while those memories brought a smile to his face, he knew that he could find those pleasures elsewhere. Perhaps even better ones. Renounce his preference for the pilot, kill her crew, kill the DreamZone addict and who was there to remember who he had been, what he had done?

Yva climbed back up onto the Bridge, shattering his thoughts. "Why are we stopped here?" Then she looked out the view screen and nodded in acknowledgment as she saw the answer to her question. Waiting for the pirates here would make it easier to destroy them one at a time. "But if the *Astra* leaves on the other side of the belt?"

Zig tapped the navigational screen to full, expanding their view of the asteroid belt in several directions. A three dimensional grid of the belt appeared at his next tap, its asteroids in continuous motion. It even showed the heat from the drives of the surviving pirate ships, just as it would show the heat signatures of any other vessels in the area. He cocked his head at Yva and she jerked her head in reluctant admiration. Nothing to do now but wait.

And until he was done waiting, he'd review his original plan, making the necessary adjustments. Zig watched the grid, lost in his thoughts until the end of that shift, and then the next, oblivious to Yva's departure when she left to sleep. By then, he begun to think about the best ways to employ his secret weapon: two military-grade robots that he had hidden in one of the cargo bays.

But he was not so lost in his thoughts that he missed the small signature of the *Astra*, finally drifting out of the asteroid belt. The signal was so faint that it was hard to track and he had to pilot them around several asteroids before he could pick it up more clearly. The ship's motion drew Yva back to the Bridge because she appeared next to his chair, almost before he knew she was there. He tapped the grid, expanding it so that she could see why he was once again risking the pirates in the belt.

"Time to cloak?" She asked, her voice still rough from sleep. The ship's cloaking system was clumsy and burned more energy than accelerating without it, but now that they were in system, that shouldn't matter as much. They could refuel on Electra or near it. There had to be a station close by; otherwise, how would the ships bringing clients to the lab leave the system?

He gave Yva a head jerk of assent. Cloaking should get them past the pirates as well, though it meant they couldn't fire on them. Cloak or fire, even the corp ships still had to choose. But if all went well, that wouldn't matter.

The comm link burst into static a few seconds later. The screen flashed a short code, then another. Navigation coordinates for the asteroid. Zig grinned at the screen before turning that smile on Yva; this was what they had been waiting for, or at least, what he had been waiting for. He was never sure what Yva really wanted from this trip, and had begun to care less and less as they got closer to his goals.

He saved the message, letting his programs unencrypt it. The coordinates shone on the screen as if they were written in pure gold. For a wild moment, he considered firing the pulsar array now and destroying the other ship once it was within range. But it was too soon. His contact might be lying even now, seeking to send them into a trap or worse.

They would wait and follow until they could see Electra. Then, Zig would get everything he truly wanted. He smiled as he saved the coordinates to a chip and piloted their cloaked ship after the *Astra*.

Chapter 20

T HE *ASTRA'S* LIFTOFF WAS MUCH smoother than her landing, to TiCara's relief. She kept the engines on minimum power, letting the ship drift with the asteroids, hoping they would hide the ship's energy signature. If Erol's good fortune smiled on them, they wouldn't get noticed by any of their pursuers. Now to hope there was something to that.

She extended her senses through the ship, part of her wondering if she would see the telltale signal of a communication going off-ship. Now that she wasn't with Sherin, she realized that even if she saw a signal, it didn't necessarily mean that it wasn't coming from Sherin. There were no guarantees in what she could read from the Bridge, nothing that would tell her whether or not the other woman was betraying her or was giving her tru tell, not yet, anyway.

That thought alone was enough to make her consider Sherin's position, setting her own desires aside for the moment. Once they reached Electra, assuming it had some kind of legal link to the United Systems, Vahn might not be content with locking up his former employee for the trip back. He could bring charges against her either on Electra itself or have her sent back to Kyrin.

If Sherin had an industrial espionage charge in her corp record, it would be the end of corp employment for her. Such a charge carried with it fines, sometimes imprisonment and indentures. TiCara hated to think of the other woman helpless, vulnerable to someone like Zig, regardless of everything she had done. She shivered at the direction her thoughts were taking.

The memory of Zig reminded her to scan again for the corp ship. She watched the external sensors warily, looking for any sign that would tell her that the corp ship and the pirates were still out there, waiting. But there was nothing but asteroids and space, the residue from the comet and the distant glow of the star and she breathed a sigh of relief.

It didn't last long. There was a bright glow, as if something had exploded out on the edge of the belt. It looked like pulsar cannon fire and she wondered if it was from the corp ship or the pirates. She hoped it was the latter and that they succeeded in blowing up the corp ship. Especially if Zig was on board.

Fighting the corp shop would keep the pirates occupied, at least for a little while. Zig's death, if the pirates won, would make her the happiest medusa pilot in the twenty systems, even better than serving as a distraction. All she wanted to know was that he was truly gone, that she would never stumble across him in a spacer bar or anywhere else. She sent a fervent hope out through her implants that she would get at least this one wish.

Then she added a second one that she would get Sherin too. It was greedy, but she could live with that. Especially if it all came true. TiCara grinned at her reflection in one of the peripheral computer screens, then turned that smile on Erol as he came up the ladder behind her.

"Good tell, Captain? That's the happiest you've looked this trip." Her Second took his seat in the auxiliary pilot's chair and turned on the autopilot function. His lips quirked in a small smile as TiCara unplugged from the ship with a sigh.

"Think this plan will work, Second. Just feeling good about this job for a change. I'll leave you to keep an eye on things. Vahn says these are the real coordinates, that there hasn't been any more tampering, but we'll see once we get closer. Got a whole system to cross first. Fly like a rock for now, Second." She patted his shoulder and dropped down the ladder to the next level with only the briefest touch on the rails to slow her descent.

It was only when she was down at the level of her quarters that she remembered that there had been something that Erol wanted to tell her, back before everything blackholed. For a brief instant, she thought about going back up or comming him, but the thought of Sherin waiting for her in her room was too enticing. He hadn't said anything before she left, so it must not be so very important. She would ask him again at the next shift change.

Thinking about Sherin in her quarters made her desperate to believe the rep's story, crazy as it was. Was it so improbable that Elia was behind the tracker as well as Sherin's presumably abortive betrayal? She wasn't sure. Her former mentor had had a fine head for strategy and planning back when they were still running corp jobs. Perhaps the older pilot had found a way to use her skills in a different way now that she was retired.

Something told TiCara that if she spent more time with Sherin, she might learn enough for reassurance. And she wanted that time and more, trust or no trust. They were nearly at their destination and she was done delaying gratification. If she was wrong about the rep, either way, then she'd pay whatever price she had to once they arrived.

That thought lent wings to her heels, even more than the *Astra's* lower than planet normal gravity. She didn't hesitate when she reached her quarters, not even to send out a medusa to check a cam and see if Sherin was inside waiting for her. Even she could learn to like some surprises.

The door slid open to reveal Sherin lying on the bed, eyes closed and apparently asleep. But her eyes shot open, startled and fearful, when she heard the sound of the opening door, then crinkled at the edges as she gave the pilot a tentative smile. When TiCara dropped onto the bed above her, she reached up to touch the pilot's cheek, "Any signals?"

"Not yet, but I've got the scanners set." She bent down to kiss the rep softly on the lips. Then she turned her face to Sherin's hand on her cheek. A dim memory of an old vizhistory on sex that she had seen before she got wired reminded her that the hands could be an erogenous zone. It was time to start experimenting, if she wanted to continue to pleasure Sherin without using her medusas.

Slowly and carefully, she sucked on each of Sherin's fingers in turn, letting her tongue caress Sherin's skin. She licked the other woman's palm, pleased to hear a soft gasp of pleasure, to feel Sherin's body rock a little against hers. TiCara ran her tongue from Sherin's hand down her arm to her shoulder, pausing to nip at the delicate skin of her elbow joint and showering kisses on her goose-bumped flesh.

"Speaking of triggers, I've been plugged in for whole cycles now, thinking about you, starshine girl. I want to be done just thinking." She lowered her mouth to Sherin's kissable mouth, coaxing her tongue between the other woman's lips. Sherin's warm arms slid up around her neck, pulling her down onto the narrow bed.

She sank into the silken touch of Sherin's skin and reveled in the scent of desire that now filled the room. Shifting her body around, she braced one of her legs between Sherin's and pushed gently to part her thighs. The rep complied with gratifying speed and she grinned into their kiss.

TiCara dropped her free hand down to Sherin's bare thigh and stroked upward. Sherin met her touch with a slight arching of her back and a soft groan. TiCara let her fingers play over the rep"s crotch, not entering her, not yet. She wanted to savor this moment of longing.

Sherin unfastened her suit, her hands surer than they had been earlier, despite her still healing injury. She kissed her way over TiCara's exposed shoulder and collarbone as together they pulled the pilot's blacksuit down. Then Sherin twisted around to take one of TiCara's nipples in her mouth. TiCara growled as the rep tongued her hardened flesh against her teeth, the sensation sending waves of heat through her.

Their free hands were occupied in peeling off the suit now, yanking it down so that TiCara's boots trapped it. The pilot pulled free of Sherin's mouth with an effort and stood up to pull her suit and boots off, tossing the suit into the closet so the ship could clean it. Once that distraction was addressed, she took a moment to savor the sight of Sherin's beautiful body, the sleepy desire-filled tilt of her dark eyes, the rapid rise and fall of her full breasts.

TiCara growled softly, savoring the wave of desire that rode her every nerve ending. She dropped back down on the foot of the bed, taking one of Sherin's feet in her hands. The rep giggled softly as TiCara hit a ticklish spot, then moaned as the pilot caressed her shin with a swipe of her tongue, working her way upwards, dragging her hot mouth over the sensitive skin behind Sherin's knee. Then she started licking her way up Sherin's legs.

Sherin's hips rocked up to meet TiCara's mouth when she reached her destination between the rep's thighs, distrust forgotten in the rush of longing and sensations. TiCara parted Sherin's legs with her hand and blew along the length of her wet slit, listening with delight as Sherin uttered a deep, body-shaking groan. She followed that up by running her finger over the rep's wet skin, savoring the pleading tone of Sherin's whispered, "Please..."

She caught herself an instant later sending down a medusa to explore the other woman's yearning flesh. *Not yet, not now.* She would have to do this without her implants or not at all. And not at all was no longer an option.

Instead, she drove into Sherin first with one finger, then two, letting her tongue join them in Sherin's salty wetness. Her lover was bucking against her mouth, legs spread wide and heels dug into the bed. The noises coming from her mouth were wanton and urgent, nothing like the dignified corporate rep that TiCara had met in visits to Vahn's office. She found that she liked this version much, much better.

The sounds were enough to drive TiCara to press harder, lick harder, as if she didn't want Sherin desperately already. Her fingers were buried inside Sherin now, thrusting and pushing her way further in until her entire hand fit inside. Sherin's walls were tight around her fingers and the rep clutched at the bed's memfoam as her hips heaved and rocked against TiCara's mouth, TiCara's hand. TiCara's own pussy was aching with thwarted desire as she coaxed Sherin to come and come again for her. But it was a happy ache. This, this was what she had waited so long for and it was shaping up to be everything she'd dreamed of. It pleased more than she could have imagined.

Sherin collapsed against the bed and wriggled slightly to loosen TiCara's hand. Taking the hint, the pilot slipped her hand out with a slighting popping noise and gently kissed her way over the rep's torso to one of her breasts, then the other, sucking frantically at each to coax out the last of the tremors from Sherin's body.

Sherin grabbed her, pulling her face up for a fierce kiss, devouring her tongue and licking off the taste of her own pussy from TiCara's face. And for the first time, TiCara shuddered as Sherin's fingers attentively, cautiously, twined their way into her medusas. The sensation traveled from her scalp to the soles of her feet, lighting an even brighter fire in their wake.

Sherin's mouth was on her neck, her thigh thrusting its way between TiCara's before the pilot had time to register that she had slipped her hand out of her implants, and was now resting it on her mons. Then Sherin's mouth and tongue and hands were everywhere, a sharp bite followed by a soothing kiss, hot and wet desire overpowering every other impulse until TiCara couldn't respond to all of them at once.

But she tried, oh, she tried! She wanted to savor all of it, every instant and touch and taste and smell. It might not last, and then what would she do? She tried to push that foreboding thought aside and bury it. That was the moment when Sherin's tongue and fingers entered her at the same time, and she lost herself in a bucking, bed clutching, convulsing response of her own.

Sherin rode her out, using her mouth and hands to call forth every desire that TiCara had until she was spent and collapsed underneath her. Only then did she let herself be pulled up to the pilot's face for a long kiss. Only then did she begin to sing softly in TiCara's ear, the haunting and lovely sound filling the room and taking them both back to the spacer bars when they first saw each other.

She even sang one of TiCara's favorite songs, an old spacer ballad about being lost in the stars. Sherin followed that up with a love song, something which TiCara tried and failed utterly to not find significant. Then she sang them a lullaby as they both slipped into exhausted, sated sleep.

TiCara woke up three machrons later and checked the time. She wasn't needed on the Bridge to relieve Erol, not yet. There was time to savor the new sensation of waking up to Sherin, of watching her while she still slept. TiCara drank in the other woman's face as it rested on her shoulder, admiring the curve of her cheek, the luxurious sweep of the dark lashes on her closed eyes, her long straight nose and those blackberry lips. Perhaps she did believe in Erol's fortune, at least a little.

But her thoughts soon turned to Electra and what had happened to Sherin in the labs. Was there another way to get her rewired without the credits from Elia and Zig? Her thoughts swirled and wandered, but came back with nothing.

It frustrated her, this new inability to find ready solutions to her problems. If it weren't for Vahn, she would have turned the ship around and flown back out of the system. Going back to Kyrin or one of the other big ports would give her time to ask around, to research. To take another job or three that might generate enough credits. Or at least, get Sherin away from temptation and further potential betrayals.

But most shadow trade jobs would not pay as well as this one. Vahn had known what he was doing when he made his offer. This job would be worth any three that she could find on her own. TiCara sighed quietly and Sherin stirred restlessly at her side, eyes opening slowly in a startled expression.

They kissed gently, all urgency gone for the moment, then lay still, each listening to the other's even breathing. Finally, Sherin broke the silence with the last question that TiCara wanted to answer. "Why do you hate the Ears so much? What did they do to you?"

TiCara shuddered and began to pull away, only to be held tight in Sherin's arms. "You can trust me. Tell me whatever you want to tell me." Her voice was soft and reassuring, but TiCara knew that she wouldn't be released until she told the other woman something.

She thought of, then discarded, several somethings, before settling on the truth. "I spent two years as a bond slave in one of the Ear dormitories. The one where Zig was in training." An uncontrollable shiver started in her middle, then radiated outward to her limbs, and Sherin held her closer. She slowly regained some control at the comfort of the other woman's touch, letting it put distance between her mind and those memories she never wanted to revisit.

But if she was going to believe in Sherin, Sherin had to believe in her. She had to give the other woman something in exchange for her truth. As it stood, there were still too many barriers between them, and those barriers would come back to haunt any chance they had at being together. And she wanted that possibility, wanted that so very badly, that she was prepared to revisit her own personal hell to do it.

She forced her words out. "He used to do…things to me. Painful things, humiliating things. He'd get the other Ears to do them, too. And I couldn't say no, not unless it would result in death or permanent injury. It's part of the contract that the bondslaves sign with the Ears."

Sherin shivered against her, but was quiet, letting her continue. TiCara wondered what would happen if she didn't say anything else and just stopped there. But now that she was talking, she could feel all of it, all the stories she hadn't told anyone except Elia, welling up inside her and starting to spill out, like a meteor shower.

She talked for what seemed like forever, her eyes screwed tightly shut against her tears, until her trembling settled down into a quiet numbness. Then TiCara was silent while she waited for Sherin to withdraw, to be repulsed by the stories that she had told. She didn't think that she would want to stay with someone as damaged as she was and she couldn't imagine Sherin feeling the same about her, not now. She braced herself to feel nothing when Sherin finally spoke.

But instead of saying anything, Sherin hugged her closer, kissing her gently. TiCara couldn't hold back her tears any more and they soon gave way to choking sobs. And through it all, Sherin held her, stroking her shoulders and very tentatively, her implants. Her touch was gentle, careful, and it reassured TiCara more than any words.

Finally, she ran out of tears that she needed to shed. She accepted a wipe that Sherin offered her and used it on her face, letting its cool pressure restore her, calm her to the extent she could be calmed. For the first time that she could remember, that calm extended inside her as well as out. She smiled her gratitude at Sherin and kissed her back.

Sherin stroked her face. "I'll get us something to eat?" At TiCara's nod, she put on her clothes and slipped out. A few moments later, she was back with a couple of containers that she set down on the shelf across from the bed. "Drink this." She held out a cup and TiCara took it and gave it an experimental sip. A warm spicy aroma filled her nose and she took a second gulp.

"It's good." She opened the lid and took a deep whiff of its contents. "This from New Chindai too? I think I need to make a jump to that quadrant."

Sherin smiled. "I'm not sure New Chindai is ready for you. But the food always makes me feel better. I hoped it would work for you, too." They ate in companionable silence for a few moments.

TiCara was surprised at how right it felt. She had never had this kind of time before with any of her other lovers; there had always been a ship to fly or a job to complete, not this relaxed quiet over a good meal, after glorious meatspace sex, with no help from her implants. The novelty was almost too much to process.

Sherin finished her food and reached out for TiCara's hand. She looked down at their twined fingers and said, "I have some more tell about Electra. It wasn't as accidental as I made it sound. The part where I lost my...my medusas was, of course. But I was in the lab to see what I could find. I was curious and I wanted to know what they were doing there, maybe learn some tell I could use later." She looked away, as if she couldn't bring herself to look at TiCara. "I was stupid and unlucky."

TiCara kissed her hands. "Signing on as a bondslave to the Ears wasn't my best decision, either. But here we are." She turned Sherin's face toward hers as the alarm on her handheld chimed. It was time for her to get dressed and go to relieve Erol. "Wait here for me. I'll come back when my shift is done." She leaned over and kissed Sherin again, putting all gratitude and desire that she felt into the pressure of her lips and tongue. When she left, she looked back over her shoulder and Sherin blew her a kiss as the door slid closed, sending her out with a happy warm glow.

CHAPTER 21

THE DOOR SLID SHUT BEHIND TiCara and Sherin stood up and stretched slowly. She checked the time on TiCara's computer display. Zig would be waiting for her tell. She wondered what he would do when he didn't hear from her.

But then she suspected that she already knew the answer to that. He had someone else on board this ship, someone else to give him the information if she failed to provide it. She stepped into the shower and let the pressure relax her while she cataloged everyone on the ship, considering, then discarding the possibilities.

Her former employer, Vahn, was not on her suspect list and neither was TiCara, but that left several other excellent prospects. She hadn't really met the other crewmembers, besides Erol, and she had never trusted Sammo. But that didn't mean that he would betray Vahn. She knew what Vahn had to offer him; it was not a price that she could deny, if she wanted to return home as badly as he did.

She let her thoughts drift back to her own home planet, imagining a different life. But there was nothing that prevented her from returning to New Chindai. She could go back and live with her crèche mates and follow a new path. All she had to do was admit that she had failed as a medusa pilot through a stupid accident brought on by a bad decision, then been discharged as a corporate rep because her employer charged her with betraying his interests.

She shuddered just thinking about how her crèche would react, and how that would make her feel. She and her mates had been engineered to achieve success; their funders had paid to ensure that. Failure on that scale was nearly unthinkable. Returning home would mean bringing her crèche down with her in the eyes of the New Chindai corps and she couldn't bear to do that.

Besides, if she returned home, what would happen to TiCara and what they might be to one another? The thought of the losing that possibility sent a pang through her. This was all so new, so wonderful. She wasn't ready to give it up yet, not unless she was forced to.

But what if TiCara had second thoughts about her, about them? What if no one else sent a message from the ship and revealed themselves as the other contact? Would the pilot still believe her then, want to stay with her?

Doubts tangled up her thoughts until she had trouble sorting out what to do next. Without Vahn's protection and without TiCara, she had nothing. She wished, more than anything else, that she had a neutral friend, someone she could ask for advice. The someone that she had hoped Elia would be. She scrubbed her hands over her face and groaned.

The easiest way to establish her innocence would be to establish someone else's guilt. The question was: who? And how could she find out? Her gaze fell on TiCara's monitor as she stepped out of the shower. Her hacking skills were rusty at best, but it was worth trying.

She got dressed and activated the keyboard. The ship's logs were secur-protected as she expected, but there was a code backdoor into them that didn't take her very long to locate. She still couldn't see

TiCara's captain's logs, but she could view the ship's standard logs and communications with Kyrin. She kept hunting, hoping to find a clue.

Sherin wasn't sure how long it took to find what she was looking for, but she was stiff and hungry when a communication log that wasn't ship standard rolled past. The destination address was vaguely familiar and the more she looked at it, the more familiar it became. Sirius Transport. Vahn had her send messages to them from time to time and Elia had used something that looked like this code as well. Sherin thought about TiCara's stories about Zig and what Elia must have told him and trembled with a newfound rage.

She spent some time comparing shifts and what few other details that she could see to come up with a suspect until one became clear: Erol's shifts corresponded with the communication times. Part of her quailed, wondering how TiCara would respond to an accusation against her loyal Second. Another part of her denied it at first: she liked Erol, at least what she'd seen of him.

But she couldn't accuse him or anyone else until she got more proof. A glance at the time on the computer told her that a full crew shift turnover hadn't happened yet. Erol could still be in his quarters. But if he wasn't, she might be able to get in and out before he got back. She might have just enough time to find her proof there, enough to show TiCara that there was really someone else, someone who would do what she wouldn't.

Sherin shut her eyes and pictured TiCara, remembering how the pilot looked at her, how happy she'd been when they woke up together. A delighted shiver went through her. That image went a long way to replacing the other one, the one she feared to see: TiCara angry, TiCara rejecting her and refusing to believe her.

She saved what she had found to a drive flagged for TiCara. The pilot would realize that it was something new and investigate it accordingly when she updated her logs. It would be there just in case she wasn't around to explain what was on that drive. Sherin shivered again, realizing that she had to go before she lost her nerve. She slipped out of the room, dropping the remains of their meal into the food dispenser as she passed.

Then she opened one of the security consoles that she had located when she logged into TiCara's computer and looked at the secur cam footage. TiCara had been as good as her word and she could see almost everywhere on the ship, based on what she knew of it. She checked screen after screen, looking for Erol until she found him, checking on the repairs.

For a moment, she paused. He had been kind when she had spoken to him. With all her heart she wanted it to be someone else, someone like Sammo. But if it had to be Erol or her, then she couldn't afford for it to be her.

She located the crew quarters and assignments a few moments later and closed the console. Whatever happened, she hoped that TiCara would find and understand the evidence that she had left for her. If anything went wrong. With that thought, she slipped down a ladder and then walked quietly down a short corridor until she stood in front of Erol's quarters.

The door was, not surprisingly, locked and it took her some time to override the code. Her heart was thudding its way up her throat when the door finally slid open. What if he had come back, was inside sleeping? But, to her relief, the open door revealed an empty room. Erol's possessions were arranged neatly on shelves and in a small chest, nothing on the floor where the cleaning bots might get tangled in it. A bright cloth covered the bed and a few trinkets decorated the shelves.

In a way, she was disappointed. She had hoped for a mess, something that indicated a forgetful traitor, one who would be easy to expose. Sherin sighed. She would just have to look more thoroughly.

First, she went through the shelves, finding nothing but his clothes and other necessities. On one side of the bed, there was a picture of Erol with a brown-skinned femme about his own age, arms around each other, smiling at the photobot. Sherin looked at the picture, a sinking suspicion telling her what tell Zig had to control TiCara's Second, what he might do if Erol failed to contact him.

But she couldn't stop to worry about that, not now. She looked at the chest and its old lock. It wasn't coded so it would need to be either picked or broken. She didn't have anything to break it with, so she scrambled through Erol's shelves until she found something thin and flexible enough to try and turn the tumbler system.

It took longer than she wanted it to take, and her hands were beginning to ache from the strain when the lock finally clicked open. She pulled it free of the latch and opened the chest. Its contents looked innocuous enough, but she hoped that there was something buried it in. Her hands were both inside it when the door slid open.

Sherin and Erol stared at each while entire galaxies went by outside, neither one moving or saying a word. Finally, he stepped inside. "What are you doing here?" His tone was neutral, calm even, but Sherin could see the muscles in his cheek twitch and his eyes narrow.

She stood up and backed away. She had some combat training, but Erol was a tall man in his own room. If he attacked her, she wasn't sure that she'd be able to get out undamaged. Or alive. That thought sent chills through her and she wondered if TiCara was watching the camera feeds.

Maybe there was audio. "I wanted to know more about you. You're the one sending messages to the Ears, aren't you?" She was nearly shouting her words, hoping that someone else was listening. "I also wanted to know why you told TiCara that it was me, that I was the one who betrayed her."

They were circling each other now, her standing on his bed, stepping sideways, her back to the wall. At any moment, it felt like he might lunge at her. She glanced sideways, looking for something that could be used as a weapon. Erol took advantage of her distraction and leapt toward her. She jumped off the bed, grabbing an old-fashioned chair from the corner and holding it up in front of her like a shield.

Erol's nostrils flared and his eyes went all pupil. "They'll kill zir if I don't give them what they want. I can't let you expose me, not now. I can't!" He lunged again, and this time, she hit him with the chair.

He grabbed the legs and snapped one off, throwing Sherin to the ground with the force of the momentum. She rolled over, narrowly avoiding a kick, and threw the broken chair at him. Erol ducked and Sherin stood back up and retreated back toward the door. *TiCara, TiCara, where are you?* She didn't want to make herself more vulnerable by looking away from Erol for the shine of telltale lights, but it was tempting.

"She doesn't know you're in here, does she?" Erol's voice took on an edge that made her shudder. He tossed the chair aside and came toward her, hands flexing as if to loosen them up. Sherin summoned a long ago self-defense move and lashed out with her foot, striking his leg as he got closer. He didn't leap backward fast enough and her foot grazed him.

But in a startlingly swift move, he grabbed it before she could finish pulling away, twisting her leg so she dropped to the floor with a yell. He looked down at her, his expression turning from menacing to cold. Somehow, that was more terrifying than him holding her foot and Sherin froze.

Then he shifted his grip slightly, digging his fingers into her leg, and the movement broke through the haze of fear that was immobilizing her. She tried to get through his shell. "You don't have to do this! We can find another way, give them false coordinates. It could give you more time to save your primary." She wondered if she was pleading in hopes of getting him to let her go or just to buy herself more time. But buy herself more time for what? *Please*...she sent the thought out to anyone or anything that might be listening.

Erol reached for her, dropping to his knees on top of her legs to pin them down. She grabbed at his belt, hoping to capture either his communicator or a blaster, if he had one. A sharp crackle of static made both of them jump and she yanked her arm free of his, making him struggle to recapture it. "Why are you doing this?" She shouted into the crackle of his handheld as he seized her arm.

"Because I have to." His hands were reaching around her throat now and she bucked frantically against him, trying to loosen his grip. "Because I think he's following us and I can't afford to fail. He'll kill Arnelle." He delivered his speech in a voice gone dreamy and distant, as if he were disconnecting from everything else that he was doing.

She managed a shrieking gurgle before he succeeded in cutting off her air. After that, the pain made her see stars as her vision darkened. She didn't hear the telltale whoosh of the room's door opening.

"Let her go." TiCara's voice was ice on an outer moon. Without being able to see her, Sherin knew that she had a weapon and that it wasn't set to stun. Erol's grip loosened and she began coughing and choking as her body tried to pull in enough air to recover. Erol shifted off her slowly, his hands now outstretched. "She's a traitor, Captain. She's working for the Ears." His voice took on its own pleading note. "Why choose her over me?"

"Because she's not trying to strangle you, Second. I know what they offered her to betray Vahn and me. What did they offer you?" TiCara stepped forward, herding him back and away from Sherin.

Sherin sat up, still coughing, and felt her throat. There'd be bruises, at the very least. A small tremor went through her as she wondered whether or not he had damaged her vocal chords. What if she couldn't sing again? But then, that was probably something they could fix on Electra. If she had the credits. Sherin shook her head, trying to organize the jumbled terrified mess of her thoughts and looked back up at TiCara.

The pilot and her Second stared each other down until Erol broke. His gaze shifted to the framed vids on the shelf and Sherin could see his expression shift through longing, fear, then back to rage in the blink of an eye. "Look out!" She shouted as Erol lunged toward TiCara, the desperation in the set of his face driving the speed of his hands.

The blast from TiCara's lazer blinded her for a moment but Erol's scream of pain filled the air, telling her what had happened just as clearly as if she had seen it. TiCara hauled her to her feet and shoved her toward the door. Blinking against the aftereffects of the weapon's fire, she could see Erol sitting on the floor, cradling one of his arms. His uniform sleeve was burned away and his skin was turning an angry deep red.

Sherin winced and looked away as she stepped out into the corridor. TiCara stayed in the room, gathering up her former Second's comm devices and any obvious weapons. She jerked her head over one shoulder to Sherin and said, "There's an emergency med kit in the next corridor. I'll understand if you don't want to get it but...I'd thank you if you did." The pilot's face was bleak, her eyes distant and Sherin understood a little of what it had cost her to act, to fire on someone who had once been a trusted companion.

Or more. It occurred to her that she had never asked about their relationship. Romances amongst crewmembers were far from uncommon and she cringed away from the thought in a morass of jealous sympathy. But TiCara had come for her, had fought for her. If keeping Erol alive meant something to her, then Sherin should try and help. She nodded and dashed in the direction TiCara had pointed in.

Behind her, the door closed on the sound of voices. Part of her wondered if Erol would talk TiCara into believing his tell. Wondered if she'd see the lazer pointed at her when she returned. She slumped against the corridor wall and started shaking, a rising wave of panic turning the ship's walls red around her. Her hands tightened into fists, closed so tightly that her fingers screamed from the strain.

Sherin lost herself in the racing drumbeat of her heart, the burning ache of her bruised throat. Her instincts took over and there was a moment, then two, where she imagined herself fleeing to the Bridge and piloting the *Astra* away from Electra, returning to Aliandra or New Chindai or anywhere that felt safe. But the tiny shred of self-control she still held inside wouldn't let her. It drove her to gradually calm her breathing and unclench her hands.

It took longer than she thought it would, but Sherin managed to return with the med kit. Then she held the lazer while TiCara dressed Erol's wound. She was proud of how little her hand trembled, even though she wasn't sure that the weapon was still necessary. Erol's head was tilted back and he looked unconscious. After TiCara used the injection pen on his arm, he slumped over on the floor, apparently asleep. TiCara pulled on his legs to stretch him out on the floor. Glancing up, she caught Sherin's gaze. "He saved my life, more than once. I won't kill him if I don't have to."

She straightened up and took the lazer from Sherin's hand. Something must have startled her because her voice got very gentle. "Starshine girl, you with me?"

"He said that they...that he was expecting the coordinates to Electra now. That Zig would kill zir, his primary," she tilted her head at the vids before continuing, "If he didn't get them. I think we need to send Zig some coordinates." It wasn't just about Erol. She couldn't let the femme in the vids die, not that easily. It would haunt her and she'd had quite enough of that.

TiCara followed the direction of her gaze and gave a grim nod. "Let's go to the Bridge then." She stepped outside, Sherin at her heels and paused to lock the door. "He'll sleep for a few cycles, then we'll have to get food to him. I'll let the crew know what happened after we send our message to Zig."

Sherin stroked her shoulder sympathetically and TiCara slipped her arm around her and tilted her chin up. She inhaled sharply as she saw the bruises on Sherin's neck. "I was too soft with him," she growled. For an instant, Sherin thought she was going to go back into Erol's room.

"There isn't time. We should go send a message before anything blackholes. More than it already has." She remembered what Erol had said about the corp ship, about how he thought that it was Zig. But how would TiCara handle that? She hesitated a moment too long and TiCara vanished up the ladder to the next level.

She scrambled after her. "Wait, we need to send the coordinates from his comms. Otherwise, they'll get suspicious." TiCara nodded, the movement sending her medusas flying around her head. For the first time, Sherin didn't find herself cringing inside at the sight of them. After all, she might have them herself again, sometime in the near future.

Except that she still didn't have the credits and she was pretty sure that simply stumbling into another lab on Electra wouldn't get her medusas magically re-implanted. Then TiCara had her hand outstretched for the comms that Sherin was carrying, and she sent all thought of her implants, past and future, to the back of her mind. "How about the middle of the asteroid belt?"

TiCara grinned at her. "I do like the way you think." Together they poured over the nav screen looking for just the right spot. Then

TiCara plugged in the coordinates after she saw Sherin's nod, and hit send. "Did they say there would be a response?"

"Not to me, but I don't know what they told him. I gave you Erol's comm, just in case they're double-checking the source code." Sherin met TiCara's sidelong look. "I hope that's enough. What he did isn't zir fault." She rubbed her arms to warm them from the sudden chill of her words.

TiCara nodded and gestured toward the copilot's seat. The array of screens above their heads shifted as the pilot ran checks all around the *Astra*. Sherin looked at each of them as they came up, noticing that the ship was still on minimal thrust, trying to blend in with the dwindling number of asteroids out here on the edge of the belt.

She checked the navigation coordinates and verified that they seemed correct, at least for now. She entered a course correction for several variables, then showed it to TiCara. The pilot grinned at her, sending spacedust swirling up inside her as she grinned back. Maybe they could be a team out of bed as well as in it. The thought made her white-hot happy until she considered their chances of survival.

They'd have to fire up the engines at full soon and make a run for Electra. And hope that the repairs held and that their pursuers gave them a head's start. Sherin shivered harder and sent up hopeful thoughts to anything that might be listening. She wondered when TiCara was going to tell Vahn that she had ignored his wishes and freed his former employee. She wondered whether or not Zig was actually following them, instead of waiting for word back on Kyrin.

But most of all, she wondered what the future held for her and TiCara. That thought was enough to block out all her other worries, at least for the moment. Sherin watched the pilot and the screens and wondered whether or not hope was completely illogical.

CHAPTER 22

VAHN WOKE FROM A SOUND sleep and found himself alone in his quarters. Annoyance filled him as he realized that Sammo wasn't on his cot in the corner or sitting in the chair. He wasn't paying the man to go wander the corridors of the ship, leaving him unprotected. He sat up cautiously, sorting through his various aches and pains, checking for anything new, anything worse.

It wasn't just for protection that he wanted Sammo by his side at all times. He was going to need another shot soon and he couldn't give them to himself. It was something that he thought of as a personal failing. But it was one he had to live with until his condition was cured. Vahn reached out for his handheld and sent an alert to Sammo's, holding down the button just long enough to make it unpleasantly prolonged on the receiver's end.

He regretted it the moment that he did it. He had always prided himself on being above such petty tyrannies, yet here he was, behaving like a spoiled child. For an instant, he wondered if it had influenced his treatment of Sherin, this mixture of pain and frustration and anger at his loss of control. But he dismissed the idea almost as soon as it crossed his mind. Betrayal was one thing, overreaction to perceived neglect another.

The door slid open, interrupting his thoughts. Sammo walked in carrying a small tray that he set down on the portable stand next to Vahn's bed. "My apologies, Ser. I went to go learn more about the repairs and the state of the crew, as well as to verify the status of your former rep." He tilted his head up from a slight bow to gauge Vahn's mood, then reached for the med kit on the shelf.

Vahn nodded reluctantly. Much as he wanted to hear Sammo's tell, it needed to wait until after he had received his medicine. And truthfully, it would need to wait until he had broken his fast too. He was too fragile to skip meals now.

Vahn bit back a curse at his body's failures, its incipient breakdown. When he was healthy once more and his corp profitable again, he would commission the technicians on Electra to create an alternative to Eternayouth, one he would be able to use. Clinging to that goal enabled him to ignore the pain from his shot and drove him to devour his food like a beast.

When he was done, he set the containers aside. "Give me your tell." He eased himself off the bed and walked carefully toward the shower as Sammo told him what he discovered.

"Your former rep is no longer in her quarters but, when last I saw her, was on the Bridge with the Pilot-Captain." Vahn gave a small hiss of fury. How dare TiCara ignore his wishes? He was paying her well for her services, and that should be enough to ensure that she was not countermanding his decisions.

But then, he realized a moment later, he had not told the Pilot-Captain what he intended to do with Sherin or why. His former employee might easily have convinced her that it was all a mistake. Another slipup on his part. He grimaced, then nodded at Sammo to continue.

"The Pilot-Captain has imprisoned her Second in his quarters. I do not know why. But the repairs have progressed and the ship should be nearly back to full functionality. The crew has also disguised the ship as an asteroid, but we are almost out of the belt so that will cease to be useful soon." Sammo averted his eyes as his employer emerged from the shower, Vahn noted approvingly. He didn't want anyone to see his twisted and decrepit body, if it could be avoided.

His thoughts turned in a new direction as he got dressed. It was a pity that Sammo didn't have the skills to serve as his rep, since he would need one again and soon. Sherin was to have negotiated with the techs on Electra on his behalf. He gave a discrete cough to let Sammo know that he could look up again. "I think we must learn why her Second required imprisonment and why my former employee required freedom. I am ready to go and seek those answers."

Sammo handed him the cane that he had hoped to leave behind and, after a moment of hesitation, he accepted it with an ill grace. Then he trailed after his bondarmin, limping, as his body processed the aftereffects of his shot. It was taking longer to take effect than it had when they had first begun the regimen. The realization lent thrusters to his aching feet. His time was running out.

He also had one last card to play: the final coordinates for the asteroid, the ones that he had failed to give to TiCara, twice now, wanting to wait until he was sure of her, sure of Electra. Now, he thought he knew just the right pilot to receive that information. "You have a lazer with you?" He asked Sammo, keeping his voice soft and hard to pick up on any nearby audio receivers.

The bondarmin's eyebrows twitched in surprise, but he nodded. Vahn could see him give the cane an appraising glance and could almost read the man's thoughts. He was wondering how long his employer could continue to move around the ship, to command others, without additional assistance. And whether or not they would get to Electra before his condition could no longer be corrected.

Well, he would soon learn how foolish his doubts were, as would they all. Vahn promised himself as much, one more time out of many. He sighed impatiently before speaking. "I think we must go and speak to the Pilot-Captain's former Second, to begin with. Does she put the ship on auto-pilot between shifts?"

"Yes, I think so." Sammo responded with a quick uncertain frown and Vahn gestured his understanding that his bondarmin had no good way of confirming this. It was another question that they could ask the prisoner.

They arrived outside his room with that thought and Sammo went to work on the door lock. It was just secur-locked, not like the quick hack job he had done on the door to Sherin's quarters, so once he understood the coding mechanism, it was only a few moments before the door slid open. The bright light of the corridor shone into the dimly lit room, revealing the crewman stirring slowly awake on the floor. The light and the sound drove Erol to sit up and raise his uninjured arm over his face to block it out.

His other arm was burned by a lazer, then hastily bandaged, Vahn noted an instant later. Interesting. He had more minor injuries as well and there was blood on his suit. The question was whether or not he had been wounded deliberately by another crewmember or through an accident. The tru answer to that would tell Vahn much.

Sammo had his lazer out and pointed at Erol the instant he moved. Vahn was careful not to block his line of sight as he entered the room and sat on the end of the bed. "How do you come to be here, Second? When last I saw you, you occupied a position of trust in the Pilot-Captain's estimation."

Erol gave him a sly glance and Vahn raised a hand to forestall whatever false answer he was going to give. "Perhaps our friend requires some encouragement to find truth?" Sammo reached for something at his belt, a small gray container, his face full of implicit threats. Erol's face collapsed without even knowing what he was being threatened with.

Vahn realized that he thought that the bondarmin might carry TruTell or one of the other drugs that compelled some degree of accurate information. But using those chemicals would make him an unreliable pilot and that was not the outcome that Vahn desired. Then again, there was no reason to tell him that. He tapped his fingers impatiently on his cane to indicate that he was still waiting for a response.

Erol looked down at his hands. "TiCara...the Pilot-Captain believes that I am working for her enemies. She is wrong," he looked up at Vahn and his voice rose in indignation. "I would not betray her."

Vahn raised an eyebrow. "And what of my interests, Second? Would you betray me?"

Erol looked back down at his hands, that gesture all the answer that Vahn needed. Perhaps here was the backup plan that his enemies had placed their faith in, the one that his former rep had insisted was on board. "Did you send a message with the asteroid coordinates back to Kyrin?"

He could see the other man weigh his answer before he spoke. Maybe it would be better to give him something to compel his truth after all. Something in his expression must have warned Erol what he was thinking since what he said next did not sound like a lie. "No," Erol said at last. "They locked me in here before I could finish the transmission of the false coordinates." Something in his face went blank and cold and Vahn wondered how he had been driven to betray his captain. Whatever it was, he looked like a man who thought it was too late to care.

How unfortunate. But perhaps freedom would be incentive enough to gain his trust and cooperation. If that failed, there was always Sammo and his lazer. "Indeed. Was my former rep in the Pilot-Captain's company when she left you?" At Erol's head jerk of acknowledgment, Vahn nodded, noting that the other man's face was now a mask of misery. Vahn decided not to ask why he had been replaced. "Then I will require you to perform a task that I am no longer sure that the Pilot-Captain can do. Can you pilot with your injury?"

Erol's eyes widened. Whatever he had expected when they entered the room, this request wasn't it. "Why would you trust me to do that, Ser? And what would I receive in return?" He drew himself up and stood with an effort.

Vahn hid a grin. Whatever the other lacked, it wasn't courage. "Your life, to begin with, Second. But if you do this well and we arrive safely, I might see my way to paying you the bonus in credits I had intended to pay to my rep and the Pilot-Captain. Would that be enough to earn your loyalty for the immediate future?"

Erol puffed out his cheeks as he exhaled and looked at a photo vid on his shelf. His expression turned bleak and lost before he looked back at Vahn. "It's too late. But I'm not ready to be put out the airlock yet and I can still make those…responsible pay for what they've done. I gladly accept your offer, Ser." A feral gleam rose in his dark eyes and Vahn found himself releasing the catch on his cane, the one that would turn his walking stick into a weapon even a decrepit old man could use.

But other man didn't move, didn't lunge forward the way it looked like he might be contemplating. Instead, he made a questioning gesture toward the door and Vahn used his cane for its originally intended purpose, leaning heavily on it to maintain his balance. He checked the computer's time on his handheld; by his estimation, the shift change had already occurred. The ship should be moving at full speed while its Pilot-Captain rested.

Sammo made Erol lead the way and together, they all went down the corridor and up the two levels to the Bridge. As Vahn expected, it was empty and the ship was on autopilot. "Disable the alerts that might rouse the Pilot-Captain, Second." Sammo gestured at the board and they both watched as Erol made some changes.

"Now enter these coordinates." Vahn handed Erol a chip and watched him plug it into the nav computer. A sharp intake of breath disturbed the quiet as Erol noted the difference in degrees between the current coordinates and the ones he had now. Vahn smiled; whatever information Erol or Sherin had sent to the Ears, it wouldn't get them to Electra.

"You have seen the previous coordinates for a decoy asteroid which orbits a nearby planet. The technicians on Electra have a number of safeguards created to guard their location; this is but one. Now, please reset the autopilot when you are done, Second. I do know what that looks like so please do not try to trick me."

Vahn seated himself in the co-pilot's chair with a grimace of distaste at the hookups for medusa implants. It had always seemed to him a disgusting thing that humans would link themselves so closely to machines. Though even he had to admit that they had their uses. He shrugged the thought away and hung over Erol's shoulder until the autopilot was set once again.

"Now please reset the alarms for the Pilot-Captain. I would not want her to miss any genuine crises that may arise." Erol did as he was told, shooting him a questioning look as he did it. "Once that is done, you will monitor the computer and together, we will watch the screens and see if your erstwhile friends are still following us."

Erol's lips thinned into a fine line and Vahn wondered if he planned a suicide mission if the corporate ship reappeared. Nothing he had seen of him so far suggested such a course of action but it was wise to be prepared for everything. "Would you not rather live to rejoice in your enemy's downfall?" He asked the question softly so as not to startle Erol, but the man's small flinch was noticeable, close as he was and hard as he was watching.

After a long moment, TiCara's former Second nodded and reached out slowly toward one of the displays. He hesitated before touching it, his eyes flickering from Sammo's unwavering lazer to Vahn's face, clearly asking for permission. There was a moment of silence, of all three men studying each other, weighing the consequences, before Vahn signaled his assent. Erol modified the control and all the display screens showed a panoramic view of the Gathwaite System.

As Vahn had suspected, they were well outside the asteroid belt now and moving along at a good speed. There were distant moving lights that suggested that they were drawing near some interplanetary trade routes that connected the planets and any outlying stations. None of them looked close enough to become a problem, with the exception of one moving point of light behind the *Astra.*

All of their attention was soon fixed on that point, which grew brighter as they watched it. "Does this tub have weapons, Second?" Vahn's voice had taken on a note of barely suppressed fury.

"Yes, Ser. But not many, only one pulse cannon, nothing big enough to take on a full-size ship. Especially not if that's a corp ship or pirates. Once we fired a few shots, the *Astra* would be dead in space and out of fuel." Erol was looking at him warily, as though he feared that an old man was losing his sanity.

As, indeed, perhaps he was. "Ready the cannon to fire. You will put up the best fight that this tub of bolts is capable of before running. Do you understand, Second?"

"Ser, it's suicide. They would have to get very close to be within range. By then, they would be close enough to capture us in a beam or to blow us up. And we would be out of fuel. It would be better to run now." Erol was pleading, all attempts at artifice gone.

"And can this ship outrun a corp ship?"

"Yes, Ser. For some distance. We can't carry enough fuel to outrun a big ship forever, of course. "

"What about that one?" Sammo's voice startled both of them. "Can you outrun it?" The ship was definitely coming closer, entering hailing distance. Or cannon range. But no signal or call came from it; a merchant, mining or security ship would have hailed them by now.

"Let me call the Pilot-Captain, Ser. I'm not wired, I can't fly this ship as well as she can for battle or escape. She's our only real chance." Erol's hand hovered above the alarm, a bead of sweat making his forehead glow under the Bridge lights.

"I think that your skills are sufficient, Second. Fire on them with one cannon pulse and if two shots are too much, then run." Vahn settled back into the chair, fastening the safety harness around him. It was a risk, of course. Erol might be right about TiCara's skills but Vahn wasn't ready to trust her again, not when she was so close to his former rep. He looked at the forward display; they were not so far from the coordinates he had Erol enter. It would be enough. It had to be.

Erol bit his lip, clearly unhappy. He reached for the board with both hands and the ship shook from a cannon blast as the sharp ping of an alarm sounded through the Bridge's audio system. His fingers blurred as he reloaded the cannon and fired again, coming closer to their pursuer this time, but still not hitting the bigger ship.

The pursuing ship pulled in closer and a bright glow under the other ship's nose filled the rear screen. Erol tilted the controls hard to one side, trying to avoid the hit. He was an instant too late and the Astra shuddered hard. The ship rolled over, anything loose shooting upward to clang against what had been the ceiling and was now the floor.

Then the empty starfield in front of the *Astra* exploded with lights and energy bolts. It was so sudden that there was barely time for Erol's shrieked curse, for the tell tale scramble of feet and shouts in the corridors below that told of the crew trying to take control of the ship again. The *Astra* and its pursuer were plunging down into...something he couldn't see.

Vahn stared out at the thickening cloud that was now filling the forward screens. This was Electra: they had found it and were about to meet it head on. This, then, was his death, the one that he had tried so hard to avoid. He pulled himself up in the chair, closed his eyes and waited.

CHAPTER 23

ZIG HAD WATCHED THE ROCK that his ship's sensors said was the *Astra* drift out of the asteroid belt, wondering if he was wrong about what he thought he had seen. Yva had to point out the heat signature to him when it accelerated slowly, her tone laden with mockery. It had not endeared her to him. In fact, he wasted valuable seconds imagining the consequences of killing her immediately.

She must have seen something in his face though, and he found himself looking at the blaster in her very steady hand. "No one will miss you, little Zig. Cease to be of use and I'll fry you. Understand?" Yva grinned at him, showing her pointed incisors, reminding him of how much she now outranked him in the Ear hierarchy.

He'd wanted those for himself, once. They were a reminder of all that she'd done, all that he feared to do. All that he *had* feared to do, until now. But he was ready and everything was going to change. Just as soon as she no longer held him at the point of a blaster that would fry him before he hit the floor. He hit the controls that would send their ship after the *Astra* and turned away from Yva as if she didn't pose a threat.

That way, she couldn't see how much his hands were shaking, how much effort it took him to turn his back on her. Every instinct told him to duck behind the nav board and hide. Nothing he knew of her suggested that she was not completely serious in her threat. She probably had authorization to do it. In an effort to distract himself, he focused on the small ship flying in front of them.

He wondered how close he could get before TiCara noticed that they were there, and realized that with all her maneuvering and hiding, he could still find her. He hoped that she knew that it was him and that his face haunted her dreams. Her terror and loathing had always been sweet.

He would miss that feeling when she was gone. But it would be easier to destroy the ship and her with it than to try and capture her alive. He repeated the thought to himself, allowing it to become more convincing. The fewer people who survived this expedition, the better for him. Every death would make those coordinates more valuable.

All he had to do was wait to be sure that he had the right ones. As if it could read his thoughts, the comm speaker set off the sharp chime that announced incoming communications. Yva shoved him aside and waved the other crewmember from the Bridge. Then she hit the button to play the audio. A series of beeps filled the room and she turned it down, letting the codes feed into the computer.

As the computer recognized the signal as nav coordinates, it fed them into a processor. When the final beep announced the end of processing, Zig hit the controls and a three-dimensional schematic hovered above the nav screen, planets in a brilliant dark blue, asteroids in a light yellow and the star, Gathwaite Six, in a deep red. One asteroid drifted at the edge of a much smaller belt than the one they had just exited.

It was colored a medium purple and Zig found himself smiling at it, as if it was an old friend. A close old friend, in this case. They could reach it in a few cycles based on the distance in the schematic. He could hear Yva let out her breath in a quiet hiss, as if she'd been holding it in anticipation of this moment.

But there remained a chance that TiCara had somehow found out, had managed to coerce her Second into revealing his compromised loyalties. He checked the source code against his records. It had come from Erol's comm. And it had better be tru, at least if he wanted to see his primary again.

Of course, that wasn't going to happen anyway. But Erol didn't know that yet. He spared a moment's consideration for Elia's little protégé, the corporate rep. No word from her, which suggested that her desire to have her medusas restored was less urgent than Elia thought, or, possibly, that she'd been exposed and was not in a position to send a message. Not that it mattered because she wasn't going to get rewired either. For a wild moment, he savored that sense of power, of control over so many destinies at once, like a new narcotic.

"What are you smirking about?" Yva's voice made her use of the archaic word grate even more than it might have from someone else. "If the tell is tru, all we need to do is to confirm the coordinates and send them back to headquarters. We don't have any other corp work in this system, or with that ship. 'Stand me, Zig? Don't know what you're hoping for, but it doesn't happen on our corp's cred." She was watching him, her weapon still in her hand.

Meeting her gaze, Zig had a visceral reaction, a feverish brew of hatred and fear and something like desire, that nearly boiled from his pores. It made it hard to think, harder to react. But not impossible. He lurched out of his frozen tableau and lunged for her and they grappled for the blaster. She tried to sweep his feet out from under him, only to have him step back and use his longer arms to hold her off.

They struggled for what seemed like a full planetary cycle, but Zig gradually got the upper hand. She clawed at his face as he released her hand to close his around her throat. They flailed and struggled for a few more minutes as he tried cut off her air, then he threw her backward as she drew blood, sinking her teeth into his arm. The crunch of her head striking the edge of the comm console was deeply satisfying. Yva dropped to the floor, limp and unmoving. He could see her breathing so she was still alive but he would ensure that wouldn't last long.

He grabbed for the fallen blaster to fry her, then paused to think. She might still have her uses. If Yva lived, she could still be given to their corporate masters as the fool who had tried to betray them. If he damaged her enough, she wouldn't be able to tell them otherwise. He grinned as he bound her arms and legs and gagged her with the safety harness he cut from the co-pilot's chair.

Then he turned his attention back to the *Astra*. It was speeding up, increasing the distance between them. Zig sped up as well, checking the schematic as he did so. From the information that Erol had sent him, they should be at Electra in a few cycles. He sent a message to the small crew operating the weapons array to power it up again.

He kept watching the little ship until he could almost see its pilot's face superimposed on it. His imagination let him hear her pleas for mercy, hear her offer him anything he wanted including her body. It aroused him until his erection ached against his blacksuit and he gave the schematic a distracted look, wishing he had time for the VR mods for a quick release.

The shots from the *Astra*'s pulsar cannon took him completely by surprise. He rolled his ship over to avoid the fire. He didn't hear the telltale thud of a strike or the clamor of an alarm, so he thought they were still unscathed when he righted the ship. But he didn't stop to savor the sense of relief. Instead, he signaled the weapons bay to fire once, then again.

His ship rocked from return fire and suddenly the space around both ships was alive with lights. Something was materializing just underneath them. And that something had weapons of its own. Now, he heard the sickening thud of a hit and the shriek of the alarms. His ship began to follow the *Astra* down to whatever it was, into a giant cloud that gradually redefined itself as a small moon. Electra 12. He'd found it.

Now he just had to survive it.

CHAPTER 24

TiCara woke up to the howl of the *Astra*'s alarms in her ears. She rolled free of Sherin's arms and into her blacksuit with a couple of fluid motions. Sherin was still sitting up when TiCara hit the button for the door and bolted out into the corridor. What had gone wrong? And why hadn't the ship or Erol told her about it sooner?

She remembered that Erol was still confined to quarters with a jolt. Thinking about his betrayal sent a sharp pang through her. A part of her still couldn't believe it. Yet here she was, racing for the Bridge while her ship bucked and surged around her and its alarms screeched, but with no loyal Second at her heels. Something must have gone wrong with the autopilot, but what? Another lurch and this time, she knew that the ship was under attack, almost certainly hit. Pirates or corp ship? Both? Neither possibility boded well for their continued survival. She grabbed for the ladder going up to the Bridge only to be hurled off the rungs by the ship's sudden motion. Her stomach lurched with the shock as she rolled head over heels across the corridor. They must be going down, but going down where?

The asteroid? Had Vahn lied about the coordinates again? Were they were going down on one of the Gathwaite planets? But they weren't close enough to any of them. Or they hadn't been. She scrambled to regain her footing and shoved her medusas out of her face. They were swirling around her head in a cloud, confused by her terror as much as by her sudden and unexpected movements.

Then, the smash of sudden impact shook her to the core as her head hit the nearest wall. Everything went black as the *Astra*'s power failed, but she was still seeing a rainbow of stars when she was able to open her eyes. It took everything she had left to crawl toward where she thought the ladder was.

The dim light of the emergency power clicked on as she found the bottom rung of the ladder by hitting her hand on the metal. She dragged herself upward, rung by rung until she could stand on her unsteady feet. What had happened to her ship? To Sherin, her crew and her passengers? A sick dread filled her and for a long moment, she didn't want to know what was waiting for her on the Bridge.

But she put one foot on the lowest rung and then the next anyway. This was her responsibility, her life, and she wouldn't just let it go. The hatch was closed, something she hadn't seen from the floor below. She shoved at the cover, trying to force it open. But it was stuck, bolted or blocked, from the other side. She'd have to find something to use to force it open.

TiCara slid back down the ladder and ran for Engineering. She found Ji-min there, sitting up slowly and staring groggily at the damage around them. "Captain. What tell?" They turned their head to one side, then the other, as TiCara checked them for injuries. They flinched as the pilot grabbed a medkit from storage and slapped a patch on their bleeding head wound. Ji-min stretched experimentally, checking for more injuries. Then they stood up, with some help from a nearby console cabinet and TiCara. "Rest of the crew, Captain?"

"Don't know. Can't reach the Bridge." TiCara frowned at the broken equipment and sparking wires around them. "Came to plug in. See if you can find a comm?" She went to look for an undamaged console. A few moment banging on a panel got it open and she plugged herself in, letting the ship's pain and distress wash over and through her.

The *Astra* began, sluggishly, to tell her things: they were on a planetoid of some kind, the ship was too damaged to fly right now and there were still some living life forms aboard. Her heart thudded into her throat as she checked for life signs. Two on the Bridge, one in her quarters, one in the crew quarters, Ji-min and herself. But how badly were any of them injured?

She commed Sherin while Ji-min checked on Vijay. A burst of joy filled her at the sound of Sherin's voice telling her that she was bruised and cut, but otherwise not hurt. That she would check on Erol while TiCara checked on the passengers.

Vahn. There was one life sign missing from her count. And there were two on the Bridge where there should have been none. She triggered the emergency controls to unlock the hatch and pulled free from the computer. "I need to go check on the Bridge. Vijay?" Ji-min was already at the door, a medkit in their hands. The engineer nodded reassuringly and TiCara gestured at them to go, with a sigh of relief.

She went the opposite direction, swinging herself up a level and jogging down the corridor. If they were on Electra, she wondered how much time they had before the lab security showed up to find out who was on board. Then she wondered what they would do with anyone they found. The answer would be even worse if they'd been hit by pirates; she had to remember that. If that had happened, Vahn was the only one worth keeping for a hostage.

They wouldn't have much time before they found out either way. She grabbed a piece of broken metal as she raced for the Bridge, hoping she could use it as a lever if the hatch was still blocked. She hit the hatch hard, the sound echoing around the floor. It still held and she hit it again. "Need help?" Sherin was climbing up the ladder on the opposite side, her body pressed against TiCara's, with only the rungs to separate them.

TiCara kissed her, desire and relief and joy all packed into the touch of her lips. "Erol?" She asked as she pulled back a little.

"His room was open. I don't know where he went. Ser Vahn's quarters looked empty too." Sherin tilted her head back and looked at the closed hatch. "Think all three of them went up on the Bridge?"

TiCara looked up from the jagged piece of metal in her hand to the closed hatch. "Let's find out." Together, they shoved against it until it opened slightly. As they opened a little more, they could hear someone on the other side, moving around. Then the hatch swung open to reveal Sammo's face looking down at them.

"Pilot-Captain. I am pleased to see that you are well." He stepped back as they climbed up the ladder. If he was equally pleased to see Sherin, he didn't say so. But his hands stayed at his sides and he didn't reach for his weapon, so TiCara nodded her acknowledgment.

Vahn was on the ship's external comm, talking to someone. Erol was in the pilot's chair beside him, sitting very still. There was a trail of blood under the chair, some of it still dripping from his head.

TiCara ran to his side and checked for a pulse. For a wild moment, she thought she felt one, but after checking his neck and wrist and a taking a long look at his still face, she knew that it was only her imagination. She dropped to the floor beside him and held his cold limp hand, rocking in place as tears trickled down her face. With all her heart, she wished that their last encounter had not been about distrust and betrayal. She wanted to keen her sorrow, to vent her pain in howls, but this was not the time; she would not, could not break down in front of Vahn.

When she felt Sherin's light touch on her shoulder, she opened her eyes and looked up. "He saved my life. I trusted him. He was my friend." She swallowed her tears as best she could, as Sherin squeezed her shoulder in a gesture of sympathy and warning. Grieving her Second could come later, but for the moment, Sherin's touch had pulled her back to the room. Now that she was paying attention, she could hear what Vahn was saying and could guess who he was talking to.

"I have transferred the credits that you required. I require immediate medical assistance. Do I have your assurance that a vehicle will be sent to fetch me?" The old man was bleeding from a wound on his shoulder and was favoring that side, but his voice was strong.

TiCara watched him and wondered if any of her crew would get the same assistance on Electra. She doubted it. But as long as she made sure that he paid her, anything was possible.

Vahn got whatever response he was waiting for and answered before setting down the mic. He closed his eyes and his breathing slowed in an obvious effort to recover and control the pain from his injuries..

It was time to remind him of their deal, now, before it was too late. "We're on Electra, Ser. I will need the credits we agreed upon to fix my ship and to get medical attention for my crew."

"In good time, Pilot-Captain. I will meet first with the technicians and hear my prognosis. Then I will know what I still have available." He stood up slowly.

TiCara jumped to her feet, her hand looking for the lazer in her belt that was no longer there. She cursed, realizing that she must have dropped it when she fell off the ladder. Sammo stepped forward, his weapon out and focused not on the pilot, but on Sherin. Vahn spoke for him, "Not a risk I would take, Pilot-Captain. Even if you were armed, which you are not."

"That is not the deal that we made, Ser. I thought you an honorable man, for the head of a corp." TiCara spat her words at him. Somewhere in the wreckage of her Bridge, there had to be something she could use as a weapon. If she threw something at Sammo and distracted him, she might be able to get across the room in time and get his weapon. Before he shot Sherin.

The thought froze her in her tracks and that hesitation cost her valuable seconds. That was long enough for Vahn to make his slow way across the room, staying carefully behind Sammo. He never looked at Sherin. It was as if she had ceased to exist for him. But as he reached the ladder, he turned and glanced at TiCara. "I am still an honorable man, Pilot-Captain. You have what I already paid you. As soon as I know what will happen next, you will have more."

And with that, he scrambled down the ladder. Sammo glanced after him, then back up at the two of them. He tipped them a two-fingered salute and a nod and followed his employer to the level below. TiCara muttered a guttural curse and forced her fists to unclench.

Sherin reached for her, enfolding her hands in her own. "What are we going to do now?"

"Check on Vijay. Ji-min's not badly hurt, fortunately, as far as I could see. But we need to be sure, run med scans on everyone. See how bad the damage to the ship is, make sure life support is still up and running. Then suit up, go down to the surface and see if we can get in to the labs and see what we can get from them. I think if we go in person we'll be harder to refuse." She bent down and kissed Sherin's fingers. "We starshine?"

"Always," Sherin's face was glowing a little. She reached out very slowly, touched a cautious finger to one of the pilot's medusas. She pulled away quickly, but there was a tenderness in her touch that thrilled TiCara and made her want to take the other woman in her arms and kiss her. But she wouldn't stop there and neither would Sherin, so she settled for giving the rep a kiss on the nose.

Sherin blushed and grinned as if she was reading her thoughts. "Let's go. Before we can't."

TiCara grinned back, but her smile faded as she looked around the Bridge. It was a blackhole mess, but how serious was it? She moved some of the debris around and ran her fingers over the nav console. Sherin started clearing out the area around the pilot's chair, piling broken pieces in one corner.

It was she who closed Erol's eyes and unfastened the harness holding him in place so that TiCara wouldn't have to do it. They would have to find a way to dispose of his body. She'd heard stories about spacers setting the bodies of dead crew adrift in space, but that didn't seem like something TiCara would do. Maybe she'd want to take the body back to Kraybourne and give it to his primary. It was a decision that they needed to make soon.

But one look at TiCara's face was enough to tell anyone watching that this wasn't the time. The occasional tear trickled down her cheek and she was looking very hard at the wreckage on the Bridge, never at the body of her Second. "Why don't you go check on Vijay and Ji-min? I'll see what I can do here until you're ready," Sherin volunteered.

"Ready for what?"

"I...I need to try to get into the labs, not just for the ship. For me. And I want you to go with me." Sherin's voice trembled a little with her words.

TiCara stepped over and enfolded her in a fierce hug. They held each other, swaying until it felt like they might never let go. But TiCara did let go, at last, though the look on her face said it was only temporary. "You're right. I need to make sure that they're okay before we go out there. Back soon?" She caressed Sherin's cheek with one cold hand, and added, "Will you be okay here?"

Sherin nodded and watched her drop down the ladder. Then she looked around the Bridge, assessing what could be salvaged and what needed repair. She covered Erol's still body with a tarp from a broken storage unit and went to work.

CHAPTER 25

When TiCara came back, Sherin was waiting for her at the foot of the ladder. "Let's not go back up there right now. I got him covered up and a lot of the flotsam cleaned up, but I think you should take some time before you see him again. There's a pod in one of the storage bays that we can put him later, if whatever we've got for cryo is working." She ran a sympathetic hand down TiCara's arm. "How are Ji-min and Vijay? And the *Astra*?"

TiCara's face was drawn and pale. Even her medusas felt like they were hanging mournfully around her head, limp and lifeless. "I should—no, you're right." She glanced up, then back down at Sherin, rubbing a hand across her neck. "Ji-min thinks that we hit Electra's defenses and that's what made us crash. But Vijay says that that the corp ship was firing on us, too. He's hurt but not badly. Ji-min is patching him up with the med computer's help. Apart from that, life support wasn't hit, but the engines were. We're not flying out of here without some help and hard work, more than the bots can do."

And that's not our only problem. TiCara reined her thoughts in before she could speak them out loud. Someone knew that they'd gone down and they would probably come back to finish the job. Or, perhaps, Electra had secret prisons as well as secret labs. Without Vahn's protection, they might be vulnerable to whatever version of corp law prevailed here.

She realized that she was staring down the corridor leading to the ship's main door as if she expected a small army of Ears to storm the place. Maybe they would. She hated to leave her crew to deal with whatever might be coming, but then, she had given her word to Sherin and she was going to have to act soon, possibly choosing between her new love and her ship.

Well, if nothing else, at least Vahn had confirmed where they were. There was a slim possibility that the station staff might help them since Vahn was a paying client. If he hadn't told the station something different, they were still with him. But the only way to find out what was going to happen next were to use the comm unit on the Bridge to try and hail someone or to leave the ship and go into the station.

From the way that Sherin was fidgeting at her side, she must be telegraphing her anxiety. That or Sherin was learning to read her thoughts. "Got an extra lazer?" Sherin tried to make her question sound casual but TiCara could hear the tension that underlay her tone and she couldn't bring herself to smile back.

Instead, she pulled her spare lazer from a pouch in her blacksuit and handed it to Sherin. Then she bent down and picked up the one that she had dropped earlier, checked it, verified the charge and put it in the holster on her belt. She remembered to check for the throwing knives in her boots, pleased at how methodical she was being in her preparations.

A part of her marveled at how quickly she was overcoming her distrust of Sherin. Elia had told her once that it would happen that way for her, that when she really fell in love, it would be all or nothing. At the time, she thought the other woman meant that she would fall in love with her. Now, she knew differently.

TiCara looked at Sherin with her heart in her eyes and said, "Let's go see what's out there." She sent a short message to Ji-min to let the engineer know what they were doing, and told them to arm the pulse cannon for possible attacks if they could. She clicked off before she could add that she hoped that the *Astra* wouldn't have to fire it in the ship's current condition.

Sherin grinned at her and gave her a quick kiss. They moved out to the bay that led to the airlock and suited up. TiCara made sure that they both checked their air supplies before they walked together down to the airlock door and opened it. Then, they climbed through it and sealed the door behind them. Sherin watched TiCara set the lock on the inner door, her expression wary even through the clear plasticene of her visor.

Once the lock was sealed on their side, the pilot reached out to unlock the outer door while Sherin pressed herself up against the airlock wall and trained her pistol on the slowly opening outer door. Just like Erol would have done. TiCara swallowed a lump in her throat at the thought and tried to concentrate on watching for anything or anyone that might be waiting for them on the other side of the door.

Once outside, they could see that they'd crashed on the rocky surface outside Electra's station walls. From where they were standing, TiCara couldn't see any wreckage that wasn't from the *Astra*. But at least she also couldn't see the armed welcoming committee that she feared was waiting. Maybe Vijay had been wrong about the other ship firing on them, but she doubted it. They were out there, either crashed somewhere else on the surface or waiting for them off planet.

When nothing happened, they stepped out onto the rocky surface of the asteroid. Gathwaite's star and two of the planet's gleamed above them, making for an impressive view. But even without the Ears or hostile security, they had other problems. Electra's station loomed above them, large dome and gleaming metal walls only a hundred meters away.

TiCara wondered how they were going to get inside. Vahn had permission to go in, but they might not. But then again, maybe they could still use Vahn. He probably hadn't taken the time to tell every junior security flunky not to let his former rep and his means of transportation into the station.

Besides, they were still contracted to bring him back to Kyrin and that was one deal he hadn't broken yet. "Let's go knock on the front door, shall we? Wherever that is." TiCara looked at Sherin, but the other woman was looking at something else and didn't answer. TiCara tried to see what that something was, but in the end, simply followed her when she started moving, their gravity boots clinging lightly to the rock.

Sherin led them up to one faceted side of the building, and once they were close enough, TiCara realized that she could see the outline of a door and a hidden comm unit. If she looked farther up, she could also see the station's security weapons outlined against the sky, rotating above their heads. She shivered a little, trying to draw comfort from the fact that they had been allowed to walk right up to the walls.

The crackle of sound from Sherin's helmet pulled her attention back to her companion. Sherin was talking to someone inside the station, requesting entrance and assistance. After an eternity of waiting, the doorway outlined in bright light as it slowly opened to let them into an airlock inside.

The outside doors sealed behind them once they stepped inside and they both waited silently in the airlock for the warning lights to turn green, letting them know that the air was breathable. For a moment, TiCara found herself fearing that it would never happen, that they'd be stranded out here. But the lights slowly changed and she and Sherin removed their helmets. Sherin reached over and squeezed her arm as an inner door opened to reveal an empty room with a large screen on the far wall.

The station's metal walls surrounded them, once they moved inside, and there were no visible exits. The room looked able to withstand multiple rounds of blaster fire. There was also nowhere to sit down, suggesting that their time here would be temporary, one way or another.

They stepped forward out of the doorway and the door sealed behind them. TiCara summoned her most confident air of bravado and swaggered up to tap the screen. A harried looking man in a security uniform appeared and looked down at them. "State your business. Mic is to your right."

TiCara spoke for both of them, loud enough so that her voice echoed against those walls. "I'm Pilot-Captain TiCara X273 of the *Astra*. We brought Ser Trin Vahn here, and crashed when we were attacked just above your security shield. Most of my crew survived, but we need some replacement parts to transport the Ser when his treatment is complete. I have credits that can be drawn on his account."

"Look into the camera." TiCara stepped forward for a retinal scan, then stepped away blinking as her vision adjusted.

Sherin was hanging back, her every movement displaying her reluctance. At first, TiCara wondered why, but once she understood, it was too late for excuses or any story that station security would believe.

Sherin must have realized that too, since when she finally moved forward and looked into the scanner, her discomfort was obvious.

The security officer frowned. "Pilot-Captain, I can let you enter. But Sherin Khan, you are barred from this station."

TiCara raised a hand to stop Sherin's protest before it started. "I realize that my crew member has been on the station before, but I need her help to acquire tech and assistance to repair my ship. Without that help, your client, Ser Vahn, will be unable to return to his home planet. Is there something that we can do to have the secur hold lifted?"

The security officer frowned and the comm went silent as he spoke to someone they could not see. Sherin fidgeted beside TiCara. "I never should have insisted that we come here. I should have realized—"

The mic crackled back to life. "Electra Station will require the following amount to ensure that Sherin Khan will not make any unauthorized attempts to access our tech." The sum that appeared below him on the screen made both of them gasp. It would cost TiCara nearly all the credits that Vahn had paid her so far just to bring Sherin into the station with her.

"No! Leave me here," Sherin's cry was a whisper, but TiCara heard it. Heard the woman she was falling in love with offer to sacrifice her dreams so that TiCara wouldn't lose hers.

TiCara turned back to the mic and drew a deep breath. "Agreed." TiCara found the word somehow and it freed her, as if she'd been trapped under a huge weight. It would be starshine, somehow: she would get the rest of her credits from Vahn and there would still be enough to get new parts. Hesitating now would be foolish. And from the way that Sherin was looking at her, there would be other rewards later. "I approve the transfer."

She pressed her thumb to one side of the amount on the screen and it disappeared. TiCara grinned at it, savoring the warm glow that Sherin's look had given her. It was going to be more than worth it.

The station door opened as the screen showed the security officer once more. "Welcome to Electra Station," he said. His voice had taken on a much friendlier tone and that alone might have amused TiCara under other circumstances.

"Where do we go for parts?" She asked, her tone neutral.

He gave them directions and sent them on to the next room, which was filled with sanitary facilities and storage lockers. They left their suits and lazers behind in a sealed storage locker and went down the corridor that they were told led to the repair bay. Not that they were permitted to do so unobserved. TiCara noticed cameras in the corners of the hallway and at a couple of the intersections. There were also technicians and security personnel walking the corridors, some of them lingering a little too long to be doing anything other than watching them.

"Starshine girl, you sure do make people memory you," TiCara muttered to Sherin. She regretted it the moment that she said it; her lover was pale and wide-eyed as it was. She reached out and squeezed her shoulder gently. "Parts first. Then we'll see what else we can do."

Sherin gave her a tremulous smile, but she held her head high and kept walking as if their extra company was no concern of hers. When they got to the repair bay, she backed up TiCara on negotiations and even put forward what she had by way of credits for the parts. TiCara fought her on that piece of generosity, but Sherin was adamant, and they emerged with an agreement that sent a mechanic and parts over to the *Astra* immediately.

TiCara let Ji-min know that help was on the way, then herded Sherin to the station canteen and an empty table. They sat and ate and talked about small things like favorite vids and which ships they liked flying. Nothing that would attract any additional attention from their observers. TiCara hoped that if nothing else, they'd become less alert from sheer boredom.

"I need to find Dr. Moest." Sherin murmured softly across the table, working her comment into the middle of a discussion they were having about which spices tasted best in food replicators. TiCara nodded as if she'd never thought of using curry that way and took a cautious look around. One of the techs she'd seen earlier was still lingering by the door.

"Leave one at a time. I'll go first and find you later. Set your comm to this frequency." TiCara turned the screen on her handheld where it rested on the table so that Sherin could see it. She followed it up with a brief story about over-spicing her food on the first replicator that she used. It made Sherin laugh, and that was a sound that TiCara thought that she wanted to hear more often. *Would hear more often*, she vowed. TiCara winked at her, then got up as if she was looking for the nearest sanitary facilities.

She left the canteen, and as she had hoped, the tech followed her. After that, it was just a matter of making multiple wrong turns and stopping to talk to almost everyone she ran across. She asked for directions, as well as questions about everything from the air circulation system to the station's building structure. Everything except the nano-tech labs and a certain Dr. Moest.

It was surprisingly easy to get them to tell her about the station and she quickly realized that station personnel were keeping her talking so that they could watch her medusas. No one else on Electra was wired, or at least no one that she had seen so far. The techs and other station personnel that she spoke to seemed to be both fascinated and repulsed, using any excuse to keep her talking for a few minutes longer.

The tech following her disappeared, and after watching to make sure that he hadn't been replaced, she ducked into a cleaner's alcove. Once inside, she changed into a station uniform that she liberated from an unlocked locker outside one of the showers. It came with a hood that covered her medusas, and she got it on just in time for Sherin's signal to reach her.

She was two levels away and TiCara bit back a quiet exclamation of frustration when she realized that she wasn't sure how to get there. Plugging her medusas in and checking on the station's computer clearly wasn't an option. But a few more moments of research on her handheld and some hints from Sherin and she was soon heading upward, hoping that her new uniform and the cleaning tools that she had taken would be enough to give her safe passage to wherever she wanted to go on the station.

CHAPTER 26

S HE COULD HEAR SHERIN'S VOICE before she saw the other woman and she paused where she was, listening to what the rep was saying. Not many words, not this far away, but the pleading note in Sherin's voice made her wince. Clearly, they didn't need to look for Dr. Moest any more.

TiCara took a deep breath and walked around the corner. As she suspected, she was now in a hallway lined with what looked like lab doors. The number of secur cams in the corners had doubled, so it was only a matter of time before she and Sherin attracted the attention of security personnel. If they hadn't already.

One more turn and TiCara found Sherin at last. She had abandoned pleading and was now arguing with a thin, pale-faced woman whose frown and crossed arms told the pilot all she needed to know about her response. Sherin was wild-eyed, tears brimming and ready to pour down her cheeks as TiCara reached them and laid a comforting hand on her shoulder. "Dr. Moest?" She asked the other woman, keeping her tone as formal and polite as she could manage.

The pale woman jumped back out of reach and glared at them. "I don't know who you are or what you want, but this area is classified.

I'm calling security." She gestured with her handheld and TiCara lunged out and grabbed her arm with one hand, placing the other over the doctor's open mouth. The doctor trembled under her hands like a faulty engine, but was quiet for a moment. But it was obvious that her silence wasn't going to last long.

TiCara tried to keep her tone calm. "Don't yell. Not going to fry you unless I have to. She wants her implants back, all wired and working like they were when your bots took them. And now she needs tru tell from you, what you need to do to make that happen." She waited to see a response, a shift in Moest's expression and when she got it, she took her hand from the doctor's mouth. But she kept a firm grip on the hand with the handheld. No point in being careless. "Let's go find a place for tell, nice and quietlike."

From the corner of her eye, she could see a security detail appear at one end of the corridor, both with blasters held out and pointed toward them. Without turning her head, TiCara knew from the footsteps that there was at least one other guard moving down the corridor behind her. Sherin flinched, her lips tightening into a thin line when she saw them. Moest still looked angry, but also smugly relieved.

TiCara calculated how many steps away the nearest guard was, and wondered whether or not she could reach them before she got blasted. If they got out of this, she was always going to carry a hidden lazer on her. She braced herself to throw Sherin to one side and hopefully out of range when she was ready to make her next move.

But the sudden klaxon of an alarm from the station speakers interrupted the scene before it could go any further. Dr. Moest yanked her arm free of TiCara's momentarily lax grip and bolted for the lab door behind her. The security details were on their handhelds, getting some tell that apparently overrode whatever they had planned to do about TiCara and Sherin, judging from their sudden level of distraction.

As the lab door clicked shut behind the doctor, they could hear running feet in the surrounding corridors. Then there was a distant explosion and the guards in the corridor vanished, racing back the way they had come. Whatever was going on, it was more important than capturing an unarmed medusa pilot and her crewmember. That realization didn't make TiCara feel much better, but at least they were alive and free for the moment.

Sherin looked at her, "What now? Back for the suits and our lazers, then to the *Astra*? At least then we've got the pulse cannon to deal with whatever that is." She jerked her head in the direction of the explosion, all traces of emotion gone from her voice.

TiCara noted her calm approvingly, though her heart ached a little to think what that effort was costing the other woman. She smiled at Sherin, relieved that her lover realized how much danger they were in, that the explosions almost certainly meant that the station was under attack. Even if they got out, if the repairs on the *Astra* weren't done, they could be trapped on Electra's surface awaiting their fate, pulse cannon or no pulse cannon.

But there'd be time to worry about that once they got back to her ship. "Let's go find out." She grabbed Sherin's hand and squeezed it. Part of her wanted to kiss the other woman's icy cold fingers, but that felt too vulnerable, too exposed. Later. Once they were back on her ship, she'd kiss every millimeter of Sherin's body.

She released Sherin's hand and pulled her knife from its hidden sheath in her boot. Its alloy material had passed the security scan, but it wouldn't help them much against lazers. Still, just holding it made TiCara feel better and it might prove useful, as long as she could surprise any attackers.

They loped carefully down the corridors in the direction that TiCara had come, pausing at every branch and turn to check for whatever might be on the other side. TiCara was desperate to plug in, to find out what they were up against. With a medusa connection, she could probably even hack into the security channels, given some time.

It would take too long if she didn't plug in, and something told her that time was going to be critical for them.

But there didn't seem to be much in the way of open terminals of any kind in this station and she didn't know where the Electra personnel hid the others. It wasn't as if she'd seen any other medusa pilots in the brief time they'd been here so maybe they didn't have medusa connections. Even if she could find one, plugging in would probably alert station security and bring them back again.

She closed her eyes for a moment, feeling her implants swirl around her head in confused spirals and her thoughts with them. *Bet that looks great on the secur cams. Be handy to be able to turn them to stone right around now. She* grimaced at her own attempt at a joke and opened her eyes again to look around.

As if she was reading TiCara's mind, Sherin paused, her fingers flying over her handheld's virtual pad. "I think I can get into the station's broadcast system. Not as good as wired, but better than running with no tell." TiCara jerked her head in acknowledgment and stepped up carefully to peer down the next corridor. It was empty, at least for now, and that alone was worrisome, given how many station personnel and others she'd passed getting to Sherin. Where had they all gone?

Behind her, Sherin's handheld crackled to life. Phrases like "attack" and "emergency lockdown" echoed against the corridor walls and Sherin grimaced. "Tell us what we don't know. Where are they?" She shook the handheld a little, like that was going to make the tell more informative.

"And who are they?" TiCara murmured. It could be the pirates, but why pick now to attack the asteroid? If any of the stories were true, it had been here for many revolutions around Gathwaite. Nothing they had seen made it look especially vulnerable to a sudden attack by what had to be former allies or trading partners.

There were other possibilities. Zig's face rose in her mind and she shuddered. If the Ear had followed them to the asteroid, and his ship had been shot down too, he had nothing but reasons to attack the station if his ship had been shot down and he thought he would get something out of it.

A dreadful certainty filled her the more she thought about it, even as she tried to deny it. It was him, had to be him. Erol had told her he was the one tracking their flight, the one who got her Second to betray her.

As for Vahn, he had only mentioned rivals in general, not any specific corp. Not anyone else with resources and a personal vendetta against the medusa pilot flying Vahn to his destination. But then, she hadn't asked if he knew Zig. She wondered if their orbits had intersected before and if Zig had some reason to hate him too.

She choked out her words, "It's Zig, that's who was on that ship. Maybe he has bots or had an entire crew in cryo or something to attack the station now. But it's got to be him." She could hear the rising panic in her voice, and winced. Sherin gave her a wide-eyed look, followed up with a reassuring arm squeeze.

TiCara leaned against the wall and closed her eyes as she fought for control of her racing heart. When her pulse had slowed a bit, she realized that she was holding the knife hilt so tightly that her fingers were achingly white. She loosened her grip and drew a trembling breath, letting her medusas drop down to her neck and send out a few reassuring pulses.

Her impulse to find somewhere to hide gradually faded, leaving her aware of Sherin's proximity. The other woman was watching the surrounding corridors for danger while she pressed up against TiCara, letting the warmth of her body bring whatever reassurance it could. TiCara reveled in the comfort for a moment.

Then the touch of Sherin's body brought other thoughts, too, and TiCara felt herself flush with heat. She imagined pressing Sherin against the corridor wall and letting her hands and mouth convey everything that she was feeling. Maybe Sherin was ready for the touch of her medusas now. Maybe...she clamped down on her fantasy and her libido at the same time with a wry smile, hoping that she wouldn't regret that choice later.

Sherin gestured with her handheld. "Well, Zig or not, it sounds like whoever they are, they're down by the loading bay. If it's him, that's where he must have come in. I think we can avoid that area and get back to the lockers if we go this way." She pointed down another corridor and began walking at TiCara's head jerk of agreement.

They kept moving, occasionally passing station personnel as they got to the lower levels. Apart from a quick threat assessment, no one paid much attention to them, which TiCara took as a good sign. "They know who they're fighting. He must have brought bots, not human or cyborg mercs or crew. Otherwise, they'd be shooting at us." She muttered the comment to Sherin, who responded with a head jerk of agreement.

The confirmation for that found them much sooner than either of them hoped or wanted. They were outside the canteen and nearly at the door to the lockers where they'd left their suits when Zig came around the corner, two military grade robots at his heels. Both women froze.

Zig smiled when he saw TiCara, then turned to the robot on his left. "Kill the unwired one first." He gestured at Sherin.

TiCara knocked Sherin aside and lunged for him, knife in hand. The other bot stepped forward on a signal from Zig, and raised its blaster. She dodged and rolled to avoid running into the blast range. The heat seared the wall and floor behind her.

The other bot was firing at Sherin now and TiCara glanced over in time to see her lover roll across the floor into the canteen and begin tossing around the tables and chairs together to make a barricade between her and the bot. TiCara hoped that she could find a weapon too. Now to try and gain the other woman some time.

With that thought, she slashed her knife across the leg of the robot reaching for her, aiming for some exposed wiring, and it lurched, its balance mechanism sending it backward. She rolled forward and past it, trying to get around its metal bulk to attack Zig. A whir of electronics warned her that the robot had turned and was arming, about to fire on her, and she spun up from her roll and jumped, using its armored body to brace her feet against as she leapt clear of it.

A hurled seat shot past, smacking into the faceplate of the other robot. TiCara wished that she had the breathing room to grin at Sherin as the robot staggered before re-aiming and firing into the canteen. But she had her hands full with its companion. Zig had not given it a kill order for her, not yet, so it was still trying to catch her. What Zig would do with her once his robots had her immobilized wasn't something she was willing to think about.

But it was enough to remind her of a long-forgotten piece of her training. She couldn't outrun this thing for long and she couldn't count on Sherin being able to do so either, so it was time for a new tactic. This half-remembered maneuver might be their best, or perhaps, their only chance.

When the robot reached for her, she let it pick her up. Then she shoved her face into its featureless head and sent her medusas into the gap between its faceplate and helmet. The resulting pain was agonizing and she screamed, barely able to control herself enough not to pull away. Dimly, through a cloud of red, she saw, rather than felt, her medusas connect with its wiring.

She could hear Zig yelling something, see the bright flash of the other bot firing, as she sent a wave of commands through her medusas. The effort made her black out for a moment, but she came to in a wave of heat and light that emanated from the robot that still held her. She sent the command, "Drop" through her implants with everything she had and yanked her implants free with a final self-destruct message. After another wrenching couple of moments, she felt its claws release her.

TiCara dropped to the floor in a shower of sparks and crawled as fast she could away from the robot. She could see Zig realize what she'd done and lunge in the other direction, trying to get clear before it blew itself up, possibly taking all of them with it.

The explosion, when it came, was sudden, filling the corridor with a brilliant, white flash. As she buried her face in her arms, TiCara hoped with everything she had that Sherin was doing the same, that she had seen what was happening and been able to avoid being blinded or worse. The air was full of metal, plastic and wire, showering down on the floor around TiCara and she shuddered every time a burning fragment landed too close.

It felt like the entire station was evaporating in a cloud of burning air. She sent out a fervent hope that anything vital that the station needed, like life support, wouldn't get damaged. Where was station security when they actually needed them?

Finally, everything slowed down and after a long moment of quiet, she looked up cautiously. There were two molten hunks of metal and plastic where the robot had been and the corridor was filled with dust and fine particulates. She squinted through the haze, looking for the second bot. There had only been time to tell it to blow itself up, not to ensure that it destroyed its companion as well.

Her medusas were limp now and she could tell that several had shorted out. The resulting headache was blinding, leaving her struggling for control. She wouldn't be able to do the same thing to the other bot. She needed a new weapon. With a huge effort, she crawled forward through the debris, looking for her knife or whatever else she could use.

Motion caught her eye: Zig was trying to stand up. She could see blood seeping from his wounds through the dust, but if he could stand, then he was still a threat. That sent a bolt of adrenaline through her and she lurched to her feet, using the wall for support.

TiCara risked a quick glance at the canteen as she stood up. She couldn't see Sherin from where she stood. But Zig seemed relatively undamaged and she had to deal with him first. She scrambled forward, grabbing the robot's lazer as she went. If she had any good fortune left, it was still working and the burns and damage to the casing were only cosmetic.

Zig started laughing, a hollow, eerie sound that echoed off the corridor walls and made TiCara want to cover her ears. Or shoot him. What was there to laugh about? One of them, maybe both of them were going to die. Sherin might already be dead. She wasted an instant wondering if Vahn had gotten his cure and was on his way down to the bay, or if he, too, had died in the attack. How long had they been here?

TiCara swayed on her feet from pain and exhaustion as she watched Zig, trying to force her feet to move her closer to him, to close the distance and ensure that the damaged lazer would do enough damage to kill him. He was grinning at her now, sharp white teeth shining under the shattered lights like the predator he was. His dark eyes were cold and dead, belying any joy that his laughter suggested, a cold ruthlessness emphasized by the weapon in his hand.

"Why did you land here?" Her voice sounded distant in her own ears. "You could have waited off planet or just registered the coordinates and gone back to Kyrin. None of this," she gestured around them, "was necessary."

"At first, I thought I'd reclaim you," he said and the statement hung in the air between them, like a cloud of toxic meteorite dust. "That was what I planned to do after I killed your crew and destroyed that tub of bolts you flew here in. We'd be just like we were before. Better, even." He laughed again, a dry, humorless bark, punctuated with a gasp of pain. "Then they shot my ship down and wouldn't let me to bargain for repairs."

TiCara began to shake as her memories threatened to flood back in. Somehow, she had always known this day would come. Had always known that he would find a way to possess her again. She could feel her hand holding the robot's lazer drop to her side. It was hopeless; why had she thought that she would ever be able to escape him?

From behind her, she heard the scrape of metal on metal that told her that the other robot was still there, might still be a threat. One of her still-functioning medusas sent a light spark into her neck, trying to rouse her, but she only shook her head, spinning it away from her. The walls around her tilted as the pain in her head increased.

What did it matter if the robot killed her or Zig did? Everyone she cared about betrayed her in the end. Her fingers loosened on the lazer as she prepared to meet her fate, whichever it turned out to be. The hall turned gray around her and a distant portion of her brain realized that she was gasping for air as the overwhelming smell of burning plasticene filled her lungs. Alarms clanged around them, the sound nearly drowning out everything else.

"TiCara, no! Blast him!" Sherin's voice echoed around them, despite the alarms. She said something else, but TiCara didn't catch it. There was a crash behind her as something big hit the floor. *Please let it be the bot*, she thought.

The sound of Sherin's voice gave TiCara a lifeline, something to pull her back from the dark wave of despair that was threatening to swallow her whole. Her fingers tightened on the lazer and she drew in a slow, shuddering breath.

She returned to herself just in time to register Zig's sudden motion. TiCara threw herself to one side, dodging the blast that he fired. "Don't want me back so bad, then. Don't think it'll be that starshine," she snarled through gritted teeth. She dodged behind a portion of melted robot, using it for the small amount of cover it provided while she took aim at the Ear.

A well-timed tossed chunk of melted seat whizzed past his head and he flinched away. TiCara fired, then screamed as the damaged weapon she was holding melted, burning her hand. She got rid of it by heaving it at Zig as she jumped forward, her knife in her other hand.

The pistol struck him in the face and he jerked away, raising his arms instinctively to avoid the sparks from the disintegrating gun. Then TiCara was on him, slicing upward into his shoulder to force him to drop his own lazer. The scent of his blood and the echo of his scream of pain maddened her and she drove the blade into his torso, looking for whatever the Ear used for a heart.

There was a blinding flash as her damaged pistol exploded, leaving TiCara sightless. She rolled free of the Ear in a panic; where was Zig? What was he doing? She thrust out again and again with the knife, hoping that the blade would find its mark without her eyes to guide it.

Strong arms wrapped themselves tightly around her and from a galactic distance, she heard a voice murmuring in her ear. Zig? She struggled, trying to break free. Some part of her realized that it couldn't be him, as her medusas did their best to calm her. Sherin, it had to be Sherin. But what was she saying? TiCara couldn't hear a thing and felt another moment of utter panic before her medusas kicked in with a soothing wave of pheromones.

She forgot about Zig in a dim rush of horror. What if she was seriously hurt? She didn't have the credits for tech healing, not after what she'd paid to get Sherin into the station. A shudder shook her entire body, sending shooting pains in its wake. She could feel rare tears trickle down her cheeks as her body and mind warred with her medusas.

Sherin kissed her forehead and TiCara could feel her fingers gently stroke her cheeks. She tried to speak, but she still couldn't hear so she had no idea if she could be heard by anyone else. Experimentally, she flexed the hand that didn't hurt as much; her fingers moved with only minimal agony so she reached up and touched Sherin's face. But her fingers came away wet and she began running her hand over Sherin's face and head, checking for wounds. Was the other woman injured too?

Despite her panic, she forced a trembling breath into her lungs, then another. She made herself stop grasping at Sherin and let her medusas take over, using them as rudimentary senses as she imposed control on her wounded body and mind. They couldn't replace her sight or her hearing but they could read her lover's body and assess her condition, given enough time. They could also tell her that she and Sherin weren't alone.

Sherin's body stiffened against hers. Was there a new threat? TiCara wanted with all her heart to believe that she had killed Zig. Wanted to, but couldn't. If he was still alive, they were both black-holed. But if it was him, why were they still alive? Was he stopping to gloat?

A faint yet familiar voice cut through the velvet silence and the buzzing which all that she'd heard since the explosion: Vahn. "It seems that you will be unable to fly me home, after all, Pilot-Captain. What a shame. Is the damage permanent?"

Another pair of hands touched her face, the fingers rougher and bigger than Sherin's. She could feel Sherin trying to push someone away, feel rather than hear her swear at someone she couldn't see, but who must be Sammo or some other security personnel that came with Vahn. Zig must be dead if they were spending time on checking on her instead of fighting him. But she couldn't even begin to make herself hope for that, not until she had seen his corpse. Perhaps not even then. Death was too easily faked, especially for Ears.

"Maybe." The new voice was cold, indifferent. "There are some burns, but she should recover from those. But she can't see, might be just until she gets the tech to fix it, might not be fixable. The implants could still plug in if you want her to pilot. No need for eyes then." Sammo. At least she could hear him now, though the ringing in her ears made his voice sound like she was listening to a faulty speaker.

"No. Take the Ear's ship. She's not leaving with you and you're not taking her ship." Sherin's voice was cold and clear, her tone suggesting that she'd found a weapon and would use it to defend TiCara if she had to. TiCara felt a warm glow fill her. Sherin cared for her as much as she had hoped she did. Sherin wouldn't give her up. Even if she couldn't see.

"I have everything I came for." Vahn, again, on faulty audio. "We have overstayed our welcome. My apologies, Pilot-Captain. I hope a cure for your condition is found." His voice rang around her ears and echoed through her skull as she tried to shut it out.

She could feel herself slipping away, giving in to the pain and the darkness. She hoped Sherin had a lazer, just in case Zig wasn't dead. She hoped that Vahn and Sammo weren't going to try to take her away from Sherin. She hoped that she'd be able to see and hear Sherin when she woke up. If she woke up. With that thought, she was gone.

Chapter 27

TiCara wasn't in the corridor anymore when she woke up. Wherever she was felt different, smelled different, nothing like burning metal or blood. Without thinking, she reached both hands up to her face, then winced and quickly lowered her burned hand.

With the other hand, she felt a bed underneath her and several bandages on her limbs and head. The ringing in her ears had been reduced to a dull buzzing but she could hear station sounds beyond that and sighed with relief. Cautiously, she opened her eyes, then shut them again immediately afterward.

She was in a room lit by what looked like harsh bright lights. She opened her eyes a slit, only then realizing that her face was covered with some kind of light bandage. Whatever it was, it was semi-opaque and fastened in a way that she couldn't quite figure out with one hand.

She dropped her medusas down to it, letting them explore the bandage's texture while she lay quietly absorbing the information that they were sending her brain. After a moment, she realized that all her medusas, even the ones that had gotten shorted out in her fight with the robot, were working again. A sense of wonder filled her: who had done this? Had Sherin managed some miracle to get her healed?

A beloved voice cut through her reverie and she turned toward it, trying to smile. A sharp pain burned her cheek and she pressed her hand up against it. She could feel Sherin take her other hand and press it gently between her own.

"The tell from the techs is that the damage is temporary. You did it, starshine girl, you saved us." She pressed a careful kiss on TiCara's fingers. Then, more softly, "Zig's dead. You did that, too." There was another pause before she spoke again. "I gave them tell about Vahn, said he hired Zig to steal tech, that they had a fight when Vahn decided to leave Zig here, that I thought that Vahn had taken a drive with some of their tech on it. They took the tell in trade for healing you, said they'd take it from there."

TiCara thought about asking what, if anything, they might do to Vahn, then decided that she didn't care that much. He wasn't going to pay her what they'd originally agreed to since she wasn't flying him back to Kyrin, so she didn't really owe him anything. Still, a part of her was disappointed that she didn't get to see him healed and strong. He'd been an interesting client, often a good one. Regardless of his motivations, she'd miss him, at least a little.

Of course, she could say the same of Erol, and that cut much deeper. His loss ached much more than any other. She had a damaged ship and a damaged face, and no loyal Second to help her injured crew pull through while she healed. She tried to ask about the *Astra*, the crew, but her voice came out as an unrecognizable croak. Instead, she tried to use her good hand to \ gesture to convey her questions.

Sherin didn't understand at first and asked a couple of questions, pausing to touch her hand or her arm as if for confirmation or assurance. If TiCara squinted hard through the wrap on her face, she could almost see her lover through the bandages. But that hurt too much to try for very long, so she finally shut her eyes and tried to use her good hand to respond as well as to ask. It wasn't very efficient, but Sherin must have speced what she was trying to do.

"I commed Ji-min and Vijay, gave them tell on what happened. Vijay's bots got him and Ji-min fixed up and he says they're fine. Ji-min says the ship is whole. By the time you're ready, we can fly off this rock." Sherin paused, then added, "And I still have access to Vahn's credit. He hasn't disconnected me yet. I took back what he still owed you."

A warm rush of emotion filled TiCara and for an instant, even if she could have spoken, she would have been at a loss for words. She tried to convey everything she was feeling with a tight grip on Sherin's hand, squeezing it, releasing it and squeezing it again. She felt the other woman raise it to her lips for a kiss and thought she was the luckiest humanoid in the galaxy.

But with that came another thought. If they could raid Vahn's cred, why not pay for Sherin to get wired again? A click from something mechanical nearby interrupted her thoughts and she could feel a cold fluid seep into her arm. She struggled against a sudden, overwhelming need to sleep, trying to get the words out before she slipped back under, but it was no use.

When she woke up again, she was alone. The lights weren't hurting her eyes anymore, and she teased carefully at the bottom of the bandage to see if she could look around the room. A moment later, she realized that she was examining the covering with both hands. That had to be a good sign.

The bandage around her eyes peeled back a little, leaving her blinking at the room and the lights. Her movement must have sent some sort of signal as well because a moment later the door to the room opened and Sherin stepped inside. "Leave your eyes covered for a few cycles more. The bots aren't done yet."

She was right. TiCara could feel them now, gliding over and under her skin, knitting it together again. She let the bandage drop back down again and cleared her throat experimentally. "Sherin," she said at last, her voice a dull rasp, as she felt the other woman take her hand. "Take Vahn's cred, get rewired," she choked out before she started coughing.

"Dr. Moest said she'd talk to me about it in a few cycles. The labs weren't damaged but I think they're using them to try to do an assessment of the tech that they think Vahn and Sammo had access to." TiCara could feel Sherin's shrug through her hand and squeezed her fingers lightly to reassure her. She could hear the disappointment in her lover's voice. Sherin continued, "I'll bring you with me when I go to see Moest the next time. Get some more sleep."

I don't need more sleep, TiCara started to say. But just as the thought crossed her mind, she did. She dropped back off into a dreamless oblivion.

The next time she woke up, it was because Sherin's hand was resting on her shoulder. "It's time to go see Moest. Are you ready to come with me? Drink this first." TiCara felt a metallic container pressed up against her lips, and took a gulp from it. She choked on the medicinal flavor and nearly spat it back out. Only the pressure of Sherin's hand reminded her to swallow.

After a couple of choked coughs, she looked up at Sherin, relieved to see that she could see her lover's beautiful face clearly for the first time since the fight. A moment's cautious probing with her medusas told her that most of her bandages were gone. Sherin tilted her face with gentle fingers. "The burn's almost completely healed. You might not even have a scar."

Sherin kissed her, lips soft and careful against her own. Then Sherin broke off the kiss with a gentle nip at her lips when TiCara reached up to pull her closer. "Not yet." TiCara could hear the regret in her voice and smiled at her.

She had less to smile about when she saw the state of her blacksuit. Burns and tears left it barely wearable and she wrinkled her nose at the scent of old blood and sweat. "Sorry," Sherin looked stricken. "I didn't think to have the station clean it. Getting them to fix you up was all I thought about."

TiCara grimaced. "The *Astra* will fix it for me when we get back on board. Now let's go see Moest so that can happen sooner." TiCara got dressed slowly and stood, albeit with the occasional sway. Together, she and Sherin walked out of the room and down the hallway. TiCara tried not to clutch Sherin's arm too tightly. Despite some pain and discomfort, the pilot felt as if she was light enough to be on a lowgrav world. At first, she attributed that to her feelings about Sherin. But when she thought about it, realizing that Zig was finally dead, that he wouldn't be coming after her, was a meteor's weight off her psyche.

And then there was the healing and the credits. Sherin had done a nova job sorting that out. She couldn't imagine what this trip would have been like without Sherin, now that she knew and trusted her. Once this was over, they'd...that was when she realized that if Moest could and would rewire Sherin, life would be very different.

Unless a wired pilot was in training, the tech for wiring medusa pilots was so specialized that most ships never had more than one wired pilot at a time. A medusa ship got programmed to individual set of brainwaves when a pilot plugged in; modifying that to another pilot's implants involved some elaborate reprogramming.

As she thought about it, TiCara doubted that Sherin had taken enough from Vahn to cover getting rewired as well as getting her a ship of her own. If she got rewired, they'd certainly have to get her working on a corp ship to manage the debt.

The sharp pang of impending loss swept through TiCara in a wave. To have come so far and been so close to having a primary for the first time in her life, then to lose her again so quickly, was almost more than she could bear. She blinked back against sudden tears and dropped her face into her hands so that Sherin wouldn't see them.

For some reason, the gesture made her think about Elia. Had the other pilot felt this way about her? And known her feelings wouldn't be reciprocated? Had that been part of why she had stayed so aloof, so distant? But her small pang of sympathy was replaced by an overwhelming sense of self-pity. Whatever Elia had wanted initially, it no longer mattered, especially in the wake of her betrayal.

Sherin lifted TiCara's chin and kissed her, driving away all her fears and doubts, at least temporarily. She tasted like warm spice and TiCara savored the flavor of her tongue against her own. Her battered body felt a surge of arousal and she reached out to pull Sherin closer. A sharp pain shot through her, causing her to pull away with a muttered curse.

That gasp was enough to bring a fast-moving med tech over to them, herding them into one of the rooms. Sherin moved away, going to sit in a nearby chair to wait. TiCara bit her lip to hold back a pout. After that, she had more pressing concerns as the tech checked her eyes, injecting them with a fluid that left her blinking in a haze while the tech removed the bandage from her hand. "It's healing well. You're fortunate, pilot. Your treatment will cost less than the credit limit your primary set."

TiCara could see Sherin wince despite her tearing eyes and mouth an apology. She tried to smile reassuringly, but the tech slipped between them to reach for one of the medical scanners on the shelf above her head. That was enough to make her briefly aware of the tech and her distant, cold expression. She could smell a very faint tang of fear sweat and it made her wonder what she was doing and why.

Unthinking, she sent up a medusa to feel what the tech was reaching for, and felt the woman flinch away. She withdrew it immediately, with a mumbled apology, and tried not to see the disgust cross the tech's round face. She had always had some trouble reading groundy expressions, but this one was pretty clear.

She ran the scanner over TiCara's injuries, careful to avoid reaching up toward her head and the writhing medusas. "They don't bite. Much." TiCara finally growled, forcing the tech to meet her eyes.

The tech's full lips quirked upward in an expression that approached a smile, but then she broke eye contact quickly. "You can leave today, pilot. Keep your hand bandaged for two more cycles to let the bots finish. They're programmed to die off when they're done." The tech finished rewrapping her hand, then stepped away. At the door, she turned and nodded slightly, this time meeting TiCara's eyes, her expression turning curious rather than fearful. TiCara let out a breath she hadn't realized that she was holding, as if coming to the end of a battle she was unaware of fighting.

Sherin walked over and held out her hand to help her up from the chair. She looked at TiCara's medusas and frowned thoughtfully. But she didn't say anything, and TiCara couldn't bring herself to ask, not after the tech's reaction.

She tried to kill off a tiny hope that Sherin was reconsidering being wired. Why should some groundy's phobia change her mind? And she definitely couldn't bring herself to ask if it changed how Sherin felt about her. Instead, she let Sherin patch up a few of the tears in her suit with some sealant that she found on the shelf, all in complete silence.

"Ready to try and escape again?" Sherin asked at last. TiCara raised her hand to her lips and kissed it gently. Sherin smiled at her, then reached out with her free hand, and very carefully, stroked one of her medusas. TiCara shuddered with pleasure and bit back a gasp as the other woman withdrew her hand. It took all the self-control that she had left to follow Sherin out of the lab when her every instinct demanded that she pull her down on to the bed and make love to her then and there.

That, or run screaming out the door to the *Astra* and back to a simpler life. Simpler, but less interesting. Now, it was time to see what their future could hold.

So she sent a fervent hope out to the universe that the bots would be able to finish repairing her sooner than the tech had predicted and trailed after Sherin. Fortunately, they didn't have to go far. Dr. Moest was waiting for Sherin in a nearby lab. When they got there, she gestured at them to sit down on the nearest stools before turning the screen behind her so they could see it too. Sherin tilted her head and looked at it sideways before straightening out and looking politely interested at Moest's frown.

"This is your skull," the doctor gestured at the screen and the thin white line that circled a blob of red and gray. "This," Moest pulled up a second image for comparison, "is an image of a humanoid skull before wiring." She paused, as if to let the pictures sink in for her audience. "You can see how much thinner the bone is here and here." She tapped the image of Sherin's skull.

Sherin reached out and grabbed TiCara's good hand. There were tears at the edges of her eyes. "So...you're saying that something is wrong. That my bones are too thin?"

TiCara closed her eyes for an instant, trying to hope as hard as she could that Sherin wasn't right, that the doctor was really saying that reimplanting her medusas was still feasible. She could sell the *Astra*, pay off Ji-min and Vijay, pay...but she found she couldn't go any further, let alone say the words out loud. There had to be another way. She opened her eyes.

Moest went on talking about bone density for a while longer, then, as if she was aware of losing her audience, concluded, "So I can't just reimplant them as your skull bones are now, not without permanently damaging you. But I might be able to do something else."

A wild hope flashed across Sherin's face. "What?"

The doctor went back to the images and launched into a complex explanation of how she might be able to give Sherin medusas again. It was a complicated procedure and TiCara didn't understand all of it, but she grasped enough to realize some of what could go wrong. Dr. Moest didn't explain the impact of those operations until TiCara cleared her throat and asked the question that hung over all of them. "But if you did that, wouldn't you damage her skull, maybe her brain?" Sherin's fingers tightened convulsively on hers and she heard a gasp.

"Tru tell, she'd lose most of her memories of the recent past, maybe more. There'd be some impact to motor skills, but those should rebound." Moest frowned at the images as if it was an interesting challenge. "I would like to try, but I cannot say that it would be safe." She shrugged and glanced back at them as if she had forgotten that she was talking about a living person sitting before her.

TiCara felt the blood drain from her face, leaving her lightheaded. For a long moment, she was afraid to look at Sherin. What if she agreed to this? What would be left for them? But then, what would she do in her lover's place? If this was the price that she had to pay to connect to her ship again, would it seem too dangerous to try, too much to give up?

Sherin cleared her throat. "I need to think about it. Just for a cycle. I know time is cred and that Electra wants us gone soon." Moest nodded and Sherin let go of TiCara's hand. "I'll ping you when I'm ready to talk," she added to TiCara. Then she slipped out of the room, leaving her lover and the doctor staring after her, then at each other.

Chapter 28

I T FELT LIKE AN ETERNITY to TiCara while she waited for Sherin to come back. She and Moest discussed a very short list of other options before she found herself dismissed from the doctor's lab to wander down to the canteen. Once there, she made herself drink something warm that she couldn't taste. She wondered if she could recreate the spiced drink that Sherin made for her and started experimenting with selections on the food processor until the canteen 'bot shooed her away from it.

With nothing else to do but fret, she called her crew. Ji-min told her that the repairs were completed, the *Astra* was fueled and that Electra's spaceport authority had told them that they needed to leave soon. Vijay told her not to worry so much and asked what their next job was.

That question shook TiCara loose from her spiraling nest of fears about Sherin, and got her planning about where they could go next. Her thoughts shied away from Kraybourne, even though they'd have to go there soon. She clicked off her handheld without giving Vijay a direct answer, mentally weighing the options. She imagined all the places in the known galaxy that she'd seen before, wondering if Sherin would like to see some of them with her, once they left here.

Or where she and the crew would go next, if they were leaving without Sherin. Kyrin was not an option, at least for now. Not until they knew what had happened to Vahn and whether or not Zig's corp was responsible for sending the Ear after her. After them. But, there were plenty of other planets, other systems to choose from, no need to retrace their steps.

Thinking about leaving Sherin here on Electra dulled her enthusiasm. She buried her fingers in her medusas with a groan, and felt them twisting around her hands, trying to bring comfort. After what Moest had said about the risks, she didn't want Sherin to get wired again, not any more. But it wasn't her decision to make, much as she wanted it to be. And, much as she wanted to find the other woman and talk her out of it, she wasn't going to do that either.

She pulled her fingers free of her implants with a sigh, and went through the list of contacts on her handhelds, sending messages to several. Her efforts yielded some tell about a shadow trade corps run a few systems over, not long after she sent the first message. The creds on offer were nowhere near what Vahn had offered originally, but they would be enough to keep them eating and flying for a while.

And the run's destination put them near Kraybourne. She drew a trembling breath, like a sob. They could bring Erol's body back to Arnelle, tell zir a version of what happened. TiCara sighed heavily; she owed her Second that much and more, wishing that he had finished the tell he started, had let her help him find a way out that would have kept him alive.

But it was too late for that. Now, she had decisions to make. She needed to accept this job within the next two cycles or lose it. TiCara found herself at war with her instincts, her training, her experience. If she turned this down, how soon would another job take its place? They were going to need to hire her a new Second, and cover their next trip if she used what she had left to pay the ship's debt.

She closed her eyes and focused on modulating her breathing, finding in that something that she could control. It reminded her of Aliandra and how she had always promised herself that she would go back there eventually and finish working with the masters. She wondered if she would be more successful now that Zig was finally out of her life.

Her handheld chimed and she picked it up. Sherin, at last. But with what tell?

Her lover asked her for a meeting in the observation lounge a few levels up, and once TiCara agreed, she clicked off, her tone formal. TiCara stared at her handheld, as if she could get it to reveal whatever Sherin was going to do just by looking at it. But not for long. They didn't have that much time left.

She got up, leaving her drink container on the table and walked out of the cantina, ignoring the annoyed-sounded chittering of the canteen bot scurrying to clean up after her. She tried to clear her mind of all her thoughts, all her hopes. To remember that whatever Sherin decided to do, it was Sherin's choice to make. Wasn't that what she herself had wanted when she first got wired, why she had been so eager to embrace her implants with all they brought with them, good and bad?

She hung on to that memory as she climbed up to the elevated observation deck, ignoring the gravilift next to it in favor of the stairs. The exertion hurt several of her still healing wounds, but the pain was bearable and it helped her clarify her thoughts. By the time she reached the top, the turmoil in her head had calmed and she paused both to catch her breath and to admire Sherin.

Sherin was looking up at the stars again, just as she had been the first time that they were together on the *Astra*. But this time, there were no tears and she looked serene. Whatever she had decided, she was sure about it.

TiCara swallowed hard and walked to her side, noting with relief that the few other beings who shared the deck with them were far enough away to be out of listening range. She didn't want anyone else hearing this, whatever this was. She pulled up a soft chair next to Sherin and sat down to wait.

Her medusas swirled around her in a cloud but she made no effort to control them this time. Sherin had to know that this decision affected them both if they were to be anything to each other, had to know that she was worried, that she cared.

Sherin looked down at her. "I stopped singing and became a pilot because it was what my crèche expected of me. We were all intended to succeed, to be the genetic combination that New Chindai could replicate for other crèches. What I wanted had never mattered before I lost my medusas. I wanted what they wanted because why would I want something else? Their success was my success," She paused and sat gingerly on the seat next to TiCara. Her eyes were wide and far away when she met TiCara's gaze.

TiCara almost reached for her, but stopped herself and instead twined her fingers together, trying not to fidget. Sherin continued after a brief pause, "I loved being wired. I loved being a pilot. But I loved that it fulfilled my duties to my crèche as much as I loved piloting the actual ships. Then I...lost that." Sherin turned her face away and closed her eyes.

She continued, her voice soft, "And worse, I didn't want to sing any more. I didn't want to do anything any more. Vahn found me when I had nothing else left and he hired me. That meant so much to me. Still does. But I thought that my crèche wanted more from me than just becoming a corp rep, even though nobody said anything. I just knew...or thought that I knew what I needed to be for them." She grimaced and drew in a deep breath. "And every time I talked to Elia, I started to blackhole, getting deeper and deeper. I didn't know what to do. Until all this happened." Sherin gestured around her and gave TiCara a tremulous smile.

TiCara felt her heart begin to race and tried to calm her breathing. What if she was wrong, what if Sherin had chosen to forget her? To give her up? Her hands started to tremble despite her efforts to keep them still.

"I thought about taking Moest's offer, but I knew that I would lose everything I've known for the past few revolutions. Even if she was able to wire me again, I wouldn't know if I'd be too damaged to pilot, not until it was too late. And I'd lose my memories of you, of us." Sherin looked away, her expression making it clear that she wasn't looking for excuses or explanations.

TiCara gave her one anyway. "I want to stay with you, whatever happens next. Even if you don't remember me, I want to try and give you new memories. We could start over without any of what happened with Elia and Zig. It could be--" she recognized that she was babbling and stopped abruptly and gestured to Sherin to continue.

"I don't want to lose you either. Or have to relearn who you are. Not for something I think I can live without. That I've been living with for awhile." Sherin turned to her and reached for her, catching her hands in her own.

"There's something else that Moest and I talked about after you left. She thinks she can gradually increase bone density in your skull. It still might not be enough to withstand having your medusas reimplanted, but it's a chance, not so invasive." TiCara stopped and choked. But she had to ask the question uppermost in her mind. There could be no avoiding it. "Can you be with me if I'm wired and you're not?"

Sherin paused, then nodded, as if she didn't trust herself to speak. Her eyes were full of tears, but her face shone like a glowlight in the darkened deck. She stood up, pulling TiCara with her and into her arms. They held each other under the stars, drawing comfort and strength from the warmth of each other's bodies. TiCara could feel every nerve ending in her body simmer into a slow burn.

Her breath caught at its intensity. "Let's go talk to Moest then." She whispered in Sherin's ear. "I want to get you back on the *Astra* soon." They left the deck together, fingers entwined.

Moest didn't seem surprised to hear Sherin's decision, simply nodding and explaining the bone density procedure and its side effects. She administered the first of the injections at Sherin's request, had them authorize some agreements and sent them on their way after they agreed to return in a standard revolution.

After everything that had happened so far, it was very anticlimactic. TiCara wasted several minutes trying to understand why she felt disappointed. They needed to leave Electra immediately now and it felt like they had gotten only part of what they came for. Her handheld's alarm chimed, reminding her of the shadow trade job and without thinking, she answered and keyed in her agreement.

Belatedly, she met Sherin's eyes when she looked up from her handheld. Should she have asked before assuming that Sherin was willing to be dragged along on a new run? Ji-min and Vijay would be all right with it, creds were creds and they still trusted her or so she hoped, but Sherin wasn't crew and didn't answer to her. Not like Erol and she grimaced against the aching loss that thought brought with it.

"Another job?" Sherin asked, pulling her out of her thoughts. She smiled a little at TiCara's head jerk of agreement and her apologetic shrug. "I guess I have to get used to this if I'm going to fly with you. Could you use a good rep?" She smiled wryly at TiCara.

"Yes! I need a Second too, but then we'd be piloting in opposite shifts too much of the time if you took that berth. I'm not giving up my time with you that easily, so we'll need to hire on when we get into a bigger port." TiCara smiled at her as they made their way down to the suits.

"I can make some changes to the autopilot to fix that, if you'll let me. And I've got some ideas for new trade." Sherin's mind was off and running and TiCara followed along, basking in the flow of the other woman's words and ideas. It felt like hope and possibility and so many other things that she'd only dreamt about.

For the first time, it felt like she was free, of Zig, of the corps, of the fears that had been crushing her. That feeling only increased when she put on her suit, pleased at how quickly she was healing. The tech had done a good job, despite her obvious distaste for medusa pilots and TiCara felt a brief wave of tenuous gratitude.

The trip back to the *Astra* was over almost before she realized it and then it only remained for them to meet with Vijay and Ji-min and look over the ship. A part of her was dreading this, dreading seeing the ship without Erol, seeing the damage, seeing Erol's body. Somehow, she expected to see it on the Bridge again, but when they got there, his body had been podded and much of the damage was cleared out and fixed.

It wasn't the same, though, and she had to recognize that it might never be.

Ji-min was still distant, still observing military protocols, though not as icy as they had been. Vijay was being cautious, hard to read. "I owe you tell," TiCara began, and gave an abbreviated explanation of everything that had happened. Getting them to believe that explanation took a bit longer, and she wasn't sure that they did believe her when the station gave them the all-clear to leave. She wondered if she would lose her entire crew at the next port before her tell was done.

"Need to give tell to Erol's primary," Ji-min said at last.

Vijay nodded, his eyes tired and hooded. "And you, rep? Staying aboard?"

Sherin straightened up. "If it's starshine with…all of you." There was an unspoken question in her voice. She glanced from one to the other of them, looking for permission, for assent. For belonging.

But you belong with me, TiCara wanted to say, recognizing that it might not be enough. That she might need more than that. And she wondered if she'd made that impossible.

Ji-min and Vijay looked at each other, then back at Sherin. After a long moment, Ji-min gave her the corps military salute, the one that they used to welcome new crew on board. Vijay followed, a bit slower because of his injuries, but he added a smile and an outstretched hand. Sherin clasped it in hers and gave them all a radiant smile. They all turned to TiCara, their faces expectant and wary.

TiCara answered with, "We have a new job, one that goes near Kraybourne. We need to take him back to Arnelle, tell zir what happened. Sound all nebula? For now?" They each gave her their assent in their different ways and she nearly sighed with relief.

She still felt as if she was sleep walking until she plugged into the ship and let the soothing rush of the nav computer fill her mind. Part of her wanted to reach out and joyously caress the navigational array when it popped up. Her ship, her crew and her shadow trade job, almost everything in her life back where it should be. Sherin's face rose on the small screen when she scanned the ship and she grinned at the image. *Their* job. Their ship, maybe.

She had piloted them away from Electra and into the asteroids by the end of her shift. After conferring with her crew, she decided to stop for a few cycles on the same asteroid that had sheltered them before. They could hide from the pirates until TiCara was fully healed and Sherin was ready to fly the ship on her own.

A quick scan of the belt showed no pirates in the vicinity and, even better, no corporate ships. TiCara set up the alarms and gave the crew leave to sleep or otherwise entertain themselves. Then she climbed down the Bridge ladder and walked to her own quarters, bouncing a little in the ship's grav. As the door opened, she revised that thought to *our* quarters.

Sherin had cleared out all trace of Vahn and Sammo and set up her meager possessions. She had put them away as unobtrusively as possible, but the small room seemed more homelike, if a bit crowded.

She was also sleeping in the bed, her face glowing golden in the dim light from the hall. TiCara slipped quietly out of her damaged blacksuit and tossed it into the alcove for cleaning and repair as the door closed behind her. Then she lay down next to Sherin, trying not to wake her.

But Sherin's eyes opened slowly as soon as she lay down and she pressed against TiCara with a fierce kiss. Tired as she was from her shift, the heat of Sherin's warm skin against hers was enough to help her wake back up. Soon, she was exploring Sherin's body with her mouth and hands and Sherin responded in kind.

TiCara still held her medusas back, flat against her skull and unmoving, vowing not to use them unless Sherin told her to. Instead, she relied on the rest of her body to arouse her lover It seemed to be working. Sherin's hips rocked against hers and the scent of her desire filled TiCara with a desperate longing of her own as she slipped her leg between Sherin's. She ran her hand up Sherin's bare thigh, reveling in the goose bumps that followed, but stopping just short of her sex.

Instead, she licked her way down to Sherin's breast, nibbling on her collarbone, then tonguing one hardened nipple against her teeth, then the other, sucking until Sherin writhed against her, moaning. TiCara lost herself in Sherin's body, tasting, biting, licking, stroking.

She wanted to find every nerve ending that would pleasure the other woman before she was ready to climax.

It was several moments before she felt Sherin's hands in her medusas, tentative at first, then caressing. She let them twine themselves in between Sherin's fingers, stroking her skin very gently. For an instant, she nearly let them release their pheromones, but that felt like cheating. This might be all that Sherin was ready for and they had plenty of unaided chemistry between them already.

Sherin pulled her hand gently away and ran her fingers slowly down to her breasts. The medusas echoed her own pleasure and Sherin's, amplifying it and feeding it directly into TiCara's brain until she thought she would explode from the sensations. Then they led her mouth down Sherin's body to her slit, sending gentle warm sparks into the sensitive skin of her belly and thighs.

Once TiCara was between Sherin's thighs, with her mouth on the other woman's clit, her medusas caressed her skin, sending a torrent of sensations through both of them as Sherin bucked and moaned. She went rigid and TiCara worried for a horrible instant that Sherin might want her to stop, might want all of this to stop. She held her breath waiting for her lover to speak or give her another sign.

Then Sherin's hips shot upward, rocking against her mouth, pulling TiCara's fingers further inside her. She moaned, clutching the sleeping pad on either side of her thighs. A wave of pure desire washed over TiCara as her medusas amplified what both of them were feeling and together they both howled out their mutual release.

TiCara rolled off Sherin to lie beside her as they gasped and quivered in the aftermath. She grinned at Sherin and her lover grinned back at her. "Was that…are you…? I mean…" she fumbled, looking for a less silly way to ask the question. "Using these?" She ran a hand over her damp implants and her whole body quivered from the contact.

Sherin laughed and reached down to pull TiCara back on top of her. They embraced and TiCara kissed her. Then they were a tangle of arms and limbs and implants, a symphony of sounds as their damp bodies slid together, craving more.

TiCara found her way back between Sherin's legs, this time twisting her finger up Sherin's ass while her mouth found her clit and her medusas sent tiny shocks into the trembling flesh of her thighs. Sherin's fingers dug into the bed and her body convulsed under TiCara's and the pilot paused, wondering once again if she had moved too quickly. Then, between gasps, she heard, "More." And she complied with everything she had.

Sherin had barely stopped quivering when she twisted around to slip her hand between TiCara's thighs. She used that leverage to pull TiCara up, tugging the pilot into position so that she knelt on either side of Sherin's face, Sherin's parted lips. Sherin's hand thrust into her while she licked her until the motion of her hand and mouth made TiCara howl her own release soon afterward.

They collapsed side by side, exchanging eager kisses until they both slipped into exhausted, sated sleep, wrapped in each other's arms. Waking brought another round of lovemaking, their exploration of each other's bodies continuing until hunger drove them to the nutrient dispenser.

Sherin spooned a warm spicy mixture into TiCara's mouth, laughing when she missed and put a dab on her cheek instead. "I need to work on the autopilot, you know. I don't want to leave the belt until we get that done," the words came with a caress, "A few adjustments to the nav controls and you'll think you have a new ship."

TiCara grinned and stretched, before they got up to spend a last few precious moments showering. Then she escorted Sherin up to the Bridge and left her there with a hearty kiss. It was time to go back to being the captain again.

The *Astra* was overdue for a thorough inspection before they left the system and she'd want Ji-min and Vijay to double-check Sherin's work on the computer. Not because she had any doubts about the other woman's intentions, not now, but because her crew knew the ship and what she needed. Sherin would learn that too, with practice, and once she did, they were going to be the best crew she'd ever worked with, on the best ship, flying free through the known systems. And perhaps, on to some new ones someday.

As she dropped down the Bridge ladder, she could hear Sherin start to sing.

ABOUT THE AUTHOR

Emily L. Byrne's stories have appeared in such venues as *Bossier, Spy Games, Forbidden Fruit, First, Summer Love, Best Lesbian Erotica 20th Anniversary Edition, Best Lesbian Erotica of the Year Vol. 2, First, Witches, Princesses and Women at Arms, Blood in the Rain 3* and *The Nobilis Erotica Podcast*. Her collections, *Knife's Edge: Kinky Lesbian Erotica* and *Desire: Sensual Lesbian Erotica*, are available from Queen of Swords Press. She can be found at **http://writeremilylbyrne.blogspot.com/** and on Twitter at @emilylbyrne.

ABOUT
QUEEN OF SWORDS
PRESS

Queen of Swords is an independent small press, specializing in swashbuckling tales of derring-do, bold new adventures in time and space, mysterious stories of the occult and arcane and fantastical tales of people and lands far and near.

Visit us online at **www.queenofswordspress.com** and sign up for our mailing list to get notified about upcoming releases and offers. Or follow us on Facebook at the Queen of Swords Press page so you don't miss any press news.

If you have a moment, the author would appreciate you taking the time to leave a review for this book at Goodreads, your blog or on the site you purchased it from.

Thank you for your assistance and your support of our authors.

www.ingramcontent.com/pod-product-compliance
Lightning Source LLC
Chambersburg PA
CBHW071511110726
47908CB00003B/806